KEITH HEALING

Visitation

The Burnt Watcher 2

Copyright © 2021 by Keith Healing

All rights reserved. No part of this publication may be reproduced, stored or transmitted in any form or by any means, electronic, mechanical, photocopying, recording, scanning, or otherwise without written permission from the publisher. It is illegal to copy this book, post it to a website, or distribute it by any other means without permission.

First edition

*This book was professionally typeset on Reedsy.
Find out more at reedsy.com*

To my wife and chief nit-picker, Penny. Thank you. I could not do this without you.

Contents

Acknowledgement	iii
Reflections	1
New Pleasures	6
Thoughts and Remembrances - Leaving Oxford	12
Tea with the Deacon	16
The Lady Jennifer	20
Captain Haydon's Log	26
Preparations	32
Thoughts and Remembrances - Pestilence	38
The Road South	42
Erthcott	48
The Albino	54
A Change of Direction	59
Of Stone and Road	64
Days of Thought	68
The Child	74
Separating	79
The Road North	85
Wood Bay	90
The Pale Visitor	95
Aftermath of Ink	100
Return	105
Gloster	110
Meetings	115
The Harbourmaster	120
Entry One	126
Tanney	127

Blessings	133
Thoughts and Remembrances - The Church	138
The Lightness of Pigment	141
Sight of a World Long Gone	144
The Darkness of Pigment	146
Aldermen	149
The Decision to Cut	154
Entry Two	160
Practice and Application	161
The Doctor and the Mark	167
The King and the Promise of Iron	173
Fires on the Shore	178
Entry Three	184
Curfew	185
The Queen Calls	190
Rite and Fire	196
Blood and Iron	203
Testing	210
The Masked Dead	217
The Yellow Crown	221
Sunset	227
Return	228
Epitaph	234
Notes and Thanks	236

Acknowledgement

Huge thanks go to Nimue Brown and Cat Treadwell, who have been happy to read early drafts without complaint and who have given endless encouragement and support.

Reflections

Master Grey, I think to myself, you are too old for this heat.

It has been relentless for the past week; scorching during the day and oppressive at night. My left leg and arm are tight and sore and the oil I apply is thin and soaks into my clothes rather than my skin. I am aware that I am short-tempered, but then so is everyone.

The heat is also making sleep unwelcome, as it is fuelling dreams of the burning of Stonehouse. It seems that every night is now accompanied by the sound and smell of conflagration, the yells of villagers, and the foul presence of Thomas Waverley and the Yellow King.

There are nights when the images change and, instead of this horror, I am walking a city of cool stone. This brings no relief as the walls are sat at strange angles, they follow lines that no builder would, or could, manufacture, and they curve and fall in on each other at random. As I walk through the narrow lanes I catch occasional glimpses of the sky, which offers no comfort as the stars are black against a white dome and two dark suns rise over a distant mirror-still lake.

There are nights when the dream ends with me standing by the lake, but there are others when I become aware of something following me, a feeling rather than a sight or sound, and no matter which route I take there always comes a time when tendrils of yellow, oily smoke curl and snake their way along the walls. They test and feel their route, always towards me, and their groping is terrible to behold.

These are the worst nights, the ones where I wake sweating coldly and refuse to sleep again in the sure knowledge that the probing and hunting will continue. On these nights I make my way down to the small kitchen and make tea, keeping the fire as small as possible to avoid heating the room too much. Once made, I take it outside, sitting on the wharf and allowing it to cool before sipping, allowing the bitterness to occupy my thoughts.

This morning, following a night of tiring dreams, I am sitting on the edge of the wharf, dangling my legs over the side, with a pot of tea. I am wearing the housecoat I made, ragged and odd though it is, as it scrapes my burns only slightly and leaves my left arm completely free of cloth. I have applied the scented oils to my burns, and I am hoping that sitting still will allow it to work into my skin. The wharf opposite the Excise Committee, Bateman's, is used by smaller ships and tends to have a quick turnaround, and the one currently docked is only around sixty feet in length.

Some of the larger ships, which require a deeper dock, are three times this length and are magnificent things indeed. Campion tells me that these massive vessels are capable of navigating the huge seas between here and Merica, although the voyages are fraught with danger. The storms that sit in the Great West Ocean are so vast that they would cover the entirety of Britain, and can produce waves taller than the masts of the ships themselves. The very best tea and opium come from Merica, and these beasts can carry nigh on five hundred tons, so it is worth the risk. They are fast and well built and, utilising a mixture of sail and up to six Stirling engines driving air screws, can make the crossing in under a week.

The ship I am looking at is, I guess, for coastal haulage, being shorter and squatter than her sleek sisters. Even so, its prow towers above me as the river is at full tide. She has finished loading and the captain is waiting for the crew to complete the job of securing her cargo. They are poised, however, ready to unfurl her sails to catch whatever breeze may be had once she hits the centre of the river. I cradle my cup of tea and ponder what a life aboard would be like. Not for me, that much is certain, as I have never been one for following orders.

A slight breeze gives me hope that the weather will break, but it carries only warmth despite the early hour. There is a series of mechanical clicks and thuds, and two gantries are swung away from the hull, propeller blades unhinging and clicking into place. I stand and step back, resting against the wall of the Excise Committee, as I know from experience that getting caught in the wash when they start is not a good idea. They should not really fire up until away from the wharf, but with no wind at all, they have little choice.

There is a shout from the captain, and the propeller closest to the wharf begins to rotate, rapidly picking up speed, and the ropes securing her to land are cast away. Slowly, so slowly, the ship begins to move, turning away to head out into the wide, slow water. As soon as she is facing into the river, the second engine is engaged, and the wind from the blades pushes me back into the wall. I do not move as it provides a welcome breeze.

Within a minute she is clearing the docks and I can take my position next to the river again. The sky is beginning to lighten over the hills and the heat of day will soon be upon us again. Hot summers are fairly common, but they tend to consist of a few days of increasing temperatures and humidity and then a terrific thunderstorm. This year there has been no storm.

My time in Gloster has, so far, been quiet and I have enjoyed getting to know the town. Both myself and Alice have become friends with Edward Madikane, the purveyor of Old World goods, and try and meet with him at least once a week for a meal. His company is, for me, particularly pleasant as he is extremely well-travelled. Alice and he are especially close, as her thirst for knowledge and his patience and quiet manner are well suited.

Alice and I have maintained a close contact, although she treats me warily. There are times when I feel her distrust of me, but these are tempered by the others when I know she wants to talk over the events in Stonehouse. Which is something I am unwilling to entertain, as I believe it will do neither of us any good, and do not wish to break the fragile bond of friendship we share.

She splits her time working with Master Evenright, making and repairing the mechanisms he designs, and learning the Watcher's ways with me. Campion expressed some dismay when she suggested that she learn, but I have privately assured him that the knowledge I pass on will only be that which may protect her. Recognising where danger lies is of prime importance, especially given her recent history. I suspect that she will still be one to leap into situations and I know that I will not always be there to help.

There is no need for her to learn how to Test or carve runes.

Campion himself has settled back into his life within the Judiciary and we have worked on a few cases together. Nothing has been particularly taxing and I have needed to Test only one. He presented no problems and pissed himself when I made the first correction to his lies. He was executed three days later. Gloster does not hold public executions so it was a small affair. He actually died well, and I believe he was welcomed by the Queen.

Gloster is slowly making itself known to me. I was somewhat overwhelmed when I first took up office. The town is so large, at least compared to Enfield and Stonehouse, and houses so many people that I believed there was no way I would ever be able to understand it. Over time, and as a result of many hours of walking, I am beginning to map the town in my mind.

The Wharfs, like the town, increase in status the further up river they go. To the left of the Excise, down river, lies Black and Tan Wharf, historically where the goods required for tanning were docked. The barrels of urine, fats and skins were unloaded and then to the tanneries in the dark, narrow streets of the Shambles. The stink of the leathering would sit heavy on the town and, when the river was dredged and more docks built, the tanneries were moved away. The Shambles however, stayed, dark and mean. They are not necessarily hotbeds of crime, but they do provide cover for those who prefer the night. One of the biggest trades coming into Black and Tan now is opium from the west.

The grandest wharf is Queen's. It sits directly in the centre of the riverside, where Queen's Wharf Road hits the river, coming up from the Square. Queen's is unique as it is the only wharf that exists for a single cargo. That cargo, loaded once a week, sails across the river and is deposited on the opposite shore, to be burned with full ceremony. The ships that set sail from Queen's Wharf are the ships of the dead.

Coming from a small village where labour is shared and people learn skills as needed, I am still astounded at the way Gloster organises itself. Skilled craftsmen tend to occupy the southern quarter between Eastgate and Southgate, nestled along Queen's Drive and the wall. Master Evenright is set up here.

The north east quarter is rich. Large properties, large egos and large politics sit here. It is at this point that Wharf Road leaves the city and the great air-boats dock in the fields outside the walls.

And so I sit, watching the sky warm up while the wake of the ship washes the wood beneath my feet. Today will be hot, I shall be tired, and the summer will extend by another day.

New Pleasures

In the months I have lived here I have found many things which bring me pleasure, despite the best efforts of my memory to disrupt them. First among these is the food. Gloster is the first large town I have lived in, and I have chosen well as it sits on the main trade routes from the south of Urope, being the hot countries where spices are grown. Those spices then find their way into the mutton and beef dishes that are cooked to mouth-watering perfection in the stalls on the market. It has become a habit of mine to sit there at least twice a week, over time working my way around the different vendors and having my face recognised, becoming known. The slow-cooked, spicy, fruity Tajeens are a particular favourite.

Along with the food, the wines have been a revelation. I still enjoy beer, particularly the pale, hoppy varieties brewed here. In both Statfield, where I spent my first years as a child, and Enfield, where I lived before coming here, the preference is for dark, powerful brews, and I still enjoy them when I can find them, but the wines brought up from the south west is glorious. And it is a perfect partner to the food.

Not everything I enjoy is food based. One of the greatest surprises has been the discovery that I appreciate art. I have always loved fine craftsmanship as, being unable to produce anything of merit myself, I believe that I appreciate it more in others. There is a difference, however, between craftsmanship and art. It is a fine one, and I have had many discussions with various people over the exact nature of that difference, but it essentially, at least to me, comes down to use.

Art is useless.

And that is its power, for it is created without the constraint of purpose other than to convey emotion.

Beautifully designed and manufactured devices and tools are a joy to handle and use. Beauty can be built into the structure of these items, but, if they then have a specific use, a reason for existing other than for the sake of existing, they are not art.

It is fair to say that I have, much to my own surprise, become appreciative of this useless, pointless, emotional pursuit.

There is artwork in the churches, of course, but it is there to convey a specific message, a story or a moral, and, because of that, it ceases to become true art. It is illustration, there to aid in the appreciation or interpretation of scripture. I have always enjoyed seeing the images, particularly when rendered in stained glass, and my appreciation of the skill required in their manufacture has not diminished. However, after stumbling upon the studio of Jacob Perez on Ness Row, I am aware that they are simplistic scribbles, however beautifully made.

Ness Row is a crooked street that runs broadly parallel to Southgate and is the haunt of printers and printing-block carvers. There are workshops and paper-presses, many of which have studios in the roofs, where light can be admitted. I have walked the Row a few times, checking that printed pages do not contravene Church law and that licenses are in order. I like the industry and the skill required to carve pages of text from boxwood blocks is quite remarkable.

It was while slowly walking the street that I noticed a door, set a little way back in the wall, that had passed me by before. A small plaque, "Jacob Perez, Artist", was attached to the door, which was slightly ajar. Curiosity got the better of me, and I pushed my way in.

A dark staircase led up, and I stumped my way, deliberately making noise with my feet and stick so as not to startle Master Perez, should he be present. At the top was a single, open door which I gently pushed wider.

Skylights in the roof allowed daylight to flood the space, which was surprisingly large. It was full of colour and the softly acrid smell of oil paints. Around the walls, stacked and leaning against each other were wooden panels, canvases stretched on frames, loose papers and bound books. In the middle of the room, beneath the skylights, was an easel, a slim man working away at the canvas.

I coughed quietly and he looked around, his face breaking into a wide smile when he saw me. That was two months ago and I have been back every week since to see what delights he has produced.

Over that time we have developed a firm friendship, and I enjoy the time I spend in his studio. Sometimes we talk for hours, sometimes, when he is working, we sit in silence. I think he likes the fact that I am happy to be quiet, while I enjoy the peace of the sound of his brush on canvas.

His art is astonishing. He tends to prefer portraits and makes his money from commissions, requests to paint those who are important, or, more often than not, self-important enough to think that a house would be improved by having a copy of themselves glaring down at guests. And his portraits are very good. They appear to be copies of the individual, frozen in time against a dark cloth, so real one could almost feel their breath should one place his cheek against the pigment lips.

What he *enjoys* painting, however, is the same people in strange and fantastical surroundings or situations. His work is deeply satirical, and when he is commissioned to produce a portrait the contract also allows for him to produce other works without the client's approval. Such is his reputation that there seems to be no shortage of people willing to be subject to his vicious wit and, I would say, cruel, knife-sharp insight. Very few of these additional pieces are taken by their subjects. Those that are, I imagine, are kept locked away, simply to prevent anyone else from seeing them. There may be a few that are displayed proudly, but I imagine they are a rarity.

Over the time we have known each other I have flicked through the works that he has kept and have found myself chuckling at his take on the few figures I recognised. Occasionally I would be shocked at the presumption or viciousness of his art, but mostly my reaction is one of admiration, for he applies the same talent to these pieces as he does to the ones sold.

These pieces differ from the official portraits in one other detail: they are not on black backgrounds. Instead, each is sitting in front of a complex scene demonstrating the characteristics Perez sees in them. In most this is representative of the town where they live, but distorted to fold around the sitter, placing them in the centre of their world. However, when examined there are myriad little details that show this ego-feeding to be a lie.

I laughed out loud when I found my old friend Campion in the pile. His picture was glorious. Campion, fat, red-cheeked, his hands grasping his robes of office as he puffed his chest out to make himself as large as possible. Around him, Gloster bent itself while criminals showed him their bare arses. At his back, I recognized the tiny form of Alderman Colston, busy unpicking the seam of his robes, a knife poised to cut the threads.

I asked him on one occasion where he got the idea for these caricatures, and his answer intrigued me.

"I started out hoping to be a true artist, painting what came to my mind and people flocking to buy my work. It only took a few months for me to realise that this is not how the world works." We were sat in the Town Square, drinking hot, bitter coffee. From memory it was the first warm day after winter, and the square was busy with people enjoying the warmth.

"I realised that rich people would pay to have their ego stroked, and so I practiced and, after a while, began to gain a reputation. This paid my rent and fed me, but I was angry at myself for becoming little more than a copyist. And then I came across an Old World book in Edward Madikane's shop." My Watcher's ears pricked at this and Jacob laughed softly. "This was after he obtained the extension to his license, there is no need to get over-excited, but the book was wonderful. It was, and is, extremely fragile with many pages missing, and a lot of the existing text and images redacted, but what is left is exquisite. It details the art of many centuries ago, long even before the Conflagration."

He sipped his coffee. We were sitting on the long bench that runs along the south side, leaning against the wall and, I imagine, looking as relaxed as we felt. At this point, however, he leaned forward, excited by what he was telling me.

"The artwork is astonishing. It is really simple with flat colours and a very basic, stylised design, but the artists worked their art into letters and the margins of text, wrapping strange beasts and plants around the strokes. What really amazed me, however, was the playfulness of the thing. Little figures, completely out of scale with the rest of the design, worked within it, tending to plants or fighting with the animals. As I read further I then discovered that many of these were satires on the political figures of the time, and in some cases, none too gentle in their attacks. the artists had sneaked them into the pages without their targets ever knowing."

He leaned back, and I said, "There is quite a jump between a hidden satire and a painting of vicious wit."

He grinned. "Well, my first attempt at subversion was included into a portrait: a merchant who buys and sells spices. Horrible, puffed up little fellow. I placed some subtle statements into the stitching on his, very beautiful, robe. I do not know to this day whether he ever found them."

He took another sip, and said. "He has never been back, though."

I laughed.

"The next one I remember was an unpleasant little fellow, who complained and moaned constantly during the sitting, and then paid me half what we had agreed. I was so angry I painted a caricature and posted it up on the south gates of town, high enough to be both visible and difficult to remove. He paid the balance within two weeks. And that got my business going. It also sealed my reputation. I have never been short-changed again, and I get the opportunity to express my imagination."

And so, here I am now, sitting as still as possible, while Jacob Perez sketches. He has been badgering me for weeks; apparently, my face, with its scars and ink, is worthy of his attention. He has promised not to undertake a caricature, and I will hold him to his word. It is hot and stuffy, and he wanted me to wear my robe, so beads of sweat are running freely down my back. Luckily, he is quick and within a couple of hours has the drawings he requires. I shuck the robe from my shoulders and we head out to get some food.

"How long will it take to complete," I ask as we walk into the square. He waves his hands non-committally and says, "A week or so. I have one commission to complete, but I shall work on this while it is drying."

My friend, with whom I have shared everything bar anything important, is going to paint my portrait, and I feel slightly odd about that. Is my ego so in need of stroking? Alice, I know, will laugh at me.

Thoughts and Remembrances - Leaving Oxford

The town of Oxford sits very close to its Old World origins, and the ragged, broken tooth walls are visible from the first floor windows of the Excise college. It serves as a constant reminder of the world we face and I remember standing, staring from the window and wondering what horrors might slither and pulse in its dark, overgrown streets. Of course, I was never allowed to find out, but that only increased the clarity of the visions in my imagination.

I had been taken on by Master Isaac Chang, a Watcher younger than his face showed. I was relieved, as several students were never accepted by a Master, and they left the college to return to their families. There was no shame in this, at least not officially. The Watcher's path is not easy and many do not learn to accept it, despite the call by Pale Mary, and they would be welcomed back into their community with tears and relief. I am sure there were some for whom the decision to leave was also a relief, but for most it was devastating, as despite the obvious dangers, the life of a Watcher was seen to be a considerable improvement on that of, say, a farmer. The role of the ego should not be overlooked in this, and I know that I would have struggled with the walk home should I have not been chosen.

But chosen I was, and by a Master who could not, I believe, have been bettered. There were some who were more well known, of course, and I was initially jealous of Jasmine Creed who was picked by Master Laura Percival, a Watcher who had made a name by rooting out and dealing with three Fear-Ridden in one village. She bore her scars well, I remember.

I was fourteen when we left. March 562 was a cold month. Frosts were still *occurring most nights. I do not suppose you remember, but that year was terrible. Summer heat never really came and I remember walking past fields with crops rotting in them, and the winter of 562 to 563 was truly awful. However, it is only in hindsight that years are awful; when one is living through them they are simply something to be endured. And when one is fourteen and has lived a sheltered, if dangerous, life, one knows not the terrible things that famine and disease may do.*

I am getting ahead of myself. Master Chang and I left Oxford and headed east, crossing the Great Forty Road and continuing along the drover's tracks. Being cool, the walking was easy, despite the weight of the packs we were carrying. Master Chang walked easily but kept his pace slow in order to allow me to retain my energy. Being young I was built more for explosive action than long-distance hiking, and I found the first days hard. I looked forward to each stop, and became adept at lighting fires.

At the end of the second day we camped at the foot of a great escarpment which ran north, rising several hundred feet above the level we were at and I was not looking forward to climbing it the next day. The camp we set up was cradled by woodland which spilled down from the land above us. A track wound its way up through the trees, and we had hoped to gain the top this day, but my legs were not able to carry me further. Master Chang gave me a look, but said nothing. I set the fire. We had caught a couple of rabbits, which I cleaned and skinned and, with some sorrel and the remains of bread we had from Oxford, we ate well.

I remember that evening as being one of the most pleasant of my life. Master Chang and I chatting softly, sucking the meat off the bones, the sun setting in our eyes, colouring the land golden red. I slept well for maybe three hours until I was suddenly awake. I went from deep sleep to sitting upright instantly. I had no idea why, but I saw my Master standing, alert and watchful. Without looking around he gestured me to stand. I tried to do so, but my feet tangled in my bedding, and I struggled for what felt like minutes. The look that Master Chang hurled at me was worse than any shouted insult.

Eventually I was standing, knife ready. I was shaking uncontrollably, a mixture, I think, of fear and embarrassment when the reason for our sudden awakening became clear. From behind our camp, deep in the woods but difficult to pinpoint, came a scream. At first, I thought it was a fox, but it rose in pitch and continued for many seconds before stopping abruptly. I was terrified.

At that, Master Chang, who had turned to be by my side, took my arm, and said, firmly and quietly, "Runes."

I nodded, but my feet would not move. In order to carve staves to protect the camp, I needed fresh wood, which meant heading to the trees from which the screaming had come. As I hesitated he pushed me to. As soon as I grasped a branch to cut, the scream came again, closer this time, and I heard the trees a way off shake as if blown by a fierce wind.

I managed to control myself long enough to cut the branch, and that seemed to give me some purpose, something to focus upon. Within a short while I had cut three more and was starting on the fourth when I heard my Master shout for me. I ran back to the camp, accompanied by another, louder scream that seemed to come from but yards away. Again accompanied by the terrible shaking of the canopy, I was certain that there might be one more before whatever it was burst from the trees and we would have to fight.

I ran back to Master Chang, who had also collected staves. He had split his and motioned me to do the same. While I drove my knife down through the branches, I could see him bent over, carving runes into the freshly cut wood and muttering the Protection. He finished and moved swiftly a few feet from the camp, ramming his knife into the ground to dig a hole deep enough to support the stave.

I continued to split the wood while he ran back to me and quickly carved another Protection bindrune. When I had finished splitting the staves I carved a bindrune myself, my hands shaking and unsure, while he carved and ran, carved and ran. Eventually he took mine and placed it at the end of the arc of staves that provided a barrier between us and the trees, and came back to stand with me, panting and alert.

The scream came again, this time right before us, and the trees whipped back and forth, thrashing as if in pain. This scream did not cease for many minutes and within the shaking boughs I could see something darker, as if the shadows of the night were taking form and giving vent to their anger.

How long we stood facing that thing I do not know, even now, looking back over so many years, it could have been minutes or hours, but eventually the raging in the trees subsided.

I did not sleep any more that night.

Come the morning our camp remained in the shadow cast by the escarpment, but I could see the lightening of the sky and I breathed more easily. In truth, I had no idea whether what had come for us would be dissipated by the light, but I clung to the belief that it would.

Tea with the Deacon

The day starts with the remnants of a loaf of bread, smoked ham, cheese and tea. I have awoken early, as I tend to since Stonehouse. I slept surprisingly well and feel pleasantly refreshed, despite the early hour. The sun is only recently risen and I have opened the door and shutters to allow what little breeze there is from the river into the house.

Although I have not slept well for the last few months, I generally enjoy waking before the town rises. On many occasions I take a platter outside to break my fast on the wharf, watching the ships coming in or preparing to leave, depending on the tide. This morning I feel that there is a little coolness to the air, a freshness that has been missing for weeks, and I position myself next to the open window, enjoying the peace and savouring the food.

As I am spreading butter on another slice of bread there is a quiet knock at the kitchen door, and a soft voice calls my name.

"In here", I reply, and the tall, thin figure of Deacon Mustaine stalks into the kitchen "I hope I am not intruding," he says in his low, calm voice, "but I saw the door was open." He smiles and I indicate the chair opposite me.

"Please, join me for a bite. We do not have much, but I can supply you with as much tea as you can drink."

Mustaine is Deacon of the Church of the Bone White Mask, the large church-cum-hospital on the corner of Eastgate and Pale Mary Way. He and I have spoken on many occasions, and I like him. He is intelligent, quiet and capable of both listening and talking to suit the occasion.

I pour him some tea and he cuts himself a slice of bread. When he takes the cup he closes his eyes and offers a silent blessing. I feel slightly guilty for not joining him, but I can not. Stonehouse has shaken my faith in these small rituals. For his part, he simply butters his bread and takes a bite.

"I often walk in the morning," he says, "I enjoy the peace along the river front. I saw your door open and worried that something had happened to you." I look at him, and see the little light in his eyes. I lean forward, fixing his eyes with mine and say earnestly, "Lying is a sin."

He laughs softly. "Very true. But lying with the aim of eating with a friend is forgiven."

"I do not recall ever seeing that in The Redemption."

Mustaine winks and helps himself to some ham. We spend some time talking quietly. Secretary Reddick, the old woman who kept the Excise building running before my arrival, lives her days later than I, and I am keen to let her sleep on, as her temper is much shorter if she is woken before she is ready. She can become surprisingly sharp. I think she has spent so long by herself, looking after the Excise, that she has found the transition to sharing somewhat difficult. She is of an age where, I believe, she does not see the point in changing her routine now.

As a consequence we see each other most often in the evenings, by which time I am tired and she is looking forward to spending time reading. We share a meal, and I am becoming a reasonable cook. I have taken to experimenting with spices and dried fruits, trying, sometimes successfully, to replicate the delicate flavours of some of the dishes I have encountered in the market.

The Deacon makes small talk, and I enjoy it. Even though I slept well last night, the times when I sleep poorly outnumber the good, and my mind now finds it difficult to remove the visions of that strange, unsettling city. I do not know whether Alice suffers similarly. Perhaps I should ask one day.

We sit in silence for a while, comfortable in each other's company. Eventually, as the final piece of cheese disappears he says, "When will you tell about Stonehouse?"

I finish my mouthful and consider his question. The truth is that only Alice would ever understand what happened, and my experience is lesser than hers. Even Campion has remained ignorant as neither of us are comfortable with going over the events, so I am certainly not going to talk with someone I do not know overly well. However, there are things I do wish to discuss with him.

"Forgive me, but I am not going to answer your question. However, I do have one for you."

He smiles and raises his eyebrows.

"How many gods are there?"

His smile fixes a little, and he sips his coffee. His answer, when it comes, is a little disappointing. "You have read The Redemption. What does it say?"

I sigh, but he looks hard at me. "I know the Redemption," I say, "that there are no gods but the Queen."

Mustaine nods, "And you find this answer unsatisfactory." It is not a question, but a statement of fact. I decide to be honest, and say, almost apologetically, "I know it to be false."

Mustaine breathes deeply and leans in, clasping his hands, and quietly, softly, says, "What did you see in Stonehouse?"

"Do not ask again, please. For the moment, suffice it to say that I now find The Redemption questionable."

"Be careful who you say this to. Such talk is not approved of."

"I know, and that is why I can not tell you more."

The Deacon's long fingers drum together as he thinks. Finally, he reaches a decision and draws breath. "Officially things are as described in The Redemption, however, there are scholars who look at texts from the Old World. It is known that other gods were worshipped, and, although it might be considered blasphemous to say, I find it difficult to believe that everyone who worshipped the old gods did so in the knowledge that they were really worshipping phantoms. Indeed, there are several religions from before the Great Conflagration whose gods commanded that they were the only ones."

This puzzled me slightly, but the ways of the Old World were strange. However, is this so different from the current situation, where a god claims to be the only one while, in a small village, something quite different is being worshipped?

"And what about now?"

Mustaine considers and then replies. "There may well be communities, cut off from the main towns, where belief goes astray, leading to the concept that there are entities other than the Queen to worship, I am sure. Traditionally the Church has been lenient on such belief, so long as penance is observed."

He looks at me, his head slightly to one side. "I get the impression I have not answered your question."

I do not know what answer I expected, but he is right. This feels like sophistry or propaganda and it does not help, but I feel that to push further now could lead to an argument, and I do not wish to fall out with my friend, so I say, "No, no. It is as I expected."

"So," I continue, with a forced smile to my voice, "what are your plans for the day?"

He looks at me a little quizzically, but decides against pushing things and is about to answer when there is the sound of shouting from outside. This is not uncommon, as when ships dock there is a lot of communication between the sailors and porters, but this sounds different, more urgent. The shouts rise in intensity before a terrible crunching, splintering sound drowns them all out.

Both Mustaine and I rise quickly, and head outside. The cause of the noise is not hard to fathom, as, a way off to our right, a great ship, her prow rising perhaps ten feet above the boards of the quay, has crashed whilst trying to dock at Ropemaker's Wharf. The thick oak boards have pierced the hull, splintering wood and sending men onto their backs. The ship has driven itself deep onto the Wharf, and has only just come to rest when we step from the Excise.

The Lady Jennifer

Deacon Mustaine and I make our way along the wharf towards the ship. Her prow has ridden up somewhat and there are porters crowded around her. A small knot of people are huddled together where the ship and wharf meet and, as we near, I realise that someone is either trapped or injured.

The ship is still over a hundred feet away, and my leg prevents me from running. Deacon Mustaine is not hindered, and he runs ahead. My slower pace allows me to appraise the scene, and the force with which the ship has struck the wharf is apparent. It looks as if she made no attempt to slow, but rammed into the dock at high speed. The shouts are mixed with cries of pain, and I fear that there may be many casualties.

Sailors have thrown ropes from the deck to the quay, and porters are securing them. It occurs to me that any rescue attempts must be made swiftly as the tide is on the turn and the river will drop by several feet, potentially causing even more damage to the ship.

When I finally arrive at the scene, and the walk has seemed to take months, there are many more people around. Warehouse workers, local shop owners, market traders have all run to the scene, some to look, but many to offer assistance. Carts are being commandeered. The Deacon is kneeling with the little knot of people I had seen earlier, and I push my way through the crowd.

Even before I reach the front I know there is a serious problem, as I can see a pool of blood, fresh and slick, dripping through the gaps between the thick oak boards. The cries have subsided to a constant moan and, although

Mustaine is busy tending to the victim and blocking my view, I am aware that what I can see is bloodied and shattered. My guess is that a porter had the poor luck to be standing exactly where the ship hit, and one of his legs must have been caught, either between the ship and wharf or by the oak slabs as they splintered and snapped.

In truth, it matters little, as his leg is crushed to a pulp. Mustaine is working quickly and effectively, binding his wounds with strips of cloth ripped from his own robes. He gives orders to people close by and one of them quickly shouts for a cart to be brought close. Within seconds the injured man is lifted carefully onto the cart, which is then hauled swiftly away. Immediately the Deacon stands, looking around and calling to see if there are other injuries.

There is little I can do here, so I walk around the ship, taking care to keep away from those people working to make the scene safe. As I make my way along Ropemaker's Wharf, which runs perpendicular to the main river frontage, I see that a gangway has been placed to allow access to the ship, which, I note, is named *Lady Jennifer*.

I am about to board when a couple of men run down it from the deck, almost knocking into me. The first runs past, but the second looks back, shouting "Sorry, sir". They catch heavy ropes thrown from above and secure them onto the huge cast bronze hooks on the wharf.

The gang plank wobbles alarmingly and there is a cracking sound from the prow as the ship settles deeper onto its scars. Once aboard, I am almost overwhelmed by the sense of activity as, out of sight from below, the entire ship's crew are busy. Sails are being struck and secured and, in the background, I hear the sound of steam being released and I assume that the boilers for the Stirling engines are being dowsed. A couple of the crew are sitting on the deck, minor wounds being tended. I can see no-one with serious injuries, and I hope that the main issues from here will be practical rather than medical.

I know my skills, and there is nothing I can do to help, so I turn towards the cabins. This ship is a heavy, short beast designed for hugging the coast, carrying goods from port to port and spending large parts of her life in the harsh waters of the north, and her wheelhouse is fully enclosed. Stairs run down to the lower decks on either side. A cursory glance of the wheelhouse confirms that it is empty of people. Charts are scattered on the floor, along with a beautiful sextant.

What is missing is any clue as to the cause of the crash, so I head down to the lower deck. I choose the right-hand stairs and they take me into the fire box where the heat for the Stirling engines is generated. Two fireboxes are supported by large cast brass supports, and a host of pipes and dials run around the walls. The fires have been extinguished but I imagine this room is almost unbearable when the engines are operating as it is not large. An engineer is checking the machinery, and he looks up when I walk in. He starts when he sees my robe, but quickly gets back to his dials.

"What happened?" I ask, but he shrugs. "All I know is that I never got the command to reverse. I can not see anything from down here." He is extremely angry, and is busying himself in his work. I look around and see a door leading forward towards the bow.

The door is slightly stuck and requires a kick to open it, evidence of the damage done to the hull, I think. It opens into a dark corridor along which are a couple of doors, with another door at the end. There are hatches along the exterior wall, and I open them to allow some light in. The first door opens into a simple room with some hammocks stretched between the walls, and, following a quick check, the next room is the same. That leaves the door at the end of the corridor.

It dawns on me that I have not yet seen any of the officers. There seemed to be no-one giving orders on deck and I have neither seen nor heard anyone down here. The door at the end opens into a reasonably large cabin, with a cot rather than a hammock, a table on which a log lies open and rolls of maps. It, like the rest of the ship, is devoid of officers.

I look at the log, but the writing makes no sense to me.

When I return to the deck the activity has lessened, and I click my way to the men standing at the prow. One of them looks my way as I approach and heads towards me. As he nears he half turns and calls back, "Be ready to give slack as the tide retreats." There is a general murmur of agreement from the men, and I note that they are holding ropes.

The man nods in greeting, and I can see a cold fury in his face, along with a deep weariness. "Osiah Jansum," he says, "Loadmaster for this ship."

I introduce myself and then enquire as to the whereabouts of the senior crew. Jansum, a large, muscular man with very short-cropped dark hair, swears. "This is a small ship, sir. We go from port to port and most of us have been on her for some time. The only high-ranker was Captain Haydon."

"Was?"

"Yes, sir." He still looks furious. "He jumped overboard about ten minutes before we hit the Quay." As he says this the import of what he relays seems to hit him, and his face falls. It is as if his anger had sustained him and, as it leaves he seems to change, becoming thoughtful and even a little shaken. "He set course, locked the steering, and jumped into the river. We were running at full speed, such as it was, and he locked off the steering and jumped."

Before I can say anything the ship gives a lurch and a mighty creak. Jansum turns swiftly and runs back to his men, barking orders to let out more rope. There is a terrific splintering sound from the bow. Jansum turns back and shouts to me, "You had best get off the ship."

As the deck gives another splintering crack I move as fast as my stiff leg will allow, back down the stairs. I hobble along the corridor, aware that the ship has moved and settled again as I constantly find myself stumbling into the wall. As quickly as possible I grab the log and return to deck. As I am disembarking I see that the holds have been opened and porters are removing crates as rapidly as possible, piling them up onto the wharf in an attempt to lighten the ship.

The wharf is extremely busy now, and there are hundreds of bodies either unloading the *Lady Jennifer* or working to make the wharf safe. I squeeze past porters and longshoremen laden with boxes and crates, all working extremely quickly to try and save the cargo while the ship is still safe to board.

I have to push my way through, and several times I almost lose my footing whilst attempting to hold onto the heavy book with one hand and keeping my stick from finding the slight gaps between the boards. Eventually, after what feels like hours, I am through and able to breathe more easily. I walk a little way away, heading towards the Excise, and then turn back to watch the proceedings. The pile of crates salvaged from the hold is being moved further onto The Wharf, where a senior Longshoreman is ordering them into warehouses in order to clear the thoroughfare. Their efforts are bearing fruit, as I believe the ship is riding slightly higher, but with low tide on the way, there will be no let up in their work. I am no expert on such things, but I imagine the *Lady Jennifer* will be stuck there for some time.

As I stand and watch, a familiar figure sidles alongside the warehouses and joins me. "Well, that is a bit of a mess," says Alice, a slight grin on her lips. "More so than you know," I reply, and she looks at me, her face falling and she tilts her head quizzically.

"I need you to read something for me, and quickly."

She responds with a drawn out, "Very well," that is more sigh than reply.

"Can you take a little time away from Master Evenright?"

"I can. The work he is doing now is so intricate I feel that I am pretty useless." She seems a little saddened by this.

"Surely not," I say, trying to help her see a brighter side, "I know your work to be excellent."

She blushes slightly, and says, "Not compared to him. He is currently working on something special." I open my mouth, but she is already cutting me off, "About which I can say nothing, other than he has begun using parts from the Boat to make it."

"In that case, would you please go to him now and ask him to give me the day with you, and then come straight to the Excise." I scan the crowd, looking for a particular person. "Is your uncle here?"

She also looks around, standing on tiptoe to try and see better, "I expect so…yes. Over there, close to the Henderson warehouse." She points and I can make out Campion's grey robe through the constantly moving bodies.

"Ask him to come to me, and please be as swift as you can." She nods and moves away, lithely skipping through the throng, moving with a grace I could not have equalled even in my youth. I see her talking with Campion and then pointing in my direction, but then porters carrying a large case block the view and, when I am able to see past, she has gone and Campion is walking towards me.

He arrives looking dark and quietly furious. "This is going to take ages to sort out. Honestly, I have never seen such a reckless act of atrocious seamanship. The captain will be treated harshly for this."

"He will not," I say, and he looks at me with barely disguised anger, "He is dead, or, if not dead now, he shall be soon. He jumped overboard in the middle of the channel after setting the ship on its collision course."

His eyes widen. "This was deliberate?" he asks, incredulity in his voice, gesturing towards the wreckage.

"It was, but there is more." He swings his head back round to me, and his expression is one of cautious expectation.

"I spoke to the Senior Loader, and the captain's actions sit badly with me. I know there will need to be a full enquiry, but," I show him the Log, "I need to go through this now. If there is something more to this I need to know immediately and put a plan into action. You shall have it back within a day or two."

He looks from the book to the organised chaos around the ship and back to the book. I can see he is thinking hard, weighing, no doubt, his responsibilities as an Judiciary against his past experience with me. "Very well. I pray you find nothing, but either way I must have it back tomorrow. Someone will swing for this."

Captain Haydon's Log

A little time later I am sat in my office, a pot of coffee brewing, shutters closed and Alice leafing through the Log. What I originally took for a single bound book is actually hundreds of loose leafs held together by brass pillars. As well as the day-to-day record of weather, tides, headings and crew rota it also includes cargo manifests and a personal diary, and Alice is ploughing through the pages of small, dense writing. I have asked her to start a month before today, in the hope that whatever caused the captain's breakdown will come to light. If not then we shall look at the previous month.

The writing is superficially beautiful, elegant and neat with extended risers and descenders but, as Alice's grunts and pauses attest, all this additional prettiness makes it difficult to read. She is following the text with her finger, mouthing words quietly to herself, making copious notes and occasionally screwing up her eyes and exclaiming things like "Oh, learn to write, man."

Eventually, after several cups of coffee, she looks up, her face pale. "Well?" I ask.

Alice breathes heavily, and swallows hard before speaking. "Something happened on the last section of their voyage. I shall read the last few entries."

I grind more coffee, boil some water, and settle down to listen. From my, admittedly limited, understanding, the *Lady Jennifer* is a shallow draft ship built to do short hops along the coast, picking up and dropping cargo as she goes, and then docking at a larger port in order for larger, more robust, ships to take certain items further afield. Her shallow draft enables her to access the small harbours and communities that would otherwise have to rely on land-trains to trade, even navigating up some of the larger rivers. It also makes her rather prone to rocking horribly in rough weather, leading to her class of ship being known as "upchuckers".

Some years ago it was hoped that air-boats might take on the mundane trading routes ships like this run, but the weather has deteriorated and storms are now commonplace all year. The boats can not fly in anything but a light breeze and the loss of three large vessels last year has made owners wary of their use for all but the most time-critical of voyages.

Alice clears her throat and, finger tracing her words, begins to read.

June 12 576AGC

Trevoze.

Spent the night anchored off Trevoze. Slept well. Crew caught many fish and we enjoyed them with fresh bread from the village.

Navigating away from Trevoze is not easy. The choice is to run between the two islands, which tidal race can reduce the day's sail by two hours or more, or skirt around them. The crew have stowed the cargo well, and the ship is running smooth, so I ran the race. The Lady behaved beautifully, the hold being full enables her to drive through chop more efficiently and we ran it without recourse to engines.

The sea, once we cleared the race, was calm, and what wind there was soon died and we had to fire up the boiler. I am concerned about the amount of fuel we have as we have had to use the engines far more than I calculated.

The next port of New Clovelly, there to pick up dried fish and wool. I shall try and source some coal, but it is in precious short supply here.

Docked at New Clovelly in the early evening. It is always unnerving, as the Old World stone harbour wall is still in place. The ship goes silent as we pass.

June 13 576AGC

New Clovelly.

The village clings to the steep, wooded slopes, straddling a clear river which runs to the sea, culminating in a waterfall, beside which we moored. Despite the proximity of the stone harbour, this is as pleasant a spot as I encounter, and I always look forward to docking here. The Lady can come almost to the beach so it is worth rowing to land where we can set a decent fire and enjoy the hospitality of the villagers.

We ate well, roasting a whole sheep supplied to us and drinking the excellent beer made in the village. We were all in good spirits and I slept well on the beach.

June 14 576AGC

New Clovelly to Wood Bay

The warmth and stillness continue. We took the barrels of dried fish and sheepskins, paying slightly over the odds, but worth it for the welcome we always receive, and cast off mid-morning. This is a short hop, being only some 30 miles, but the lack of wind is very troubling. There was no coal available at NC and our stocks are low. If there is none at Wood Bay we might have to put in at Flatome and pay the extortionate prices for a barge to come from Brean.

The coast as we head north is rugged and quite majestic. It only eases at the mouth of the estuary at Appledoor, into which I have sailed in the past, but the sands have shifted over the last few years, meaning that even The Lady with her shallow draft can no longer make her way inland. What will become of Appledoor itself I do not know, as the estuary wharf is the only way of getting goods in or out in quantity, it being sat within an island formed by the collapse of the land to the south. My guess is that the village shall die.

The journey to Wood Bay is uneventful, if slow, as we are reliant entirely on our engines, and I am trying to eke out our fuel.

We pull in at Wood Bay mid-afternoon. I have never been here before. I was asked to carry a crate by means of an advanced, pre-paid docket handed to me when we left Gloster in May. Skins and salted pork, to a weight of 130 pounds. The bay is actually nicely suited to ships like The Lady, but the steep sided, heavily wooded cliffs make any meaningful approach from land impossible.

A signal fire had been lit to help guide us in and Hopgood and Mortimer rowed ashore, returning with a large, heavy crate. I could see poor houses in the bay but no-one came to help them. In small ports this is not unusual, as the arrival time of ships such as The Lady can be erratic.

By the time the cargo had been secured it was too late to leave for Gloster, and so we settled in for the night. A good, long day tomorrow should see us back in civilisation.

June 15 576AGC

Slept poorly. Very restless. So much so that I gave up the attempt before dawn and spent time on deck. The sea was glass-smooth, and a bright moon shone, which should have made the scene quite beautiful, but my eyes could not appreciate it. It was like something brittle, a facade behind which a terrible vision sat.

When the sun rose the feeling dissipated somewhat, but it soon became apparent that the crew were also not as rested as they should be, and we were very keen to leave for home. I have encountered this before, and it is not uncommon towards the end of a trading leg when everyone is tired and looking forward to some time with their family. However, it soon became apparent that the act of leaving Wood Bay did not lift our spirits. We were still becalmed, and I realised that we would indeed have to stop at Flatome, something I was loathe to do but, unless there was a breeze, also something I had no choice in doing.

This meant a delay and the crew grumbled, even Mortimer, who is normally as easy going a chap as is possible to meet.

The mood of the crew when we pulled into Flatome was bad, especially as it had taken longer to reach than anticipated. A failure of a bearing had reduced our speed to 4 knots, so it had taken seven and a half hours to cover what should have taken under four.

Once anchored, I sent up the black flag to indicate our requirements, knowing that we would be here for the night.

June 16 576AGC

I am unsure whether I slept. If I did my dreams were horribly vivid. If I did not then my mind is finding its way to places it should not go. The details are unclear, but the stars were black in a bright sky. I have spent the time since raising the flag in here, away from the others with their whispers and foul faces. I feel that if I were to stay with them I should wish to strike them, or worse.

I heard loud arguing at some point in the night, and found myself hoping that whoever was involved would succumb to their instincts and one another. I knew they were arguing about me and my decisions, that they believe we would never have had to dock here had I not been in command. The truth is that their laziness and lack of basic ability has cost us time and fuel and I shall waste no time in getting rid of them once we make Gloster.

The supplies can not come soon enough.

Update: Come nightfall no barges had appeared and no coal delivered.

June 17 576AGC

Still no sign of the lazy bitches from Brean, so we sit here unable to move. The anger within the crew boiled over last night, and Wilson took a beating. I do not know the reasons behind it, but there is little doubt he deserved what he got and, had I not feared such treatment myself, I would have gladly joined in.

There is a lake in my dreams, into which the twin suns sink at night beneath black stars. Behind it all is a thing whose face is pure white and I am blessed above all as Queen Death herself has come to me. If she comes tonight I shall open myself to her.

Update: Coal delivered late, so we can slowly prepare for our final journey.

At this point Alice stops reading. I have been engrossed listening to her and it takes me a while to realise she is not continuing. "Is that it?", I ask. She shakes her head slightly, and there is something in her eyes that makes me pause, so I gently ask, "What is it?"

She inhales deeply before answering, and when she does her voice is quiet, nervous. "I know where this will lead." She pauses and I remain silent, allowing her time to collect her thoughts. "I know that you will need to follow it, and that I will have to follow you, and I am frightened as to where it will lead."

I draw my hand across my mouth. "It will lead where it leads," I say, "whether you need to come is up to you." Anger crosses her face, and I hold up my hand, "But, I will do everything in my power to protect you, whatever you decide. I need to hear the rest, though."

She looks down and mutters, "Read it yourself, then," under her breath. She taps her fingers on the table a couple of times, shakes her head, and continues to read.

June 18 576AGC

Finally on the way to Gloster. The crew are sullen and there is an undercurrent of suppressed violence, but the thought of home is making them work. The noise of the broken bearing resonates through the hull, a constant drone that hurts my head. I can not wait to be off this ship, to be away from those stinking men. We are still only making four knots, so the journey will take eight hours.

"I think the following were written at different times," Alice mutters, "and they become difficult to read."

I closed my eyes for a few minutes. The white mask was there, close to me, obscuring the lake. There is a stench on the ship that I can not place.

Alice pauses again, in part, I think, because the writing has become spidery, as if the author is writing hastily in order to commit his thoughts to the page before they disappear.

It is a fearful thing, to fall into the hands of the living God. The mask was close and a foul hand reached up and slipped it off and the Queen was revealed to me, a face of corruption and pus. Stars wheeled in its yellow hood and my screams were drunk as wine.

She looks up, and I understand why she is frightened. "Did they bring it here?" I think hard. The most likely explanation is that the captain was Fear-Ridden, that he was infected by something brought onto the ship which was then released. I remember my old master telling me of rituals that may build Fear and project it to a focus, but I have never seen it. If that is the case then the crate is now no more than a wooden box as its evil will have been used to ride the captain. Even if the box were full of shaped stone its effects would not have been that quick. No, my guess is that there is something in Wood Bay that needs dealing with. The amount of damage it has already done suggests that it is powerful, and the illusions it cast into Captain Haydon's mind are worrying indeed. That it exists on a shipping route is of concern, and I am also aware that I have not heard of a Watcher south west of here in many, many years. There is also the fact that this captain has been suffering similar dreams to myself, and I am aware that my desire to face the Yellow King and kill it is clouding my judgement. However, I also know that, unless I attempt it, I shall not sleep well again. I also know that I would rather not go alone.

Preparations

Alice and I stare at each other for a while. She, I am sure, knows exactly what I am thinking, and before I say anything, she says, thin-lipped, "You want to go to Wood Bay." I nod, slowly. "And you want me to accompany you." Neither are phrased as questions.

Alice sighs heavily, and I can almost see the argument she is having with herself. I give her a few seconds, and then say, "I can not guarantee your safety, but I think it is important that you accompany me." She looks at me and I see anger behind her eyes.

"You can not guarantee my safety? Really?"

I raise my hands in an attempt to placate her, but she does not let me get a word out. "You failed to protect me in Stonehouse, so why should I expect anything different now?" She leans forward, her finger jabbing at me as she speaks, her voice raising. "You want me to go along as a buffer, in case you run into someone you can not deal with. You want me to be a shield, someone to step before the King while you carve some runes and convince yourself that there is no more you can do while it rips into my head again." She is shouting now, face red and mouth flecked with spittle.

Her anger is infectious, and I shout back at her, "Yes. You are right. I want you to go to help me. What do you expect? I am old and burned…" She cuts me off swiftly.

"Do not try the sad, pathetic old man routine with me."

"Very well, " I say, quietly, "what if I train you as we travel? That way you will be as prepared as you can be when we reach Wood Bay."

She stops, her finger still pointing at me. "What?" She looks sideways at me, her eyes narrowing and I sigh long and deep.

"I can train you in ways to protect yourself."

She looks harder at me. "Uncle told me that you had said you would never train anyone again."

"Well, things have changed," I reply, gruffly. "What I actually said was that I did not want to take on an apprentice. This is different. And you are right." At this she raises an eyebrow. "I do need you to be there should I run into something I can not deal with. You are the only person I trust enough."

As Alice is considering a reply, Secretary Reddick pads softly into the kitchen. "Do not mind me," she says as she walks towards the pantry, "carry on shouting at each other when I am gone." She loads a plate with bread and cheeses and potters out again, no doubt heading to her study chair.

Alice lowers her finger. When she speaks it is with a voice that is quiet and determined, hiding the fear, just as I am trying to do. "I do not want to face the King alone again."

I shake my head. "If I knew what had happened to you I would have come for you immediately. If I could have gone in your place, believe me, I would. I do not know how you bear it." I falter. "My dreams…" I can not continue with the sentence. Telling her that my dreams are horribly similar to those of Captain Haydon would be giving too much of myself away.

Alice takes a deep breath. When she speaks again, she is calm, more herself. "I will come. And I will hold you to your word."

"Thank you."

"How far is Wood Bay?"

"I do not know. It can not be that far as it was only a couple of day's travel. Maybe eighty miles."

"That will be several days by cart." She does not say so, but the implication that it will also be several days in close proximity with me is evident in her expression.

"Plenty of time to teach you the basics," I say, with forced brightness. Alice does not even smile.

A while later, Alice is securing a horse and cart and I am sitting with Campion in his office. The day is still fine, but there is the beginning of a cooler breeze coming in off the coast. We have been talking over the Captain's Log, and he agrees with me that I should investigate Wood Bay. His belief, like mine, is that Fear is localised and that investigating such a strong infestation is necessary. He has agreed to check the shipment while I am away. He has also given me leave to take what supplies I need and to charge the town for them.

As we sit, listening to the sounds of the town outside, I broach the subject of Alice. When I first mention the idea of taking her he shakes his head firmly. His objection is one borne of love for his niece and all I can do is try and reassure him. The difficulty is that he knows both the dangers and my own personality.

"You become obsessed, too focussed on the quarry." I try to raise arguments to do with my age and mobility, but he waves them aside. "These only make you more dangerous to those around you, " he growls, "for you send others in to soften the ground. Makes you a good Watcher." He pauses. "And a poor companion."

I huff, and he continues. "I am also aware that she is an adult and more than capable of making her own decisions. So, if you do take her along there is little I can do to prevent it. But know this," and here he leans in, his voice menacing and firm, "should anything happen to her I shall hold you responsible."

I bridle, but in truth I expected nothing less. Campion is a creature of show and bluster, although a decent Judiciary, but I do not doubt that the threat is not made lightly.

"I promise I shall look out for her."

Campion grunts and I take that noise as acquiescence.

My last meeting is with Inigo Evenright, Alice's part time Master and a skilled engineer. His workshop is on the south of the town, just off Queen's Drive, the wide street that curves around joining Eastgate and Southgate. The town is busy today, and the walk is slowed by the crowds of people. I am looking forward to leaving this jostling, noisy place, and my temper is short due to the heat and the events of the morning. When I am barged into and almost sent sprawling by a young lout pushing his way through the crowd I lash out with my stick, catching his legs and making him fall. He slams into the ground hard, dropping his sack which lands with a crashing sound. He regains his feet quickly and, fists balled, looks around for the cause of his fall.

When he sees me standing firm, stick in one hand, the other resting on the hilt of my knife, he baulks and backs away. Without a word he picks up his sack to the noise of what sounds like broken pottery, turns, and runs.

Master Evenright's workshop takes up several shops along Queen's Drive, and I have been here a few times, each time keen to discover exactly what new device is being worked upon. Evenright seems to have no boundaries to his mechanical and artistic skill, as he ranges from apparatus to heat houses to delicate mechanical insects that operate by springs and scuttle across a table when wound up.

He and I have spent some time together in the past, chatting happily over wine, but his reaction when I walk in is subdued. I assume that Alice has been here and told him that she is leaving for a while. He is sat at his workbench, bent over a drawing, pen in hand, which scratches on the page. Without looking up he says, "You have already taken my horse, what more do you want?"

I stand still, my mouth foolishly working silently as I try and get my mind around his words. Before I can formulate an answer he laughs, and he looks up at me, winking as he does so. He places the pen into a little cup and stands up, walking round his bench to greet me, holding out his hand, which I grasp. I shake a finger at him, "You swine."

"What I said was true," he laughs, "Alice came a little while ago to take my horse and cart."

"Ah. I am sorry."

He shrugs, and then says, "So, what can I do for you?"

I reach into my robe and pull out my rune-knife, handing it to him. Inigo takes it carefully and immediately starts examining it, lowering his face and slowly turning it over and over.

"Could you make one like it? Not the same, but the blade of iron is vital."

He looks up, his eyes peering at me through raised eyebrows. "For Alice,"

I say. He keeps his eyes on me, but they narrow slightly. "Why would Alice need a knife like this?" he asks, his question quiet. I decide not to tell him the full answer, but simply say, "For her protection."

Inigo looks down again, turning the knife over slowly, thoughtfully. "Any knife can be used for protection, and Alice is hardly defenceless."

I decide to keep my silence. If she wants to tell him about Stonehouse and the King, that is her prerogative, I will not do it for her. So I ask, "Can you?"

He hands it back to me. "Of course," he says. "A week?"

"Thank you. What will the charge be?"

He shakes his head. "Nothing. If Alice needs this then it shall be a gift."

I leave him and head back to the Excise. The day has warmed up and the slight breeze has gone. I hope that it will be a little cooler out of the town, away from the crush of bodies and the walls. A little voice in my head sings at the prospect of getting away, of being on the road again and doing what I know. It is a treacherous little voice as it knows it is putting Alice in potential danger, but it cares little for that. It repeats instead that the journey is necessary, that there is little chance of encountering anything particularly nasty and that it is a good teaching opportunity. I do not like this voice, but it is persuasive.

The following morning, while I am pondering which items will be necessary for me to take, I hear the door open and someone enter. On going downstairs and looking out of the door a large, two-wheeled cart is sat close by, with the biggest horse I have ever seen between the shafts. Its shoulder is taller than I am and when I walk close to it, it looks at me with deep, docile eyes. I reach up and pat the side of its massive head, scratching its cheek.

"You have met Harrold, then." Alice comes out of the building, carrying a large draw-sack. She hefts it around me and heaves it into the cart, climbing nimbly up and tying it beneath the seat. "Harrold?", I ask.

"Master Evenright's horse."

I look into Harrold's eye, gently blowing his great nose. "Hello Harrold." He looks back at me and I am instantly taken with his gentle demeanour.

I tear myself away from Harrold, and head into the Excise. Upstairs, in

PREPARATIONS

the room that I had allotted to be my study but which is simply a place to store old possessions, I find, after not a little sweat and swearing, the canvas tarpaulin and supports that I can use to cover the back of the cart, in case we need to sleep in the wild. In theory we should be stopping at Way Stations, at least until we leave the main roads, but one never knows what a journey might throw up. It is, however, heavier than I remember, so I have to drag it downstairs, bumping it noisily on each tread. Secretary Reddick is watching me carefully from the kitchen door. I know that she will examine the woodwork when I am gone.

As I drag the bundle outside, Alice calls down to me. "I have picked up bread, waxed cheeses, dried ham and a couple of bottles of wine."

"Well done," I grunt, lifting the end of the tarpaulin for her to grab. Between us we manage to manhandle it into the cart, where it is stowed. We take stock of what we have, and while deciding whether to add to our inventory, Campion appears, a roll of parchment in his hand.

"Thought you might need this," he says, and offers the roll to me. I unroll it on the back of the cart. It is a map, covering Gloster and the country for many miles to the south west, almost to the border of the Cornish lands. I look closely, and see that it marks roads, areas of forest, rivers and, most importantly, Old World ruins. The detail is exquisite. As I trace the southern coast line of the River Severn I find Wood Bay. The map does not show much in the way of ruins around it, which gives me a little hope.

"This is remarkable," I say, a little breathlessly. "It is based on an Old World osmap," he says. "They covered the whole country in meticulous detail. We do not have all of them, but luckily we do have the ones that cover this area. This copy was made some years ago. Try not to damage it."

I thank him, and he walks away from me, stiff and unsmiling. I am not sure when, or if, he will forgive me for taking Alice with me. As I watch them hug I question my motives again, but it is that treacherous little voice that answers, and I feel content in my decisions.

Thoughts and Remembrances - Pestilence

My mother died when I turned fifteen. I was still in training with Master Isaac Chang and had received my first tattoos, the protection runes across my face. I remember the pride in receiving them, I do not remember the pain, but that may be simply because of what happened soon after.

Master Chang was kind, calm and efficient at dealing with Fear. We had been slowly making our way from Oxford east, with him teaching me as we travelled. This was time to learn away from the rigours of the school, and I was enjoying it. He instructed me on how to carve runes; it is very different carving in a safe environment compared to the wild when protecting a camp might be the difference between sleeping and fighting the night away.

We had been on the road for three months, meandering our way from village to village, re-cutting Way Markers if required, and carving runes to help those settlements abutting the Old World. I remember that as being a very pleasant summer. Master Chang was very patient, and I enjoyed his company. I found particular pleasure in fishing when we settled next to rivers, and still retain a fondness for fire-cooked fresh fish.

I was under the impression that our route was random, that we were simply going where his whims took us, until I realised that I recognised the landscape. I remember that feeling very clearly, the joy that I knew where I was, that within a day I could be with my parents, who I had not seen for many years. I asked Master Chang whether we might visit my family, and he smiled and nodded. The fact that the following day would be my fifteenth birthday merely added to the excitement I felt, and it only occurred to me much later that my Master must have planned it, plotting a route that would enable me to go home when I entered manhood.

The countryside around Statfield is thick with the Old World, and the road passes north of the broken and desolate villages. The land is flat, and therefore visibility is somewhat restricted by trees and hedges, so the village is almost completely hidden until one walks through a thick stand of trees.

It lies a little way to the west of a major road running north/south from the London Glass all the way to the colder, wilder lands far to the north. Sections of it are almost perfectly straight and were, I have been told, laid out many hundreds of years before the Great Conflagration. It occasionally has to detour around a shattered town, but it is, for the most part, wide and well maintained.

Statfield provides a good staging point for travellers, as it sits at a junction of the North Road and the route we had taken towards the west. The road heads further east, and eventually finds its way to the coast, and the trading ports at Landermere. The village is surrounded by fields segmented into well-maintained stock yards by miles of wooden fences. A few times a year it is the home of massive animal auctions.

And now it is quiet.

We walk together into the village. House doors are closed and the windows shuttered. The few people we see are stooped, weak and look sick. I recognise no-one. Statfield is built around a crossroads with a few streets branching off, which means I have a clear view of the whole place as I move slowly through. My parent's workshop is just off the main north road and when I reach it the place is shut. Even the front door, which I remember as always open. I stand in front of it, afraid to open it, and the other thing that is wrong, that has been prodding my brain since I walked in, manages to make itself heard.

The smell.

There is a smell of corruption, of death, and it is undercut by a slight saltiness. Master Chang is standing silently by me, and he speaks quietly, "Hobb, touch little, eat nothing, drink nothing. This is cholera, I have seen it kill whole towns."

I stared at the door, either unable or unable to open it, I can not remember which. Eventually, Chang reached around me and thumbed the latch and, as the door swung inwards the smell that hit me made me wretch. The darkness inside seems to be thick with the stench of shit and the sweet, heavy stink of rotten meat.

The door opens into the workshop, where my father made and repaired boots. His reputation had carried for many miles, and there were traders who would stall the purchase of new boots until they could get to see him, and the workshop was always spotless, but homely. I loved the smell of the leather, and the sound of the thread being pulled through it, but now it is dead and dark and the smell is no longer comforting.

A soft groan issues from the room next door, and when I push the door with my elbow, I am greeted by a sight that has never left me.

Lying on the floor, his arms around the grey, lifeless body of my mother, is my father. His eyes are sunken, skin pale and sweaty and he is in a pool of liquid that stinks of rotten fish and looks like rice.

Amazingly, he survived, but the disease ripped through the village and slaughtered nine in ten of the populace.

Master Chang and I stayed close to Statfield for two weeks, during which time my father's health improved. Cholera, it transpires, hits hard but dies fast once it has done its awful work and, if one survives the initial attack, recovers well after a few days.

So many did not survive the onslaught, many dying late in the same day they fell sick, that it was impossible to bury them, and a great pyre was built in the centre of the market fields. A memory I shall never lose involves carrying people, many of whom I knew, from their homes to that vast construct of logs and tinder. We layered the bodies and wood and, by the time we had brought everyone, it stood ten feet high and contained near a hundred people. The stench was truly horrific, for the weather was still warm and many bodies were decomposing. That, coupled with the cause of their death, created a stink that sat like a blanket on the village. One could move a few hundred yards away and smell only the warmth of the fields. There was a threshold, however, and once crossed, no smell beyond corruption held sway.

At that time, Watchers were able to perform services should the need arise, and, once we were certain the infection had run its course, Master Chang agreed to carry out the Committal. The nearest town with a Deacon was Bedford, a day's *ride away, and it was deemed, after meeting with the surviving villagers, that this would be too great a risk. Fear has been known to inhabit the dead, and there were so many potential homes that any delay in dealing with them could have been even more appalling than the situation we were in.*

Master Chang was, I hope to have established, a good man. He was relentless, but gentle with the innocent and as good company as I could have wished for. However, when he donned the Bone White Mask and began to intone the Committal, accompanied by the murmured responses of the survivors, grouped around the pyre on that late autumnal evening, I appreciated, for the first time, how much theatre a Senior Masker put into the rituals.

I think it was that realisation that pulled my mind away from the fact of dealing with a terrible situation, to understanding that the world, at least my small part of it, had changed forever. My mother, the kind, gentle woman who had given me my first lessons in life, had been taken by the Queen.

Not simply taken, but ripped from her life in pain and degradation. Taken by a god who cares not for our fleeting sorrows, but who has, like the Watchers, a terrible purpose. Looking back, I think this was where I lost my compassion for the Fear Ridden. I understood the Queen's place in the world with a new-found clarity and saw my place at her feet. As I allowed tears to fall for my mother, my heart hardened.

The Road South

The town is barely stirring as the cart trundles through the square. Harrold seems like a good, solid animal and settles into a steady walk which, I believe, he can keep at for hours. The cart is comfortable, the wheels being sprung, better to protect any delicate machinery Master Evenright needs to transport. Most useful is the large box beneath the seat, in which is locked my case. Given that the lock is of Master Evenright's design I am certain of its security.

Alice has recovered her usual cheeriness, happy to be on the move again.

I admit I am slightly apprehensive. My last trip away from home hardly went smoothly and, given the reason for this excursion, I am not entirely convinced there will be no similar trouble. However, such concerns are for the future. The day is bright and the road is long.

We leave Gloster, passing through the huge gates and earthen ramparts, and very soon are surrounded by open farmland. The crops, corn, wheat and some sort of cabbage, are all looking a little forlorn; a result of the recent incessant heat. Indeed, the temperature is building already and I look as far ahead as I can. There seems to be a sign of cloud on the southern horizon, but it is many miles from here. Even when cloud has built in recent days it quickly disperses and only adds more humidity to the air.

After a couple of miles the road slowly turns south, and I know from earlier in the year that we shall soon join the Emfie Road, the great trackway left behind after the Conflagration which runs for many miles to the south and north. We reach the crossing where, if we were to continue, we would soon find ourselves in the burnt remains of Stonehouse. I fancy I can see a little dark smudge in the distance, but that is surely my imagination for there are many turns of the road and stands of trees between here and there. Without pause I steer Harrold to the right and we start down the long slope to the Emfie. Alice, I note, turns to look towards Stonehouse, keeping her head facing towards it as we trundle away.

The road is wide and well maintained, for, aside from the coastal trade lanes, this is the main route for travel from the south-west to the north. Wool, cloth, salt meat, raw materials and fuel are all transported along this road, and traders often form long caravans for company and protection. Bandits may attack a small, heavily loaded wagon, but few will tackle twenty such vehicles.

Even as we start on the Emfie, a caravan of eight wagons grumbles and creaks its way past, pulled by oxen. We nod to the drivers as we pass, and are greeted similarly in return.

The road surface is made of hard, compressed stones, sunk into the ground and trampled flat by years of use. As the stone is unworked it does not attract Fear, and it is relatively smooth. Harrold keeps a steady pace, and we cover the miles very pleasantly, the reins resting lightly in my hands.

After a few hours, Alice reaches back and pulls a pack to her, opening it and removing a package wrapped in waxed cloth. Inside is bread, cheese and a couple of earthenware pots sealed with wax. Potted meat, I think, which makes me very happy. The weather is warm and I feel sweat starting to form beneath my robe. I might consider removing it if it were just Alice and I, but I am not prepared for the stares my burnt skin will attract.

Alice places the cloth and food on the seat between us, and we share the food as we move on. The road passes through a wide, open area where heavy stands of trees are kept away by constant clearing and management. Even so, the vegetation to our right is thick. To our left there is a swathe of scrub before the trees take over, and I have heard that this marks the original width of the road. If that is true it was truly enormous. As the road now stands it is easily thirty feet wide, but it must have been near a hundred feet. How much traffic pounded such a construction?

Shortly we pass a place where a great bridge must have stood, and I shiver as we plod through the gap between the ragged remains of great smooth stone supports. Even though the stone is cracked, broken and succumbing to the ministrations of brambles and trees, it is still evident. Many feet thick and with no visible joints, it almost appears as if the stone has been melted and re-formed to a sharp edged regularity. Both Alice and I feel the slight, almost imperceptible chill of Fear as the Shortly we pass a place where a great bridge must have stood, and I shiver as we plod through the gap between the ragged remains of great smooth stone supports. Even though the stone is cracked, broken and succumbing to the ministrations of brambles and trees, it is still evident. Many feet thick and with no visible joints, it almost appears as if the stone has been melted and re-formed to a sharp edged regularity. Both Alice and I feel the slight, almost imperceptible chill of Fear as the

Shortly we pass a place where a great bridge must have stood, and I shiver as we plod through the gap between the ragged remains of great smooth stone supports. Even though the stone is cracked, broken and succumbing to the ministrations of brambles and trees, it is still evident. Many feet thick and with no visible joints, it almost appears as if the stone has been melted and re-formed to a sharp-edged regularity. Both Alice and I feel the slight, almost imperceptible chill of Fear as the cart creaks its way past. Harrold does not seem to notice anything, and I find that I slightly envy him. No doubt there will be plenty more such constructions along our route, so maybe I should learn to be more Harrold than Hobb.

Both Alice and I have been largely silent, occasionally pointing out things of interest, but largely enjoying the simple pleasure of easy movement and fresh air. I had not realised how thick with stink the air in Gloster was until now. I must have noticed it when I first moved there, but the nose becomes accustomed to smell easily, and I am relishing how clean it is away from the thousands of bodies. In truth, the infrastructure the Council has organised for keeping the town clean is remarkable, but I much prefer this.

My assumption that Alice is quiet for similar reasons is broken when she speaks.

"Master Grey?" Her voice is quiet, and when I turn to look at her she is hunched forward, hands clasped together. She looks towards me, and I know what she is thinking.

"I fear the coming days."

"I know you do." I take a deep breath, and say calmly, "I shall protect you this time. I only want to see what the Captain encountered, so that I may know what further action to take, if any. You have my word that if there is the slightest hint that events similar to Stonehouse are underway, I shall keep you apart from them." I attempt a smile. "At any rate, you shall be better prepared as I intend to teach you protections you did not have last time."

She smiles half-heartedly, and nods. "Please, try to put your mind at ease. I shall not let anything harm you. I am prepared this time, and will be harsh on anything that threatens you."

She forces herself to relax. I do not know whether my assurances have helped, but I am fully prepared to take severe action against anyone I suspect of dealing with the Yellow King.

Over time, the gentle movement of the cart and the heat of the day begin to take their soft toll and, while Harrold keeps plodding, Alice climbs into the back and settles herself in the baggage to sleep. My head starts that terrible deep nod that signifies impending sleep. Although we are rarely truly alone on the road, the other travellers are spaced out enough for us to feel as if we have the landscape to ourselves for much of the time.

After a few hours I see a track leading off from the road, and a sign by it showing a crude image of a horse drinking and, although Harrold looks like he could go for many hours more, I gently point him down the track. After a short walk through tall bushes and trees which offer welcome shade, we come to the side of a lagoon. Several travellers are stopped here, their animals tied to posts close to the water. I find an empty place and steer Harrold towards it. When he finally stops I go to climb down from the cart, but find that my legs are stiff and painful. I make assorted old-man noises as I try and work some life into them and am aware that Alice has woken up and is watching me with a small grin on her face.

She quickly jumps down and deftly unhitches Harrold, leading him to the water. He is drinking before I can slither gracelessly from the seat. Alice shouts across to me, "Do you need a hand, old man?"

I bend, rubbing my left leg hard to try and get some feeling back into it, and shout back, "When you are as old and damaged as I then you may smirk." Eventually, I start to walk around, the pain in my leg slowly easing, and I realise that, jesting aside, I *am* feeling decidedly old. I will need to take breaks during the day, something I had not factored into the journey.

Alice is walking around as well, and I am fairly certain that she is feeling the results of the hours on the cart, but being considerably younger she is able to shake them off quickly. After a few minutes, during which time Harrold is enjoying the cool water, she approaches and we stand together, surveying the other travellers.

There are a couple of large wagons being hitched to oxen, the huge beasts standing calmly as the traces are attached. One of the drivers waves an acknowledgement to us, and Alice nods back. The sun is high and I realise that I am hungry, despite the food we had earlier, so I lean over the cart and rummage through the packs, eventually finding a large pie, which I pull out and place on the ground, spreading a cloth out to sit upon. Alice joins me after grabbing a large bottle of small beer.

I cut the pie, delighting in finding it full of mutton, dried fruit and potato, and we settle down comfortably to eat. Whilst chewing Alice asks how far I think we have come. I stand and retrieve the map that Campion gave me, smoothing it out between us. I can trace the Emfie Road and after a short while I find the lagoon we are sat next to. It looks as if we have covered around half the distance to the first Station, which is where we shall bed down tonight, so around three hours travel should see us there.

After this brief rest we continued. The landscape through which the road runs is largely flat, but with hills fairly close to our left. To our right, in the distance, lies the Severn, wide, brown and slow. Alice and I chat initially on leaving the lagoon, but we soon lapse into silence, both content, I think, to simply enjoy the rhythm of Harrold's steps and the rumbling creak of the wheels.

Eventually, the land begins to rise and we work our way up a long incline, taking perhaps a mile to reach the top, where the land again flattens out. To our left we have a glorious view across many miles of terrain, and I see smoke rising from the little villages and hamlets which must lie within the copses and forests. Large areas are clear, providing fertile fields in which I can see neat rows of crops. Sheep, small, white spots on the green, quietly graze on grass.

After perhaps another mile we reach the end of the plateau, and the road begins to descend again. If I peer, I can make out the Station in the distance at the bottom of the hill, a collection of buildings and stockades. The Emfie turns a sharp left at the Station, adding many miles to its original route, in order to avoid the dark mass before us. Sitting in the distance, squatting like a poorly healed scab, is the huge bulk of Old Bristol. At the centre of the broken, Fear-filled streets which cover as far as I can see before me, is the Bristol Glass, glinting in the sun; black, hard and covered in grey mist.

Erthcott

It is a quiet and sobering journey down the long incline. If I keep my eyes towards the left I can almost fool myself that there is nothing other than the green, lush countryside, but my eyes are drawn constantly to the darkness before us. Living in Enfield I was only around twelve miles from the great expanse of the London Glass, but it was never visible and I thought nothing of it. In Gloster it is easy to live one's life completely free of the idea that areas like that exist. Here, however, it is inescapable.

As we continue, heading ever lower, I try and take in the sheer size of the old town. I can see the shattered walls, covered with shrubs and creepers, sitting darkly amongst trees and extending from the bottom of the hill all the way towards the horizon. The road curls around to the left and disappears behind trees. Further in the distance, it reappears, skirting the enormity of the ruins, which extend for miles. They continue all the way to the Severn, which, at this point, is enormous, easily a mile wide and flat and brown and sluggish.

Alice is equally enthralled, and I feel her shudder slightly. "How can we ever be safe when there are places like this in the world?" she mutters, a small voice in the quiet of my contemplation. In truth, I do not know what to say. Given what was lurking in the centre of Stonehouse, which would sit, lost, within the smallest section of Old Bristol, I am similarly unnerved. The only consolation I can muster is that the very size of this place would work against it, at least as far as snaring people might go. Stonehouse was terrible simply because there were routes to the centre that were direct. They could be taken without having to spend too much time walking through the ruins. There could be no such short cuts here, and I believe that madness, or whatever foulness lurks in such places, would take a traveller well before they reached the Glass at the centre.

As I am mulling Alice speaks up.

"I have never seen such a huge expanse of the Old World before." She points towards the centre, where little glints of light shine against the darkness. "Is that Glass?" she asks.

"It is."

"Have you ever seen it up close?"

I shake my head, and say no. The thought of doing so even before Stonehouse was terrible, now it is unimaginable. "How was it made?", she asks.

"The official story is contained within the Redemption, as you should know. Queen Death saw the depravity of the Old World and sent fire to cleanse it. It was the first act of the Great Conflagration, which cleaned the Old World and halted the Fear."

Alice looks at me, and her face is quizzical. "I know the official line," she replies, "I want to hear your explanation."

I consider before answering. "There are aspects of the Redemption that I find inconsistent. I believe that the Fear rose from the Glass and Old World after the Conflagration."

"Why do you believe that?"

"Glass, ordinary glass, is made by heating sand to enormous temperatures. The Conflagration, whatever it was, turned whole towns made of stone and brick into black Glass. It did not happen to small towns or villages, and it did not even happen to every large town. There are many that are simply ruined by time. I believe that the Conflagration was accidental, wrought by men, and that the Fear rose from the ashes, also by accident. If it is this Yellow King, then he took advantage of a society that had been shattered."

"And the Queen?"

"She appeared after, a counter to despair and Fear, and has guided us ever since."

She nods, and then looks away from the Old World. As we travel further down the hill, the view of the ruins narrows and, by the time we reach the bottom, it is hidden by trees and shrubs. The road curves gently to the left and, after a few more minutes, the buildings of Erthcott Station begin to appear, peering round copses and bushes. The Station is huge, comprised of several large, two-storeyed buildings with steeply pitched, thatched roofs. Fences extend for many hundreds of yards, creating enclosures for cattle and horses, many of which are occupied.

Even from this distance, and we are still several hundred yards away, I can see the place is busy. People are milling around the buildings, and I can make out others in or near the pens, either tending to animals, or walking slowly around. These, I assume, are guards.

As Harrold pulls us slowly closer, a large wagon, heavy, painted black and pulled by four horses similar to ours, trundles out onto the road and turns towards us. After a short while we pass, and Alice and I lower our heads and cover our eyes as a mark of respect. This is a church transport and is heavily armoured, and escorted by well trained militia. I guess that it is carrying valuables to Gloster and beyond. The church acts as guarantor to merchants and businesses who deposit monies and are given Bills of Trust in return. These Bills may be used anywhere providing they are counter-signed and carry a code given to the holder at the time of deposit. This means that merchants can travel from town to town without carrying large sums of money, and still access their funds wherever they are.

The funds themselves are occasionally transferred from town to town in these imposing wagons. They are heavily constructed and guarded, but I feel that is more for show than real protection now, as anyone foolish enough to attack one would have the entire might of the church come down on them, let alone the wrath of the merchants and guilds - something that no-one could survive.

We round a low stable block and find ourselves in a large quad with three storey half-timbered buildings on the remaining sides. The whole place is about the same size as the market square in Gloster, and, just as there, stalls are set up around the edges. I am pleased to see that there is a Leathershodder, as Harrold will need new shoes before we set out, and I should buy a few sets in case other way stations are less accommodating.

Alice has the reins, and pulls Harrold to a stop when a stout man with a portable desk around his neck approaches us. He stomps around to her, looking slightly flustered, and barks, "Two of you?" I can see that Alice is about to retort in a way that might not help, so I lean over and reply before she can. "Yes, overnight but separate rooms."

He harrumphs, shaking his head as he runs his finger down the list on his desk. After a short wait he shakes his head more emphatically and, without looking up, says, "No. I can put you into one room or you can sleep in your cart. I can place you in the covered stable." He looks up from his papers at last, and finally notices my robes, at which point he mutters "Sorry, sir."

Alice answers before I can, "We shall take the room." I look quizzically at her and she shrugs. "This way we get beds and you know how restless you are." My expression must have gone from mild annoyance to embarrassed fury, and I swear she can feel me getting ready to explode. The administrator's face is switching from her to me and back rapidly, no doubt thinking all sorts of questionable things about our relationship, and Alice turns to me and says, with a wide grin and a shake of the head, "Mother used to say exactly the same thing."

I am now unsure whether to be angry or laugh, and the look of dawning understanding on the administrator's face does not help. He gives us directions to the room, and then hands over a set of keys kept inside his desk. As she gently guides Harrold towards the stable block she giggles, quietly.

The stables are massive and, as we approach we are stopped by a young man who asks for our stall number, which is stamped onto the key.

"Thirty two," says Alice, after a quick glance.

He waves towards a couple of lads who run forward. "The stall is for your horse only," he explains, "we shall unhitch the cart and it can stay here." He points to a selection other carts, all lined up against the outside wall and locked to the building by a padlocked bar through the wheels, which is fed through thick cast brass hoops driven into the ground.

"If you have anything of value then we can help you secure it."

"Thank you."

Alice jumps down, as do I, after my own fashion. The lads are efficient and it is not long before Harrold is settled in a warm, comfortable stall with thick hay and fresh water. Alice and I leave him munching happily and are pointed towards the large building to our right, which rivals anything in Gloster. Huge oak trusses rise thirty feet to a beautiful thatched roof, which is golden in the lowering sun. Wooden masks, each at least three feet high, their white paint only slightly pitted, sit either side of the large doors, which are hooked open allowing a steady stream of people in and out.

Inside, once my eyes have adjusted to the dark, I am stood in a huge Inn. I do not know how many tables there are, but it must be close to a hundred, and most are occupied. The noise is remarkable, a constant rumble of voices with the occasional barked laugh which rises and falls as if choreographed. Servers walk deftly between the tables, carrying jugs and platters. I stand, rooted to the spot. I am uncomfortable in crowds, my burns seem to become far more visible and I become clumsier, at least, that is how it feels.

Alice, I think, realises my discomfort, and points towards the far corner. "There is an empty table. I shall secure it." Before I can say anything she scoots away, almost dancing between servers, patrons and tables. I keep my eyes on her until she stops, and then start towards her. It takes me considerably longer to make the journey than it did her, but I make it without incident. The table is nestled up against the wall, in a dark alcove, and is as far away from the bustle of the main hall as possible. It is lit by oil lamps which cast very deep shadows and I am glad Alice has seen it As I am removing my robe to sit down, I notice that we are not alone. There is a man sat in the corner, in the darkest spot of an already dark table, a mug in front of him. I can not put my robe back on without appearing extremely rude, so I sit, hoping that the shadows will hide my pink and shiny skin.

Alice's expression offers an apology, but in truth, I did think it was extraordinarily lucky to find an empty table, and I smile that I am happy. As I sit I let out an involuntary groan, stretching my left leg for the first time since we stopped to allow Harrold a drink.

The figure pulls back his grey hood, revealing skin so pale as to be almost silver, long, pure white hair, and eyes that reflect the light with pink irises.

"Getting old is a young man's game," he says, a slight smile turning the corners of his mouth.

"It is that, " I reply, holding out my hand to shake. "Hobb Grey, and this is Alice Malville." He takes my hand, "Ren Lockwood." His hand is covered in tattoos that I do not recognise, and he grasps mine in a strong grip. He looks intently at me.

The Albino

It takes only a few minutes for Alice and I to secure food and drink from the constantly active staff, and spiced mutton, cheeses, bread and a large pitcher of weak red wine are soon being slurped. Lockwood helps himself after first raising a quizzical eyebrow. There is so much food and we have intruded upon his table that it would seem churlish indeed to refuse.

Over the course of our meal, and with the wine making conversation increasingly easy, we find out a little more about our strange new company. Ren Lockwood is what my parents would have called a shar-man. He travels the countryside as an itinerant healer and setting wards around the ancient stone circles which litter the land. His voice is gruff, as if he has spent the last twenty years shouting into the wind.

I was warned about them, these remnants of a people that were ancient even before the Old World, but there are so few in the east that the warnings could be forgotten. I understand that there are more in the west, and some truly enormous ones in the cold islands way to the north. Efforts were made to destroy them, but they resisted and are generally well marked and avoided.

If Lockwood is telling the truth, his life must be hard and dangerous indeed, for while there are many individual standing stones that would be easy to ward, some of the circles are large, many yards across, and it would take many hours to ward something that size.

Warding a site like that is not the same as protecting a temporary camp, as the circle itself is a site of terrible Fear. As he speaks I look more closely at his tattoos, and I can begin to make out the runes and binds he has used. His skin is heavily lined and scarred, but his eyes are young. I guess that he is in his late twenties.

I have only seen a few circles, but those I have seen have struck me with unease, and one in particular rises in my memory.

It is a set of three separate constructions, some twenty miles from Oxford. There is a ragged circle of many stones, each around three feet high and looking more like broken teeth than stone. A little way away is a group of three huge stones, leaning towards each other, for all the world as if they are whispering dark secrets. The group is completed by a single, tall stone a few hundred yards from the others, sitting on a slight rise, known as the King's Stone. I never paid much thought to the name before, but now, it chills me.

They are avoided, no settlements close by and farms are fenced well away from them.

"So what brings you here?" I ask Lockwood. Up until this point he has been cheerful, but his smile falters a little. "Well," he begins, "I have a set route, touring the land and securing what I can. Normally this time of year I would be a little ways south of here, but…" He takes a deep breath before carrying on. When he does, he stares into his mug of wine, slowly swirling it. "I would meet with Pen Unsworth, another Stoneguard, and we would head over to Abiri Great Circle and ward it together."

Alice asks the obvious question. "Where is she?"

Lockwood sighs. "I waited for two weeks. I have the feeling," he says, with forced brightness," that I am the last of my kind." His smile is brittle-bright, and Alice reaches over and rests her hand on his. His smile drops a little, and he looks at me. "You must know how that feels."

I am taken aback. "What makes you say that?"

He holds my gaze, "I can not remember the last time I met a Watcher, is all. Judiciary are in every town, but real Watchers?" He shakes his head.

"It is true that our numbers have declined somewhat, but…" And my voice tails off. Could he be correct? I can not allow myself to entertain this thought, especially not now, so I bring the conversation back to him.

"Tell me about the Great Circle. It is not something I have heard of."

Lockwood smiles grimly. He knows why I have changed the topic of conversation. He takes another gulp of wine.

"Abiri sits some thirty miles east of here. It is a massive construction of earth and stone, nearly a mile around. The stones are huge, ten feet tall, and the whole place is sat in dark woods that hide it from the outside. There are good markers, kept clean and bright by the local villagers, but the wards are set close to the stones. I can feel it pressing against the wards sometimes."

He suddenly looks downcast. "Not a job to do alone."

He sips more wine, and then the forced smile breaks his face. "And what of you? Where are you heading?"

Alice and I tell him of our journey and its destination, and his face falls again. "You be careful, Watcher, you and your apprentice. The world is not what it was but a few years ago, and the west, I believe, has it worse than most."

Alice and I exchange looks. When I embarked on this journey I hoped that it might simply be an opportunity to stretch my legs, see a bit of the country that was new to me, and maybe teach Alice a little to help her peace of mind. It had occurred to me that we might find something darker, but I was resolved to deal with it alone. Now, with the words of this strange, pale, pink-eyed man I was not sure at all what I might find. His assertion that I was the last Watcher also hit me hard, for I had lost track of others. Even my appearance in Gloster was unusual.

Before I can marshal my thoughts, Alice begins to speak. "Master Lockwood, we encountered something a few months ago…" She speaks in fits and starts, her voice dropping to a whisper and the three of us sit with our heads almost together, the atmosphere around us becoming darker and more tense despite the warmth and noise of the inn. I do not know how long it takes her to finish her story, and I do not fill in the areas she omits, but by the time she falls silent the food and wine have gone and the room is considerably darker, oil lamps having been lit around the walls. A lamp has been placed on our table, but I have no recall of it happening.

Lockwood looks from Alice to me and back. Eventually he begins to speak, keeping his voice low. "I was born pale. My skin burns easily in the sun and my eyes hurt in bright light. Summer is a trial to me, particularly when it is hot as I must wear thick clothing. I have seen one other like me, and she died thanks to lesions that ate her skin from exposure to the sun. As a consequence I learned to travel and work in the dark. Even on moonless nights I can navigate and carve well enough to do my calling." He breathes heavily, a sigh that works its way up from the base of his soul.

"I do not know about this "King", but I do know that I no longer work in the dark as I used to. The Fear is too strong now, close to the stones. I have passed villages abandoned in the west, those that sit close to Circles. The towns are still safe, and the little stories that have filtered through are dismissed, but I," and here he taps his eye, "see the truth. There are few of us remaining, possibly none. I am heading to Abiri, and there is a good chance I shall die there. Even if I survive, I shall not be going back to the west." He leans back on the bench, stretching. "My part is done."

He looks suddenly old and tired. His face, half shadowed by his long hair, is lined and drawn. I can not imaging the life he has led. Mine has not been easy, the Queen knows, but I have always acted with the weight of the Judiciary behind me, the knowledge that what I do is sanctioned not only by law, but by the organisations that support it, the courts and the church. Lockwood has been alone, even when acting with a companion, and doing a job which exposes him to the worst impact of the Fear. It is true that I have seen the worst things the Fear may do through agency, but I have rarely dealt with it directly. Indeed, the work in Stonehouse is the closest to the real Fear I have been for many years. This man, this haggard, smiling albino, has withstood its malevolence for decades.

"Can I ask," I say, and he sits forward, smiling again. "Where does the Queen sit in your life?"

He barks a short laugh. "Well now. Just as I have never seen your King, I can not say that I have seen much of your Queen either." He glances around and then leans in again. Alice and I follow suit. "When you get away from the big towns, people do what they must, and the Church does not tend to venture far from the main roads. You saw that in the place you went to, and that was only a few miles from Gloster." He drinks, and points from me to Alice and back, his finger moving slowly before tapping his forehead. "Think what it is like down here, or further west, where the Bone White Mask does not get seen. And where you are going, up to the coast, well, there are villages there that have been left alone for hundreds of years. They believe what they need to believe, and when you are faced with the might of the sea, that belief can go vicious. There are hundreds of gods being prayed to, and as long as the trade continues and the towns flourish, the Church cares not." At this he leans back a little, smiling. "See, to me, no gods is real. All there is, is Fear and us. And we are losing the ways of dealing with it, so after a while all there will be is Fear."

"Do you think it is growing stronger?" Alice asks. Her voice is matter-of-fact.

"That, or we are growing weaker. No, wrong word. Complacent. And that means that we become prey."

We spent the rest of the evening with Lockwood, talking in ever more hushed tones as the tavern grew quieter. Eventually, we bade each other good night and Alice and I searched out our room. As I settled in on the somewhat lumpy, thin mattress I mused over what he had said. I have never heard of anyone warding the old Circles, although, in truth, I have never really given any thought to it.

His assertion of his lack of belief does make me think, but I can not conceive of a world without the Queen. Even the people in Stonehouse still believed in her, they had just added something else to the mix, something more immediate. The fact that it was, to my mind, evil, is still an assurance of its existence.

"The only difference between a freedom-fighter and a terrorist is whose side they are on" sprang to my mind. It was something that one of my old Masters would say to me when we encountered something terrible that a Fear-Ridden had done. I never questioned him, but now I pondered the words as I drifted off to sleep.

A Change of Direction

We leave Erthcott Station early the following morning, trundling away from the stockade with the sun peeking above the hills. Fog sits, greying the world, and I find that I have to wrap my robe around me to keep warm. This is the first time I have felt anything other than unpleasantly hot for many weeks, and I am trying to convince myself to relish it. The truth is, of course, that my body has no memory of things past other than the pain of fire. Attempting to tell it that the cold will soon pass and be replaced by sweat-inducing heat again does no good.

We picked up supplies of food from the Station, and bread, fruit cheeses and pies sit cosily wrapped in linen behind us. Alice has been quiet, saying nothing as we ready the cart and hitch Harrold to it. She only speaks when we pull away from the buildings when, on turning right to continue our journey south around Old Bristol, she happens to look to her left. She nudges me, and I see a tall, thin figure in the mist, white hair streaming down its back, striding away towards the east. We both watch it as it disappears into the grey, and then I shake the reins and Harrold continues his steady plod.

"Have you ever heard of someone like him before?" Alice asks. Her voice is quiet, as if speaking loudly in this silent, half-formed world would be somehow rude.

"I have not," I reply, equally quietly. "But if what he says is true he has a harsh life indeed. I could not maintain his good humour."

Alice chuckles. "You can not maintain his good humour living the comfortable life you have now. If you lived his life you would be the most miserable man alive."

I can not argue with her, and laugh.

The road begins its long curve and, as we plod ever onwards, I become aware of old world ruins around us. The road is still wide, but we have left the original course, so it is down to perhaps twenty feet across. The verges have been kept clear, and they add perhaps another twenty feet either side of clear ground before the bushes and shrubs begin. To my surprise the weather stays cool the stillness of the day only increases the further we travel. We pass travellers and merchants heading in the opposite direction, and the niceties are shared, but we are all wary. There are very physical dangers which may lurk, hidden, in such conditions, and, although robbery on the Emfie is relatively uncommon, let alone dangerous for the perpetrators given mine and Alice's differing skills, desperation can drive men to stupid actions.

Over the course of the morning, the mist clears as the temperature rises, although not to the heights of the last few weeks, and the journey becomes rather pleasant. The countryside is lush and green, and small villages sit close by the road, no doubt hoping to pick up trade from the traffic. Our mood lifts, and we chat aimlessly and happily. Little rivers snake through the land, and we clatter over wide wooden bridges.

Our peace lasts until the road passes between two Old World settlements. The buildings are close enough to be visible on both sides, albeit hidden in thick woodland, and both Alice and I become quietly introspective as we trundle past. We have been heading south west for a while, but the road turns almost directly west once we have cleared the ruins, and we quickly find ourselves back in open country. I am aware of the mass of Old Bristol to the north of us, but it is not visible and it would be easy to believe it did not exist. However, my right side tingles constantly, and my skin occasionally rises in gooseflesh.

Over the next couple of hours, during which we pause to eat and allow Harrold the opportunity to drink at a stream, we head ever further away from the Fear, and Alice and I return to light conversation. This is interrupted suddenly and surprisingly when the road begins the slow curve northward to rejoin the Old road. The terrain here is gently undulating, with well-tended fields opening the landscape, but with copses and small stands of woodland breaking the skyline. As we pass a small village Alice suddenly shivers and looks to her left, telling me to stop the cart with an immediacy to her voice that causes me to pull hard on the reins, much to Harrold's annoyance.

I look across to where Alice is staring, but I can see nothing to warrant her alarm. Fields with wheat and cabbages surround a small hamlet, beyond which is a bank of tall trees. Alice is staring hard towards the trees, and is obviously agitated, her hands grasping at the wood of the cart. I ask what the problem is.

"Can you not feel it?" Her voice is tight, clipped.

"I can feel nothing out of the ordinary."

She does not look round, but I hear her huff. "There is something over there." She points to our left, but all I can see is the wide expanse of fields and small copses that stretch for miles.

"Well," I say, "I can neither see nor feel anything and we need to reach the next station before dark, so…" Before I can finish she leans across and snatches the reins from my hands, pulling Harrold round so that we begin clattering along a track between fields of corn.

I am about to take the reins back and berate her for this rudeness when I see the set of her face and decide that whatever she feels is something of import.

The land drops in a shallow incline towards a large stand of trees, perhaps a mile away.

We trundle onward, slowly decreasing the distance to the trees where, I assume, the object of Alice's interest lies, for there is nothing in sight that warrants such action. Eventually, we come to a halt, all but nuzzling the trees.

Alice leaps down, almost bouncing in agitation. "Can you feel it now?" She looks at me, and her eyes almost plead with me to join her, but I can not, and all I can do is shake my head. She tuts and hops from foot to foot, all the time staring into the trees, and I ease myself to the ground, making sure I have my stick at hand.

"You want to go in?" I ask, and, to my surprise, she does not immediately start walking. "I am not sure. There is something there, but it is cold and dark. I both want to see it, and I want to avoid it."

"Which is stronger?"

She stands absolutely still for a short while, managing to stop her agitated jigging, before stepping forward without a word. I glance back towards Harrold, but he is happily munching on the long grass, and I have to trust that he and the cart will be there when we return.

The edge of the woodland has been managed by the villagers, so there is a definite boundary and we cross into shade. Woodlands are always places to be wary within, as they have an ability to hide the Old World, and it is extremely easy to stumble into ruins without seeing any warning. Usually, in areas of high traffic, Way Markers are cut to guide people away, but I can see none. It may well be that there is no need of them, of course, or it may be that the villagers know not to come here. Either way I proceed carefully.

In truth, however, I feel nothing untoward as we venture further into the trees. Dappled sub breaks the shade, and birds are singing in the foliage. Alice, however, is still uptight, and she moves carefully, still with grace, but without the swift, determined speed I am used to. I remain behind her, following in her wake.

Occasionally she stops, turning her head from side to side, seemingly sniffing for a trail, and then continues forward. My stick catches on roots and brambles, and I begin to fall back. After a while I can no longer see her, and have to rely on my hearing and the fact that she has not deviated from her course. Within minutes I am effectively alone, and I call her name. I am not afraid, but separating now will cost us time later, and I do not want to be on the road come nightfall if it can be avoided.

As I bumble my way forward it dawns on me that the woods have become silent. Not only can I not hear Alice, but the birdsong has stopped. The woods are still light, however, and I press on, making sure that my knife is at hand.

I begin to silently curse, whether just myself or both myself and Alice, I am not certain. I can not believe how reckless she is being, especially after her experiences in Stonehouse. Even children know not to wander into woods, and the fact that I am having to chase someone who should know better irks me.

As I grumble and beat at the undergrowth I stop when I almost collide with her, standing still and staring ahead. I am panting and my left leg aches from the uneven ground, but I remain silent when I reach her. She looks round at my approach, and, without saying anything, points ahead. I have to move my head to see through the trees, but eventually, after much bobbing of my head, I do see what she is indicating.

Perhaps twenty feet away, partially concealed by leaves and broken sunlight, is a stone, upright, about eight feet in height and the same in width. It is rough and covered with lichen, but stands in a clearing. Alice moves her arm, pointing further to our left, and I can make out another stone, similar to the first.

What amazes me, so much that it actually takes a long time to realise, is that I feel no Fear.

Of Stone and Road

Alice steps closer to the stones, moving easily now, smoothly. Everything I know wants to stop her, but I can not do so. My body refuses to move and I am voiceless. This simply can not be. Shaped stone attracts Fear, this I know, as certainly as I know that my left leg aches. Shaped stone attracts Fear. It causes the breakdown in Stonehouse, it is the reason for our uneasiness passing between Old World buildings earlier today.

And yet.

Alice has reached the nearest stone, which towers over her, its bulk dwarfing her slim body. She looks round to me, the same expression on her face as I imagine she can see on mine, and she reaches out and touches the rough surface. At that movement I am freed from my stillness and I rush forward, stick raised to smack her hand away. Even I would find touching stone that size hard, even overwhelming, and I have runes for protection, while she has none. However, as I reach her she turns to face me, and she is smiling. I lower my stick and look deep into her eyes, but all I see is her. She laughs, a little, short sound of absolute joy.

My relief at seeing her safe is quickly overcome by the anger at her recklessness. "What in the name of the Queen are you doing?" I bark.

"Can you not feel it?" she asks.

"I can feel nothing," I respond angrily.

"Touch the stone."

I stare at her, contradictory thoughts shouting for my attention. She is obviously unharmed, happy, even, and yet the idea of reaching out and running my hand across the rough, lichen covered surface, is so alien to me that my hand does not move. This is something I am not equipped to deal with, something so against everything I have been taught, that there is no way I can counter it.

The fact that I can sense nothing is also troubling me. The problems at Stonehouse were a result of Fear building steadily over the course of months, but I have known it to hit hard and fast, overwhelmingly so. I have seen the effects of attempts to build but small furnaces, have seen the pain and distress of family as their loved one is taken, gibbering, into madness. And yet, here, by this massive stone placed into the ground, there is nothing.

I can not bring myself to follow Alice, and I step back.

She also pulls away, looking at me quizzically. I open my mouth to explain, but she just smiles and then heads off towards the other stone. I follow her, and, as we move past the first huge stone, I see others, sitting within the trees. These are smaller, probably between four and five feet tall, but as I become accustomed to their shape, I can make out many of them, describing an arc that disappears into the trees. If they continue around then the circle they make is enormous.

Alice is walking slowly from stone to stone, running her hands across each in turn. I can not bring myself to follow, and I will not enter the circle. Instead I spend time looking around the way we came in, seeing if there are any Wards or Way Markers I might have missed. The search reveals nothing, and I am left confused. When Lockwood was talking he seemed so sincere, and the idea that circles like this would be places of intense Fear makes perfect sense to me. And yet, here, there is nothing. Worse than that, Alice is obviously feeling something that eludes me, something that makes her happy.

There is nothing in my training that I can latch on to here. Nothing that makes sense to me. These stones are obviously shaped and placed. If I had made this the Fear would be strong indeed. And Lockwood mentioned that the great circle at Abiri might well be his last, when he came to Ward it. His apprehension was real, of that I am sure.

But why then do I not know of these places? It can not simply be that I was not told because I was to be stationed in the east, as Watchers travel wherever they are needed. Has something changed then? Or are some circles like this one while others are to be avoided? If that is the case, why? What regulates that difference? This place raises so many questions.

As I am lost in thought Alice returns. She smiles at me and I try to return it, shaking my head. I honestly have no idea what to say to her. Luckily, she speaks, "Shall we see if Harrold is still where we left him?" Grumpily I nod, and we make our way back through the trees.

Harrold is waiting patiently, munching grass. He raises his head when we emerge and whinnies softly, and Alice strokes his muzzle. I climb aboard the cart, and Alice pulls Harrold round before jumping up. The shadows are lengthening, and I have the nasty feeling we shall be still on the road come sun down.

As we start he long trek back to the Emfie, my mind is working hard.

"Tell me," I say, "How did you know the stones were there?"

Alice, who has taken the reins, shakes her head. "I honestly do not know. I did not actually know what I would find, just that there was something I needed to see. I am sorry."

"You have nothing to apologise for, but I will admit to finding this concerning." I turn to look at her. She is keeping her gaze resolutely forward. "What did you feel when you touched the stone?", I ask.

I half expect her to shrug, but instead she takes a deep breath, her brow furrowing as she thinks. "It is difficult to put into words. I was nervous, but when I did reach out I felt…calm. As if the Fear does not exist. As if the Yellow King is a shadow, nothing more. As if the Queen is similarly mist-like." She pauses. "As if," she says quietly, "this world is false."

"Say nothing of this when we return to Gloster."

She shakes her head emphatically. "I will not. In truth, the feeling is fading now, and I am not sure whether I shall remember it. Already my memory is hazy. Everything was so certain and immediate, but now it is dispersing." She sighs heavily.

Eventually, and much to Harrold's relief, I suspect, we rejoin the Emfie, and the ground levels out. I am pleased to see that we soon come within sight of the next station, as the light is fading rapidly. By the time we reach the stockade the sun has sunk behind the horizon and darkness is rapidly encroaching.

We are guided into a large field where numerous wagons are already stationed, and the marshall informs us that the Inn is full, so we shall have to sleep with the cart. We are manouvered to a small enclosure where there is fresh hay and a fire pit. As I sort out the tarpaulin Alice heads off to get some food and drink. The day did not heat up to the same degree as recently, and the temperature is already dropping. By the time Alice returns I have got a good fire going and the tarpaulin is stretched taught, secured by pegs into the firm ground. Looking round it is pleasant to see other fires burning, and the field has the quiet hum of people settling.

The food and drink is acceptable, and we spend the evening chatting about things unrelated to the day's events. However, as I settle to sleep, wrapped in thick blankets with the fire smouldering and the sounds of quiet conversation around me, my mind returns to Gloster, and the reason for our excursion. Captain Haydon's log troubles me, for his descent into madness was not only relatively quick, but it continued through the voyage. The more I think on this, the more I wonder whether I have made an error of judgement. Whilst it is certainly important to see where the captain's delerium might have started, it may be that I should have stayed and checked the cargo. Although the manifest contained nothing to give concern, it occurs to me that his insanity could be the result of something on board the ship, rather than something he encountered at Wood Bay.

There is little I can do about this now, and we might as well continue.

Days of Thought

Two more days of trundling and nights of sleeping in questionable lodgings sees us leaving the Emfie and striking north towards the coast. The weather has continued to cool, and we had a small amount of rain last night, but not enough to do much more than dampen the ground. At least it should reduce the amount of dust Harold and the cart's wheels throw into the air.

The road we take is much narrower than the Emfie, and the land is heavily wooded. The trees have been kept away from the road, but the visibility is much reduced. According to the map, the road should take us to Wood Bay, but I am unconvinced. It is clear that this section is quite well used, but as we head further away from the main trade routes, the poorer the state of repair will be, and I fully believe we shall need to walk the final stretch. I may be wrong, succumbing to the less than positive state of mind that seems to be my norm. I try to convince myself that, as the Bay is deep enough to accept a ship the size of the Lady Jennifer, it could well act as a trading port for the whole area. It should, therefore, have fairly decent tracks and roads servicing it, but the trees are thick and I can see little evidence of settlements. On the Emfie, pillars of smoke rise around us signalling villages every few miles, but here I can see nothing. I am sure that there are little hamlets around, and tracks spur off the main road, disappearing into the trees. Birdsong is everywhere, and, despite my mood I find myself enjoying the sounds.

The road is still fairly well maintained, although rougher than the Emfie, and Harold plods on at his steady pace. Alice is silent, and I can almost feel her brain working. I admit that the stones have unsettled me a little, but without further investigation there is little to be gained by worrying. It does strike me as strange that we met with Ren Lockwood just before encountering the stones. I have learned that there is no such thing as coincidence - everything has a cause and the strands of Wyrd intertwine to bring disparate events together - and the Fear certainly wraps and distorts Wyrd for its own gain. Indeed, I use this distortion in order to uncover the truth, pulling at strands and unwrapping them during the Testing. There are times when I have been pleasantly surprised by how nicely events have fallen, seeming to slot together in a manner that has worked to my advantage. However, I can not remember a time when external events which had no direct bearing on my work conspired so neatly to show me something new.

And then it slowly seeps in that I was not the intended audience, that Alice is the one who sensed the stones while I felt nothing. I have a slight regret about not touching the stone, given Alice's reaction. Maybe I can have a look on the way back.

There is little point in interrogating Alice as she is still processing the episode, and I do not want to worry her prior to reaching our destination, but there is so much about this that concerns me. The fact that there were no Wards or Way Markers suggests that the local villagers know about the stones and do not need to be warned. Whether that is because their knowledge keeps them away or whether they know there is nothing to be wary of I do not know. If the former, then that suggests a complacency similar to Stonehouse, and if the latter then that suggests something more fundamental, something that I had never suspected.

Could it be that not all stone is dangerous? That some shaped stone is safe? If so, then that means that not only is my training incomplete, but that the Redemption is lacking. And if the Redemption is lacking, what does that mean for the Church?

Alice and I have been eating rations bought at the last station, a poor, grubby affair of few clients. Travel here is much reduced, and the snippets of conversation I listened in on seem to indicate that the lands further west are pulling away from the rest of the country and looking to become more independent. They have always been a little removed from the main towns, largely by dint of their remote location, but also politically. The Cornish in particular are keen to set themselves apart, and view themselves as a distinct population. As I understand it, this could cause some issues as the Cornish lands are rich in certain metals, but mining is a horrifically dangerous undertaking as, not only is there the constant danger of collapse, but the act of tunnelling can rapidly attract Fear. This has led to the cost of Tin, for example, rising significantly, and pressure has been brought onto the miners from the more populated areas to produce more, but the physical issues are restricting the amount. This is leading to increasing anger amongst the Cornish, and they have responded by pulling away from these markets and selling more into the mainland of Urope.

Quite how this situation will resolve I do not know, but its immediate effect is to reduce trade between the West and the rest of the country, with the subsequent reduction in usage of the way stations.

As we are slowly making our way through shades of green under a slowly clouding sky, Alice speaks up. "Tell me about Fear and stone."

"I can only say from my experience and what I was told," I say, "and I am now not certain how close to reality my words will be." She looks at me, a little shocked, I think, at my admission. The truth is that Alice is now the only person I can really talk with regarding my thoughts. The shared experience of Stonehouse and the more recent events at the circle are things that I can speak of only with her. Campion can not be expected to understand the former, and he would try and reason away the latter. Similarly, the thought of discussing such things with the Deacon now make me uneasy, as when examined, both point to conclusions that are at odds with official Church teaching.

"I was taught that Fear is a by-product of the Great Conflagration, a presence that appeared to take advantage of the pain and confusion. It settled in stone because it is an entity of cold and death, and when that stone is shaped it is freed, but that act of freeing sends it mad and it latches on to the nearest mind it can in order to give vent to its insanity."

Alice ponders for a short while before responding. "Is that what you now believe?"

I sigh, perhaps more heavily than intended, for that question is one that I have been mulling for the last couple of days. Were it anyone but Alice asking, my answer would, I think, be different.

"I do not know. It *feels* wrong to me now. Or, at least, it feels wrong in substance." She looks quizzically at me. "I think it is still the truth, but I think that there is more than I was told. Another layer, perhaps."

The road has been following an Old World way as it heads north west over gently rolling hills, but when we reach a junction with a small station I consult our map, and realise that we need now to turn off, heading almost due north along a track which curls away from us between steeply sided hills. The track is poor and both Alice and I understand that Harrold will not be able to pull the cart much further.

There is a small Way station here so I decide to stop for the remainder of the day, even though it is but mid-afternoon. According to the map there is about twelve miles to walk to reach Wood Bay, a distance that, if it is taken without haste, should be feasible in a day for me. It does mean that we will have to stay the night on the coast before heading back south, but Harrold could do with the rest.

The station is little more than a large house, double storied and neat, with paddocks fenced to one side and well kept fields to the other. As we pull in close to the building, the door opens and a young man steps out. He is large, powerfully built, but he gives us a friendly nod and walks over, gently taking the reins and patting Harrold.

"Good afternoon, Master," he says, his accent lengthening the vowels. As I step down he sees my red robe and his face changes briefly, a little flicker of recognition is followed by an expression I can not immediately place… hope? Possibly. Alice has leapt down from the other side and calls out, "Do you have rooms?"

The man continues to watch me, answering only after a brief pause. "We do." He blinks and then drags his eyes away from me towards her. "Good rooms and good food, if you need it."

"Then we shall take two rooms."

He nods. "Go in, Marta will see to you. I will stable your horse."

The room we enter is dark, with small windows on two sides. It is set up as an Inn, with several tables and benches dotted around and a serving area off to one side. It is empty but for a woman, young, short and fair haired, is busy wiping a table. She looks up when she hears us come in, and smiles. "Come in, come in," she calls. "If you are hungry I can feed you and if you are tired I can supply a comfortable enough bed."

Alice immediately says, "We are both," and the woman's smile broadens. "Then sit yourselves and I shall bring you some stew and bread." Her manner is open and friendly, but it falters when we step away from the open door and out of the light that has been silhouetting us and she sees my robes.

As we make our way to a table my eyes adjust to the darkness, and I can begin to see details. The room is poorly furnished, with mis-matched furniture that seems to have been accumulated over time, scratched and pitted with use, but sturdy. There is little decoration save for red ribbons that have been tied to the rafters and wooden pillars. In fact, as I look round, the ribbons are everywhere.

When we sit Alice looks around appraisingly, and I see that she is noting the ribbons as well. She leans in and whispers, "A little monotonous on the colours." I nod in agreement, but any discussion is brought short as the woman, who I assume is Marta, bustles up to us with a tray, placing bowls of hot, dark stew and crusty bread in front of us. A block of butter is also placed on the table.

"I hope you enjoy your food," she says, "I shall prepare rooms for you now. When you have eaten your fill I shall show you to them." We thank her, and she hesitates, nodding before turning and walking away. Alice, dipping a chunk of bread into her bowl, watches her go, her face displaying deep thought.

The stew is delicious, and most welcome, but the silence of the place starts to make me a little uneasy. Even though we are quite a way from the main trading ports there should be more people here, and, as I stare out of the window I watch a couple of riders pass by on the road. They actually spur their horses to get past the Way station quickly.

Alice, who has been eating while looking around the room thoughtfully, asks, "Did you see any Way Markers here?"

I drag my eyes back to her and shake my head, "No, but that is not unusual when the road is so well used." She grunts, chewing, before leaning back in her chair. Over the next few minutes we finish our meal and when the woman returns, Alice stacks our bowls and picks them up, walking over to meet her. I turn to watch as Alice has never done this in all the places we have stayed in. My curiosity is rewarded when she goes to hand the bowls over and says, "Thank you, Marta, it was very good. Tell me, what sickness has hit your house?"

The Child

The woman's face pales, and she looks close to fainting. I stay seated, but turn fully to watch her. Alice places the bowls on the nearest table and gently takes Marta's hand, leading her over to me and guiding her to sit. Alice sits next to her, taking her hand again, and speaking gently.

"I have seen the red cloth before, it took a while to remember as it was a long time ago. Someone has a fever."

Marta nods. She looks miserable indeed, as if acknowledging the problem to someone else has allowed her to see it fully.

"My daughter," she says, her voice shaking. "She became sick the day before yesterday." Alice glances at me, but I am content to remain a spectator, at least for now.

"How old is she?"

The woman gulps air before answering. "Three, nearly four."

"I am sorry for your trials. Is she very sick?"

Marta nods fiercely.

"Do you have help?"

She shakes her head, saying, "No, it is only myself and Matthew." She looks directly at me. "We did put pestilence markers out on the road, but there are no Way markers on the north. We get so few people from that direction that I thought it would not matter and that we could warn those who did come." She lowers her eyes. "And then I saw your robes."

"You think I can help?"

She looks up again, her eyes wet, " I hoped."

Alice looks at me and I shrug slightly, but her gaze does not falter. As I look from Marta to Alice I see a faint hope in one and the beginnings of questioning annoyance in the other. I sigh.

"Can I take a look at the child?" Marta almost bursts into tears again. "Listen," I say, " there may be nothing I can do. My skills lie in Fear and its effects, not in disease, but I can look and, if there is something I can do, I shall do it." Marta nods furiously, the hope in her face leaking from her eyes. "I need you to understand," I continue, "that if I can help it might not be pleasant, and if I can not then the best thing you can do is pray. Tell me her symptoms."

Marta gathers herself, taking a couple of deep breaths and clasping her hands together.

"It started with a headache and fever, which came on very rapidly. She did not sleep at all that night and was exhausted the following day, which allowed us to rest. Yesterday she was taken with pustules, small and hard and pale, that came up rapidly over her whole body, and her fever increased."

Her hands are gripped tight, the skin white where her fingers are clasping, almost as if to hold on to her fear and pain. "And that is how she is today."

"Is there any change in her personality?"

She shakes her head. This is not a good sign as it suggests that this is a natural disease, for Fear exists to cause despair. It has no truck with individual suffering. However, until I can perform a few tests there is no certainty. I stand, saying, "I need to collect some equipment, but I shall return very shortly, and then we shall see what may, or may not, be done."

I ask Alice to come with me, and we walk out into the early evening sun. Heavy clouds are colouring the sky, but they are broken and allow shafts of sunlight through and I breathe deep. "Tell me about the red cloth," I say as we walk around the building towards the cart.

"It was something they used to do where I grew up, specifically for fever. The idea, I think, was to wrap the patient in red cloth to draw the heat from them."

"I do not think the Church would approve of that," I reply, pulling the complex key from my purse. "It smacks of pre-Conflagration thinking."

The lock clicks, soft whirring continuing for a short while after I turn the key.

"That is why it changed, I suspect," Alice says. "With red cloth being hung around the house a case can easily be made that petitions are being made to the Queen."

I lift the case from its temporary home, closing the lid and locking it again, handing the case down to Alice before sliding gracelessly off the cart. "I have never heard of this practice."

We start walking back towards the Way Station, Alice carrying the case. "It may be regional, so as you spent much of your time in the east it may simply never have reached there."

As we walk, Alice slows a little. "Have you ever heard of a disease like this?"

"No," and I shake my head. "I have seen what other maladies can do, and if it is as quick to spread as what I have seen then be thankful we are far from a town." I sigh and we continue walking.

"And if is as quick to spread?"

I sigh heavily. "If it is, then it would be best to seal this house up and not let anyone in or out. Including us."

Alice sighs, the sound echoing mine. "Just as well I had no plans for the next week or so." I smile as we re-enter the building, and Marta is there to greet us. We follow her through a door and up a staircase. At the top we are shown to a small room occupied by a crude, but well made, bed. A small body lies upon it, little whimpering noises issuing from it.

"What is her name?" I ask, quietly.

"Jess," comes a whispered reply. Marta has not entered the room, but stands in the hallway. I turn to Alice. "You should stay back as well. If this is natural my tattoos will offer some protection and if it is Fear they shall offer more, but you are unprotected either way."

The room is small, and there is the thick, musty sweet smell of stale fever-sweat. I take the case from Alice and step into the room, looking around and seeing nothing bar a cloth rabbit which has fallen from the bed and now lies crumpled upon the floor. The sounds of ragged, fast breathing provide a quiet rhythm. On reaching the bed I look down at the tiny figure and am shocked at the way her face has been ravaged. Hundreds of small, pale lentil-like swellings cover every scrap of skin.

I do not want to be here any longer than is necessary, as the symptoms are so reminiscent of the terrible disease I was told of more years ago than I want to remember. It was held up as an example of the arrogance of the Old World, that the willingness to openly challenge the natural world would, of course, not go unpunished. Yet, I must admit, that if I could remove such an illness as this, should it be natural, I would have few qualms in doing so.

I thumb the Infinity Clasps on the case and open it, pulling a sharp, double ended needle, a small beaten brass dish, a brass cup which is stained dark, dark red and a thin bladed knife from it. The bowl has runes scratched around the edge and, like the cup, is stained black-red. I place the bowl on top of the case and, taking a deep, steadying breath, lean over the child. With the needle I prick one of the pustules, causing the child to cry out. I apologise in my mind, and as a small amount of pus seeps from the tiny wound, I collect it on the tip and carefully transfer it to the cup. I then turn the needle round and prick my own thumb, squeezing a couple of drops of blood into the cup to mix with the pus. This foul mixture is dripped into the bowl.

Once this is done I take the knife, settle as comfortably as possible and allow my mind to turn inward. I rest the knife blade against my left arm and, when I see the soft shimmering of the child's web, begin cutting wyrd-shapes. As I cut I pull strands of her web and wrap them around the bowl, using the knife to direct them. As they encounter the runes they play across the surface, intertwining and wrapping around each other.

The whole process takes but a few minutes and I am soon back with the child in that close, sweet-smelling room. I pick up the bowl. The blood and pus has formed streaks, snaking across the bowl, reaching for certain runes, and I have my answer, although it is not an answer I have ever encountered before, and it troubles me.

I stand, slightly shakily, I note, and speak to Alice. "Get me short staves of Willow, about eight. Split them in half. There is a stand of Willow a couple of hundred yards from the road to the south." She immediately turns and runs down the stairs. I then turn to Marta. "Do you have a fire in the kitchen?"

Marta nods and I follow her down, turning away from the main room and into the kitchen where a fire sits burning in a pit. The kitchen is surprisingly large, and I realise that they use it as the main room of the house. Along with a large table there are sets of drawers and shelves with plates and mugs stacked upon them. In a corner, sat on its own little shelf, is a small white mask. With no access to a Church the family show their devotion here.

The fire is contained in a pit lined with thick brass plates, and there is a brass gantry sat over it with a large pot hanging from it. "Do you have a long, metal spoon?" I ask. Marta quickly reaches across to a set of implements hanging on a wall.

"Perfect, thank you."

I place the needle onto the spoon and place it into the fire, where it briefly sizzles. I leave it there for a minute or so before withdrawing it. Marta stands close by, anxious, but I do not know what to say to her. I can feel her questions, and when she is joined by her husband, the unasked queries become louder. They stand close together and after a few minutes Marta leaves and goes back upstairs.

Matthew stays silent, standing as his wife had, solidly, worried.

The runes on the bowl are not the ones I carve for Testing or for Warding. These are bindrunes of Suggestion, shapes of Wyrd that tell stories, that show the shape of things that are hidden. And what they show is Fear and nature together. Intertwined, inseparable.

Separating

Alice returns a short while later, a bundle of freshly cut Willow staves in her hands, all neatly split lengthways, and I go to meet her outside. The Willow will require a little preparation and I need to speak with her before I do anything.

For her part, she obviously sees my expression and her eyes narrow. "What?" is her greeting as I guide her away from the house towards the cart, nestled in a shed. When we reach it, secure and covered by a shingle roof, I ask her to place the staves down so that they may be smoothed. I show her how to use her knife to shave the cut wood smooth. While we work I give voice to my concerns

"The test I performed is one that can show the nature of events; whether they are driven by Fear and, in some circumstances, what its intent might be."

She looks up from her scraping. "Intent?"

"Oh yes. Whilst normally it will simply latch on to the nearest or weakest member of a community, there have always been instances of more organised attacks, although they are rare. I have dealt with perhaps three, including Stonehouse. The test can help determine the best means of disrupting events, whose web to pluck. However, it will not work if the events are natural or simply the result of mundane developments."

I pick up a stave and start drawing the blade of my knife along its cut side, shaving thin splinters of green wood. I enjoy this process immensely as it gives my hands work while my mind is free to wander.

"What the Test is showing me here," I say, "is that the malady striking the girl is natural, in that the disease is a physical ailment, but it has traces of Fear associated with it. It is being propelled and fed by Fear."

We work in silence, the sounds of the world, soft and distant, are accompanied and marked by the repeated *shuck-shuck-shuck* of our blades as we smooth the wood. Eventually I break the quiet, my voice sounding coarse to my ears. "Do not go back into that room."

Alice laughs, and the sound is surprisingly welcome, "I had no intention of doing so."

Within a few more minutes more the staves are prepared and I look around, enjoying the changing of the light as the sun sits lower in the sky. A Kite, wings wide, skims over the trees close by, hunting, and a shiver runs down my back. I am not one for portents, despite being taught that the shape Wyrd can be read in the flight of birds, but the way the Kite flies, purposeful, effortless and with deadly intent strikes me deep.

I gather the staves and, accompanied by Alice, head back into the Station. Matthew is still in the kitchen, standing at the little shrine. He does not look round when we walk in, but I see his shoulders rise as he takes a deep breath. As Alice and I walk through the room he speaks up, but does not turn to face us. From the catch in his voice he is crying, and I guess that he does not want me to see.

"Can you help her?"

I do not wish to lie, but to tell him of my concerns serves no purpose, and so I use the weasel-words "I shall do my best."

I follow Alice up the stairs. If this is as I suspect I am unsure of my next course of action. Were I in Gloster, I would have notified the Aldermen and passed the responsibility of further action to them, but I am not in Gloster, I am here, miles from anywhere and alone. Just like in Stonehouse.

I shake myself. I am not alone and that thought was unfair. Although, as I watch her turn towards the child's room, I am unsure as to what my company actually is, given her reaction to the stones.

Alice stops at the doorway and I take the staves she carries from her, moving past and walking into the room. Again, the smell of sweet sweat hits me. Marta is sitting on the floor next to the bed, one hand holding her daughter's, the other cradling her head. She looks up as I walk in, and squints, her eyes slowly focusing on me.

"Leave me with her."

Marta stands slowly, and as she shuffles past she looks back at her daughter, at the wreckage that was her daughter, and that, even if I can help, will never really be her daughter again.

"Close the door behind you."

Through the narrowing crack I see Alice peering, her curiosity evident.

Once the door is closed I turn to Jess. Her eyes are closed and her breathing is fast and shallow. A slight sheen of sweat covers her skin, highlighting the terrible pustules that cover every inch. It is impossible to know what she looked like before this pest took hold, and I note that even her eyelids are marked. I am pleased she is unconscious, but even now she is whimpering in pain. A little more would not be felt.

I take my knife and make a small cut in her arm, trying to avoid touching her skin. A few small drops well up, and begin their slow descent towards the runic bowl I hold to catch them. Once done I use the knife to catch her sleeve and pull her arm over her chest.

Next I take the small oil burner from my case, and use it to heat the blade of the knife, killing any pestilence that may have attached itself through her blood. With a practised flick against my left arm, not as easy as it could be due to the scarring of the burns, I collect a little of my own blood as well.

Placing the bowl carefully upon the floor, I position the staves around the room, after wiping each smooth, white face against my wound, smearing red. I always chant a little incantation when I do this kind of work as it helps me focus on what I need to do. Some of my teachers did this, and I suspect that I do it now more from habit than need, but that is no reason to stop. Ritual is, after all, what the Church is built upon, and I feel that Deacon Mustaine would approve, even if he would prefer me to work in something about the Queen.

The staves sit against each wall, and I take especial care to cover the door and window. If there is anything here I want it to have neither entry nor easy escape. With a further stave at the girl's head and feet I settle down on the floor as comfortably as possible, although I have to keep my leg out straight. At least I can lean against the wall and still be close enough.

The Runic bowl is sat before me, and I close my eyes and begin cutting runes into my arm.

It takes a little while for my focus to narrow, closing my mind off from the room and the noises of the world, in particular the fast, whimpering breathing of the child in front of me, but when I do I can see the faint blue lines of her Wyrd, tangled and bunched around her, undecided and confused. They form a cage around her, trying to protect her from the attack of disease. The runes on the bowl are pulsing as our blood mingles and I send a strand of my Wyrd into it, where it can find the faint wisp of hers stretching from the cut in her arm.

I start probing around her, gently working my way along the strands and trying to find a way in. Eventually, after much coaxing and prying she allows me in, and I can start searching. Within the cage her Wyrd is jagged, red, pained and constantly writhing, but with areas that are blackened and still. This I have seen before, where disease is powerful and survival uncertain. It takes different forms, certainly, but the general overview is the same. With Cholera, for example, the blackness spreads so quickly it is almost impossible to track, while here it is slower, almost deliberate, and no less terrible for that.

So far this is no more than a simple malady which, although terrible, should be easily contained within this house, even given that Alice and I are heading out, we should be able to avoid contact with anyone else for the next few days, so the risk of us spreading it is slight. I fear that the house will need to be shut, however.

And then I see it. A change in the way the web lies. Deep within the coils and spikes of her pain is something else, something that is not her. It sits like a toad in a well, difficult to see but slowly poisoning the water. It is small, indistinct, like the memory of something rather than the thing itself. A footprint of Fear rather than Fear itself. A small, pale, sickly yellow expression of evil that, while not driving the sickness, is certainly enabling it.

I pull back, coming back to myself and the room. Pain suddenly flows up my left arm and when I look down I see that my cuts have gone deep, much deeper than usual, blood dripping onto my leg and the floor. My knife hand is shaking.

I stand and, holding my arm, make my way to the door. Only Alice is in the hallway, sitting against the wall, and she jumps up when I open the door. Her eyes flick from my face to my arm and back and, without waiting for me to say anything she runs down the stairs. I hear a muffled conversation and she returns with a length of clean red cloth, which she wraps tightly around my arm. The colour darkens slightly as blood seeps in, but the flow is already stopping.

She looks up at me again when she finishes, but I have not finished yet, so I simply say, "Later," and turn back into the room.

Once the door is closed again I stand, unsure as to what to do next. If this were Fear my course of action would be clear, and Alice could assist in the process by keeping the child secure, but this is different. I am fairly certain that my tattoos will give me protection, especially as I have seen that Fear is driving this, but I am also aware that the disease itself is natural, and Alice will have no protection against that. It also means that the usual methods will not work effectively. However, I must rid the child of the foulness that lurks deep in her to give her a chance of fighting off the sickness. I could use the Test to pull the Fear from her, but she is so weak that a Test would likely kill her and, while that may be her fate, it is not one I wish to encourage. It would also mean waking her, and I feel that she is in so much pain the result would be useless.

The only thing I can really do is use runes and open her Wyrd to try and smother the Fear myself. This will be hard, and given how much damage I have just done to my arm I am not sure I am in a position to undertake this.

Ah! When did I ever think the path of a Watcher would be easy? Stop wallowing in what may be and do what is needed.

I settle myself on the floor next to the bed again.

Unwrapping the bandage that Alice has so carefully bound around my arm I am able to see the wounds. The scar tissue from the burns and the many previous cuts has made furrows of my skin, and the knife has sliced through them and, while the bleeding has stopped, I am shocked by the depth of the cuts.

With a deep breath I close my eyes once again and sink into the world of moving lines and feeling that is Wyrd, finding it easier to reach than before. Again, I place my knife against my arm, making sure to avoid the existing cuts, and dip the point into the skin, carving a rune of entry. Immediately I am back in the tangle of pain and protection that Jess has thrown up, but now I know what I am looking for, and with coaxing and the gentle use of runes I soon find myself close to the foul thing at its centre.

I have been careful to leave runes of entry to stop the child closing her Wyrd around me, and, far off I can hear her whimpers. This must be unpleasant, like a robber hammering on the door, but it must be done. I switch now to carving a rune of capture. This is a rune I have used only occasionally. It was called the Wolf-hook by Master Chang, and it is well named. Using it I can pull and slice at the Fear, even as it writhes and tries to pull back, but it is small and alone and it soon succumbs to my ministrations, sliding free like an oyster, slippery, foul and formless.

Once free I am able to slice it and cause it pain by using runes of life and death. With a final burst of something that fills my mouth with the taste of vomit, it dies and I am able to pull away. When I open my eyes I am shocked to see that the room is in darkness for night has fallen.

I light the little lamp and inspect my arm again. The cuts are deep, but lighter than before and I wonder why I am being so heavy-handed. I re-bind my arm, mulling over the fact that I will be useless now for days should the need arise for more Wyrd-work.

As I stand I look at the child. Her breathing is still shallow, and I do not know whether I have done enough to save her as she has to fight this disease still. But at least it is now only the disease.

The Road North

A short while later I am sitting at the kitchen table with a mug of small beer and some bread, both of which are very welcome. My arm hurts and my right hand still shakes a little. I have been able to offer little hope to Marta and Matthew, and Alice, looking with optimism when I emerged, has settled into a more sanguine mood.

After a few good mouthfuls of beer I ask of Matthew, "Tell me, how much traffic travels north from here?"

He shakes his head, "Very little. There are a few small villages, but there is little else."

"What of the port at Wood Bay? Does that not attract trade?"

He shakes his head. "No. The bay is difficult to get to as the path to it is steep. We had a small group pass through perhaps a week ago heading north, but that was the first for months."

Alice and I share a look. "Did they stop here?" she asks.

"They did. One night and then they left. They did not return, at least, not to stay."

I sup some more beer and chew thoughtfully on some bread. "Did they have any luggage?"

Matthew shakes his head. "No. They did not speak much, and the road is not good enough for a heavy cart, but one of them did mention that they were meeting a ship." He pauses and then says, quietly, "Will my daughter by well, sir?"

A sigh escapes my lips before I can stop it, earning a hard look from Alice. I try and keep the annoyance from my voice, but my concern is not with him. "I do not know, Matthew. I do not know. I hope I have helped, but I can not cure her. I have given her a better chance." My arm is painful and I can feel my fingers stiffening. It will be days before I can work Wyrd again.

Alice pours herself a small mug of ale. "Where is Marta?" I respond with a slight shake of my head, and Alice presses no more.

The following day we leave early. Alice has ensured that Harrold has plenty of food and fresh water, certainly enough to last the few days we are planning to be away, and I pack those articles I feel I might need from my case into a backpack, along with a cooking pan and bedroll. Alice is carrying a similar load and, as we strike out, she looks back to the Way Station. She quickly looks back, saying "Matthew is at the window."

I grunt, but there is nothing else we could have done.

I found the nails in the stable, and all doors and windows have been secured. I shall check in when we return to pick up Harrold. They have enough food and drink. I push a heavy pair of pliers beneath the door-step.

I placed pestilence markers around the house to warn passers-by.

When we woke in the morning, Jess was still very sick, Marta was ridden with fever and Matthew was pale and drawn. He did not state he was sick, but he was unable to fully open his eyes and I suspect he had a severe headache.

The day is cooler, much to my relief, and it feels good to be walking and allowing my body to stretch. My arm still throbs, and a nagging little thought has taken root, to whit, am I too old to continue my work? In my youth I would shake off a Test within an hour or so, but over the years the recovery has taken longer. This is, I suppose, to be expected, and I am aware that I cut far too deep last night, although I do not know why.

The road, although relatively narrow, is in good order, and once we leave sight of the Way Station my mood improves. Birds are singing, and the sound lifts me. I never learnt to identify them, but a few I recognise. In particular is a Sky Lark, warbling and bubbling as he rises, and it is the sound of summer from my youth. Alice, keeping pace with me, although I know she would walk faster if I were not here, also seems happier once we are away.

The land gently rises for a few hundred yards and then begins a long fall through woodland, although the trees are kept well back from the road, and the going is easy. After an hour or so of the sound of footstep, stick and bird, Alice speaks up and asks a question that I am not expecting.

"Did you ever want children?"

I am so surprised that I look towards her, more for confirmation that she asked what I heard than for anything else. She looks to me, and raises her eyebrows in expectation.

"Why do you ask?"

"It has occurred to me that I know very little about you, and as we are to have nothing, not even a horse, for company, we might as well fill the space with knowledge."

I smile. She is certainly Campion's niece. He would never allow silence to grow when it could be filled with chatter.

"Do you really think I am fatherly material?"

Alice laughs, and says, "No", most emphatically. "At least," she continues, "not now, but you may have been."

"A long time ago?"

"A long time ago." Her response is also punctuated by a slight laugh.

"No. Not through conscious decision, merely lack of opportunity." I cast the lie easily, and I know that Alice hears it. I also regret it. The truth is that I have always slightly distrusted children, and the work that has shaped and built my life is harsh. I tend to see the worst that people can be. One of the reasons I wanted Alice's company is simply that she sees a better side of people than I do, jaded as I am. Of course, I do aim to teach her as we go, but that is harder than I imagined, not only because of what happened at the Stones, but the simple fact is that to really train her I have to put her in danger again.

Maybe I shall keep her training more theoretical.

The day continues bright although clouds are gathering away to the west and we make good time. There are small hamlets on the road, little affairs of three, maybe four, families, the trees cleared well back to allow cultivation of crops and animal pens. The landscape is gently rising, and has been for miles, although not so heavily as to cause exhaustion.

The people we pass watch us with polite disinterest. I do not imagine they get many passing by. Occasionally we are offered drinks, which are welcome, although they do not brew ale but sida, which is made from apples and is fierce. I quickly learn to avoid it.

Towards the end of the day we reach the lip of a large bowl, heavily wooded, that leads down to the sea, blue-grey and vast. The path, cut through the trees, meanders like an old river, turning left and right to make the slope manageable. Far below, several hundred feet, is a curved bay. Dotted around are the roofs of houses, although no smoke rises. Alice and I share a glance, and then she starts on the track, while I follow.

The going is hard, but mainly because of the incline, as the track itself is relatively smooth. Where it is very steep, particularly where the direction switches, steps have been cut, and we manage to gain level ground before the sun sets.

The path, for the final thirty yards or so, follows the course of a stream which cuts a deep, narrow track, deeply overgrown with ferns and moss. As we leave the trees behind the water splashes down onto shingle, disappearing into the stones, and we find ourselves in a wide semi-circular bay with steep sides. The only way in or out, apart from the sea, is the path we have just navigated. Set around the bay are small wooden houses, five in all. Dotted around are the skeletons of boats. There are no people, no sounds of habitation, just the quiet, gentle repeating sound of small waves.

Alice says, "Well, what did you expect to find?"

I look around at the desolate remnants of a village. "More than this."

We walk to the nearest house. It is well maintained, and I can see evidence of recent repair work, part of a window frame is fresh wood and carved with care. And yet the place is silent. Alice knocks on the door, loudly, but there is no answer. She tries again, with a similar result. With a look to me for approval, she lifts the latch and pushes the door open, and I see her hesitate on the threshold. She looks back, and there is something in her eyes. She backs away, shaking her head and muttering, "I can not, I can not."

She backs away from the door and I step past her, taking the latch and pushing the door. The smell seeps into my nose and I know instantly why

Alice could not enter. I push the door wide, allowing light into the building, where it highlights the motes of dust thrown up by the sudden movement of air, the table and chairs, and the two bodies, one slumped onto the table, the other on the floor.

Where it hits skin it shows raised pock marks and terrible death.

Wood Bay

I back away smartly, catching my foot and stumbling. Alice is quickly at my side, trying to take my arm, and I shake her off. I am not an invalid, despite my age and burns and shaking arm.

"Are they all dead?"

"How should I know?" My words are filled with fear and come out with anger. I look around wildly. There are five houses, and the Queen is sitting in at least one, in as ugly a guise as I have seen. I need to check whether She is present at other hearths.

"Stay here."

I stalk across the shingle, my stick slipping against the larger stones and forcing me to move slowly despite my urge to speed.

The next house is larger, and occupied by the bodies of a family. Mother, father and three children, all together in the large, stinking bed. To find them I have to walk through the front room, my heart thumping in my chest. On leaving the house I take huge, gulping breaths of clean, sweet air, enjoying the slight tang of salt. Alice is standing where I left her, watching me.

The next house, the last on this side before the water, is small, one room at a guess. I take a deep breath before trying the latch, but when I push the door there is no smell of corruption. I throw the door open and step inside. The room is dark, despite the door, but smells sweet. There is no one here, but the house has been lived in, and recently. There is ash in the fireplace, and a bowl and spoon on the table.

I tap my stick on the floor, thinking.

As I make my way across the bay towards the other houses I look over to

Alice, who has sat on the ground away from the buildings, still watching me.

Standing across the bay, perhaps fifty yards from the empty house, stands a larger building with a covered area, in which a large boat shelters. Nets, many yards long, are hung across posts, drying, evidence again that the village has only recently died.

My mind flashes back to the day my mother died, and, despite my clenched teeth, a groan escapes me as I walk around the hovel. With no preamble I open the door and step into the darkness. The sun is almost set now and the steep cliffs throw the whole bay into shadow, so it is only the light from the sky to the north that creeps into the building.

A table and fire pit sit unused, bowls and a pitcher reside on the table, rope is strung between two wooden frames and baskets of fish, days old and smelling high, make up its contents. There is no-one here, and I head through to a door, ill-fitting but easy to open, and am met with a soft enquiry.

"Who is it?"

The voice is weak and, in the less than half light I can not even see from where it emanates. Cracks of light indicate a window, and I undo the latch and push open the shutters. Again the voice, "Who is there?"

Turning I see a cot, on which is an elderly man, the areas of skin I can see between filthy shirt and white beard are pock-marked, but the redness seems to have gone.

"My name is Hobb Grey, I am a Watcher."

He grunts, and then says, "Can you get me some water?"

"I can." I pick up the pitcher and walk back to the stream. Alice looks up, and I tell her what I have found. She looks pale, and I realise this must be hard on her. It is hard on me.

Filling the pitcher I return to the old man, pouring some of the cool water into a bowl and handing it to him. He struggles to sit, leaning against the wall, and sips at the water, making appreciative noises as he does so. When he has finished I take the bowl from him.

"How are you feeling?"

"Better than I did." His accent is thick, the vowels lengthened so that "did" sounds as "ded". Many people who live in out of the way villages like this

VISITATION

spend their whole lives in them, leaving only to attend markets, and a man of his age would find it difficult to climb the path out. My mind goes back to Lockwood, the albino shar-man, and I wonder who or what these people worship.

"Good. When did you become ill?"

He thinks for a while, forehead creasing. "Days ago. Not sure exactly. Been out for some time, just about as sick as I could be, I reckon. Is anyone else sick?"

I decide to try and question him now rather than answer his question, as I think I will get little from him when he knows the truth.

"I understand some men came here a little while ago to catch a ship."

He nods, and goes to rub his beard, something I assume he does as habit, but when he touches his face he winces. "They did. Three of 'em. Stayed a night and then set a signal fire on the shore to draw in a ship." His face clouds, and I suspect that he is trying to remember something more. "That day was when I fell sick. Terrible headache. They took something in a crate."

"Did they arrive with the crate?"

He shakes his head. "No. They got it from Izaak."

"Izaak?"

"From across the bay, opposite." He waves his arm towards the house I have just come from - the empty one. His hand is covered in pustules, now dry and scabbed. He brings his hand up to look at it, turning it to see how far the pocks have gone. They even cover his palms.

Bringing his hand up to his face, he gently runs his fingers over his skin, and his eyes show fear.

"You are recovering. In a day or so you will feel better." I say, and I believe it.

"Is anyone else sick?"

Be honest without being explicit. "They have been."

He looks towards me and understands what I mean. His face falls and he shakes a little. "Oh, but Queen Bitch has been busy," he says, his voice so heavy and cracked that I can not respond.

"I still have one more house to check; your neighbour." As I stand I look down at him. "Would you like something to eat? We have a little to spare."

He is still for a while, as if unsure of what I said, and then shakes his head. "No. Not hungry."

I leave him and close the door behind me. The sun has set and I had not realised that the world had darkened, wrapped as I was in the old man's misery. The bay is beautiful, the half-light from the deep blue sky producing heavy shadows tinged with purple and, if it were not for the contents of the houses, this place would be almost idyllic. As it is I am eager to leave. We shall use the empty house to sleep in and head back first thing in the morning.

Alice is still sitting, resting her head in her hands. I can just make her out, mostly silhouette with some highlights. And so I stomp to the final building, knowing what to expect and terrified that the disease has hit so hard and so fast. I can carve protections on the house to keep her safe.

The final building is everything I know it will be. Three bodies, all foul and filled with pus.

With a sigh I exit and head back towards Alice, and I finally realise that something is wrong. She does not raise her head as I approach and even when I stand directly before her she does not move. "Alice?"

She simply grunts, and with that grunt my stomach sinks and I start shaking. I kneel before her, gently placing my hand on her shoulder. "I shall prepare the house for us, you can rest soon." She grunts again, and I know her head is excruciatingly painful. Damn, I should have kept her well away from that child. I need to act fast now.

It is fortunate that the house is small, with only one doorway and one window, so the protection will be quick to carve. The bindrune is simple, and I quickly cut two on each post and one on the head of the door, repeating the same on the window frame. And then comes the blood. It always comes to blood. So I roll up my left sleeve and stare at the mutilated skin. Scars run across the whole surface, both from fire and knife, and there is no space left to make an easy cut. No where that would require less than permanent damage. And so, I swap hands, taking the knife into my left, where it shakes under the weight, placing the tip against the skin of my right arm and, with a deep breath held, push.

The cut is clumsy, free of the usual grace and dexterity, and the rune I cut takes far longer than it should, and the end result is poor, but it should suffice. I collect some blood in my cupped left hand and smear it into the carvings. This done I walk quickly outside to collect Alice and my pack. I gently slip my hand around her arm, pulling her upright. She staggers slightly and I can see, in the moonlight, how pale and sweaty she is. I lead her slowly towards the end house, a distance of 30 yards or so, but it takes us minutes, and she almost falls at least twice.

Eventually we make it into the building, and I settle her on the cot. As soon as she lays down she sighs deeply, a ragged sound of pain, and her eyes close.

Pulling the small lamp from my pack I click it alight and set it upon the table close by. Given what I saw with the girl, I would normally run a Test, but my arm is useless, and I am not sure that, even in the best of circumstances, it would really help.

The best I can do is protect her, not fight the disease, and that protection will change her forever.

The Pale Visitor

The soft light from the oil lamp casts black shadows that move slowly around me. The light illuminates Alice's face, and then only half of it, pale even in the yellow glow. Her breathing is shallow, and I know that the Fear is lurking around her, wrapping itself around her Wyrd, insinuating into her life and giving easy entry to the corruption that she brought with her from the child. More than that, I feel it now, here in this village, in this house. The runes I have carved will prevent its entry, but will offer nothing to what we have brought into the house with us.

The speed of her collapse has frightened me, and I need to work quickly. Pulling a chair next to the bed I take the rune bowl and begin the process of grinding the small, black ink stick against the side. I sometimes use ink to mark runes when carving is not appropriate, but now it will fulfil a different purpose. A little water turns the collected powder into a thick paste.

Have you prepared yourself, young Hobb? This will be an ordeal.

The voice of an old Master flows across my mind as I take a thin brass needle from my pack, passing the tip through the flame to cleanse it. Needles are always useful as rips in clothing are distressingly common. Tonight, however, there will be no stitching. With a soft, sharp little noise the needle is drawn against a whetstone, picked from the shingle outside, rotated along its axis a little, and drawn again.

Ideally I would have a stick to attach the needle to and tap it into her skin, but I do not have the time to go searching in the dark, so I will have to do it with less beauty in the design, and I am deeply, deeply sorry. Leaning over Alice's head I gently pull her hair back away from her temple. Moving closer

I bring the needle to her skin and begin to scratch, trying to cut deep enough without raising blood.

The pain is bearable, once I understand it, but it goes on for so long that I feel it working into my mind, becoming everything I am. It takes days.

The first set of runes, *my wyrd is mine*, is cut swiftly, the runes describing an arc from eye to ear along the hairline. I stretch my back and arms, looking down at the damage I have done to Alice's face. The first cuts are beginning to redden. And so, a deep breath and onto the next line, *as these runes are mine*, running from cheek to ear to bottom of jaw.

And nothing but me is here takes a long time to cut as the curve of her face is complex and I have to keep gently moving her head. The soft skin of her neck is particularly difficult and there are times when I do cut a little too deep, but the blood stops swiftly. I am very glad she is not awake. More so as I now begin the complex tracery which links the lines of runes, altering her wyrd to wrap around itself, fold in on itself, protecting itself. The words describe intent, the tracery links that intent to her wyrd.

As I finish, her body twitches slightly. Whether a symptom of her sickness or a reaction of the Fear within I do not know, but it matters little. I can not have her moving while I work and so, after cutting strips of the bed sheet, I bind her securely to the bed frame.

I straighten up, stretching my back, and move the lamp around to the other side, immediately throwing my work into blackness. I can now mark the cuts, smearing ink over them. It will have to stay there for a day or so until fully dry. When washed off the cuts will be permanently coloured.

And so onto the other side of her face. The runes I have cut so far are personal protection, powerful in stopping anything outside getting in, and expelling anything that should not be there. The ones I shall cut now have a deeper meaning. These are the runes of power, runes that will project her wyrd beyond herself, that will pull in power from around her, that will ward off attack and will give her her name. Cutting these is a task that I regret deeply, as these, even more than the others, should be her choice. The first runes are a protection, and are the only thing I can do to help drive the disease from her. The second are a cry to the world, a shout that Alice a Watcher, which, of course, she is not. However, it is unwise to cut one without the other, as it causes one's wyrd to curl about itself, like a shell. It protects but also imprisons. Without the bindrunes proclaiming her new self to balance them she would, over time, fall in on herself and become a husk of herself.

And so, with another deep breath, I start cutting again. The bindrunes are complex and intricate, and I take my time, trying to stave off the fatigue I now feel. I am not sure of the time, but it has been dark for hours.

My breath clouds before me and I stop the cut. I take a breath in and breathe out again, slowly, experimentally, and a soft cloud dissipates. I know that the night is warm, and yet I can feel the chill.

I am not alone.

Looking up I see nothing, the light from the lamp making more shadow than illumination, and I bend to my task again. There is a poem I was taught which aids my concentration, and I begin to repeat it. The lines are old, older even that the Great Conflagration, and are kept to Watchers. I remember when I first heard them, how the pattern of them held me, how the allegory with Fear made it easy to visualise.

"Then the dark comes,
nightshadows deepen,
from the north there comes
a fierce hailstorm
in malice against men.
From life to life, with life through life, the Watcher I am."

The first bindrune is cut, and as I start on the second the wind rises outside, quickly, rolling around the bay, rattling shingles and creaking the shutters, feeling its way in beneath the door, causing the flame to gutter briefly and then drops.

Oh, I know you. I have met you before, and you are not getting in. I have carved runes to bar you.

The needle continues its work, marking her life on her skin. The designs are universal, but the way they flow over the skin dictate the actual design, so every one is unique. They become a signature, clearer than a name, and a mark of power. A warning.

As I work the wind bellows again, and the first scream is riding it, howling as it did all those years ago, but this time I am the Master, and my runes are strong. I know this.

As the flame gutters again, trying to escape from the wind as it oils its way through the cracks in the door, the shadows create shapes in my peripheral vision, and I know, with sickening clarity, that something is there, squatting in the corner, pale, glistening and visible only in shadow. My breath is clouding again, but I can feel sweat prickling.

I do not believe it has actually got in, this is a ghost of what is howling around the building, of what sat at the core of the child, of what wants to curl itself into Alice and I will stop it. It was not expecting resistance, and it is furious and baffled. Once I complete the tattoos I can apply myself to it, but I can not stop now.

Cutting is a fiddly process and I have done it only once before, and then in almost ideal circumstances. Half way through the final bindrune a great wash of fatigue hits me. I feel it wave up from my feet and it runs into my hand before I am prepared, and my hand slips. I curse loudly, the needle skittering and then drawing blood. There is no way of erasing the mistake. All I can do is complete it as well as I can. The bulk of the rune is sound, but the mistake will have changed its powers. As for what it will do I can not say at the moment.

The wind screams again and something oily, wet and sickly writhes and flops on the floor, closer to us but soundless. I can feel it now, and my heart flutters as I race to finish the work before it reaches us. Pain in my left arm makes leaning over Alice excruciating, but I will complete this rune and, with a final flick of the needle I reach into the bowl and smear ink onto the wounds.

"I see you," I whisper, "and it is time for us to dance." I sit up, stretching, controlling my breathing, and the pain in my arm eases.

Standing, I pull out my knife, pick up the lamp, and walk over to the door. If my runes have failed I can strengthen them, but it will take more blood, which will weaken me even further. Stop whining, nobody said this life was easy.

Glancing down at Alice, at the smeared black on her face, at the knowledge of the scars beneath, at the sweat on her forehead and the ties at her wrists. At that moment the scream comes again, louder, high and low, resonances that hurt the ears and chest. I kneel at the door, checking the runes. Good and strong. Same as the ones at the window. I turn back, raising the lamp higher, and the shadows shy away from the light, creeping beneath the bed and hiding by the chair.

The pale thing has either gone, or was never there. If the former, then I do not know what it was. It did not come in past the warding, and the scream is testament to their effectiveness. If the latter, then it is perhaps time to retire.

I release Alice's bonds and settle on the chair. I am in for a long night.

Some hours later and I jerk awake. It takes me a while to get my bearings as I am pulled from dreams of the pale thing sitting, watching me as I sleep. Two things work their way into my consciousness, the first is that the screaming has stopped and I can hear the soft rhythm of the waves again. The second is Alice's breathing, which is slow and steady. Light is filtering in through the shutters, and I stand, painfully, and slowly limp my way to the window. My left leg has seized after the night in the chair, and I will need to treat it before too long.

Opening the shutters, the day is fresh but overcast with low, grey clouds covering what I can see of the sky, and I look out onto Wood Bay. I shall check in on the old man soon. I breathe deep, the air sweet and cool, but am dragged back into the room at the sound of movement from the bed. Alice turns onto her side and slowly, slowly opens her eyes.

Aftermath of Ink

Some hours later, Alice is sitting outside, looking out to the sea. I carried a chair and placed it by the door at her request. She looks pale and weak but her fever has gone and, with a little rest, she will recover well. She drifted in and out of sleep for some time after her initial waking, and, once I knew she was safe, I went across the bay to check on the old man.

It was little surprise to me that I had to cut him down from the rafters. Whether a result of his circumstances or a victim of the evil that spat its fury against the house I do not know. All I can hope is that the end was swift. I laid him on his bed.

I feel exhausted, both by lack of sleep and the excesses of last night. My arm throbs, pain lilting from fingers to shoulder, and my leg is tight. I have done a thorough application of emollient, and I hope that with a day of rest it will ease the tightness.

My concern over what was lurking in the house has not gone. The fact that it made no move is comforting, but I am none the wiser as to what it actually was. I have never seen Fear manifest directly before, and I am trying to recall whether any of my Masters made mention of it, but my memory is failing me. Given that the runes were strong and that the thing screaming around the house did not make entry, I am falling to the conclusion that it was something already latched to Alice. It may have been my mind making a representation of whatever is lurking at the centre of disease, and that is something that I can accept. If so, why have I never seen anything similar before? What is it about this woman that attracts such evil? The Yellow King at Stonehouse, the way she reacted to the standing stones, and now this.

The day is still overcast, and considerably cooler than of late, but still, and I have set a fire close to where Alice sits. A further look around the village revealed a smokery attached behind the first house I searched, with fish strung up inside. A couple are now suspended over the fire, and the smell is very good. Alice sits, staring into the flames. Her face is ragged, the ink smeared on her gives her a wild, almost animal appearance. I decide to have a good look in the house and walk past her. Her eyes follow me, but she does not speak. Something is brewing in her.

Standing in the doorway the room looks exactly as it did when I first entered yesterday. The cot, chair, my lamp. A small table with a bowl and cup on it. Nothing to mark it, and yet this place was empty. There is no body, no sickness, alone amongst the whole village. Why?

Izaak. That was the name the old man said; Izaak lived here. He also said that the visitors had got the crate they took aboard the Lady Jennifer from this man. My eyes scan across the room and I walk slowly inside, trying to take note of everything. The pits of the plaster on the walls, the scratches on the floorboards. Floorboards. the other houses had earthen floors, compacted and strewn with ferns. This house has boards.

Dropping to all fours I shuffle over to where the pale thing sat, running my fingers over the wood. A scuff and a splinter give me pause, and I look closer. The board runs beneath the bed and, if I lower my head, I can see the end but a few inches under it. Putting my shoulder to it I push the bed away and, after a little scrabbling, ease the board up. What I see beneath makes me sit back suddenly, and I swear loudly.

I am still sat on the floor when Alice appears in the doorway, looking in. "What?" Her voice is quiet, exhausted.

"Build up the fire, please. As big and hot as you can." She says nothing, but turns and I hear wood being dropped onto the fire.

Under the board is a small pit, hollowed out of the hard earth that has been placed on the shingle to level it prior to the floor being placed. Nestled comfortably inside is a piece of stone. Rectangular, perfectly smooth, as perfectly finished as anything I have ever seen. Cut into it are bindrunes, but these are ugly, vicious things. The components I recognise, at least some of them, and they are similar to the warding I have placed in the doorway, but they are surrounded by figures I do not know and whose purpose is hidden from me. I silently curse the timing as, had I suspected that I might find something akin to this I would not have cut myself to help the child and could then have divined something of this stone. And helped Alice, of course.

After a few minutes I wrap my hands in the cloth I used to bind Alice, reach into the pit, pick up the stone and march as swiftly as possible outside, throwing it onto the fire and then piling more wood around it. While I am watching, Alice passes me a fish and, as I pick flesh from it, she says, in a voice calm with anger, "What have you done to me?"

With a mouthful of fish, I answer, "Everything I could." And then, quieter, "Everything I could."

Her shout startles me. "WHAT HAVE YOU DONE TO MY FACE?"

I look up. Alice has turned to face me, her eyes are full of rage, her skin pale and she reaches up and wipes her hand across her forehead. "I can feel your marks. What did you do?" If she could she would spit the words. It must be the remnants of the Fear acting through the stone that is feeding her anger.

"I had to tattoo you. The disease was driven by Fear, just as it was in the child…"

"Jess. Her name is Jess." Her anger is deep, her mouth thin, and she hisses the words at me. Her body is tense, fists clenched and arms straight.

I nod, spreading my hands, aiming to placate her. "Yes, Jess." I rolled up my left sleeve. The cuts are scabbing over, something that has never had to happen before. The emollient has helped ease the tightness, but the pain of the cuts is still there. I turn my arm to show Alice, and say, quietly, apologetically, "I could do nothing else."

She looks down, her brow furrowing. The fire is going well, and the stone must be extremely hot by now. I walk past, picking up a small bucket which is sat at the corner of the building, and walk the few yards to the sea, filling it with water. I pick up a branch and push the stone away from the heart of the fire before emptying the bucket onto it. Steam hisses in great clouds and the stone cracks. I am sure I hear a quiet scream within the hiss, like the sounds in the wind last night, but that may well be my imagination. Fatigue swarms over my body and I feel my knees tremor. This has happened before on the completion of a Test, when Fear is forced from a person or area it seems to take energy from those around it, a small theft. In this instance, the feeling is strong, taking the air from my chest in a gasp.

"Alice," speaking is difficult, and I have to force the words from my throat, "if there was anything else I could have done, I would have done it." And then my voice fails, any further words I may wish to say are clamped in my chest.

It is as if the breaking of the stone has given me sudden, and unwelcome, clarity. I am old. I should have felt the presence of Fear in this house. I should have felt it in the child, *Jess*. I should have been able to protect Alice as a Watcher, and instead I reacted to situations without thinking. I have become impulsive and rash. Dangerous.

And you let people die.

I realise that tears are making their way down my cheeks. "I am sorry."

Alice stares at me. "How long do I have to keep this shit on my face?" Her tone has calmed a little, but I can hear the resentment. "Wash it off now. If the marks stay they will help you, if not…" I shrug.

She turns and walks slowly to the sea, kneeling at the edge of the water and splashing her face with water, rubbing hard. A sudden thought flashes into my mind, a thought that crushes me with fear and insight, and my legs give way. With a low cry I fall to my knees, the realisation of what I have allowed to happen thumping me hard, pummelling me in the stomach.

I hear footsteps in the stones which stop next to me. "We have to get back to Gloster," I say. My voice is hoarse, my throat tight, and I can barely speak. It is as if the events of the last three days have wrapped themselves around my neck and are preventing me from breathing. My chest is tight and I have to gulp to get air. The colour drains from the world around me.

I can not remember the last time I prayed, but now, silently, all the prayers I remember from childhood are repeated, and with the same childish hope and intensity.

Return

The journey back to the Way Station is not as pleasant as the one away from it. Alice does not speak, her presence is grim and brooding, and she stalks ahead of me on the track, keeping up a pace that I find hard to maintain. My left leg and arm are complaining, the leg through use and the arm through scars which are healing oh, so slowly, and by the end of the day I am limping badly.

The weather is closing in with dark clouds rising from the west, and there is a smell of rain on the air. It is cooler than yesterday, for which I am grateful, but rain, if it comes, will make travel more difficult.

It is approximately an hour out of Wood Bay when the damage Alice has incurred comes to the fore. The track winds its way down into a deeply wooded valley, executing a wide curve as it does so, I assume to skirt the remains of an Old World settlement, hidden within the trees. Such places are always a risk, providing cover for attack or thievery. Watchers are rarely the victim of such action, partly because of our reputation and partly because we generally travel light, carrying little wealth.

It seems as if such considerations have not reached this part of the country.

I became aware of noises in the trees to either side of the track only moments before two men emerge and block our path. I am also aware of a third behind us. Alice stops, perhaps five feet from the closest, who is brandishing a large knife. He is dressed in well-maintained, hard wearing clothes and I guess that this attempt at robbery is not his main source of income, but rather an opportunistic sideline. They must have seen us head north and hoped that we might pass back. Travellers on small side roads are rare, and we must have presented an almost irresistible opportunity for possible enrichment.

I lean heavily on my stick, taking the opportunity to rest and, I hope, presenting myself as older and more frail than I am. The first man to appear steps close to Alice, and says, "Your valuables or we take the gi…" He stops speaking when he looks at Alice, noting, for the first time, the marks upon her face.

With no warning or preamble, Alice moves quickly, stepping towards him, brushing his knife aside with one hand and driving her straightened fingers into his throat. As he grunts and staggers, her other hand, flat, is driven up into his nose, and I am sure I hear a crack. He collapses back, thudding heavily to the ground, knife discarded and hands clutching at his throat and face. Alice rapidly leaps over him, straddling his head and turning towards his companion. The time it has taken her to do this is but seconds, and the man she now faces is confused.

I hear movement from behind me, and bring my stick around, guessing that he will run past me to aid his friend. My stick connects well and a howl of pain causes birds to take flight. The figure staggers away to the side, bent over and clutching his arm. I turn my attention back to Alice. The man she is standing over is thrashing now, panicking, and I realise that the damage she has done will kill him as he is unable to breathe.

And so we stand, a little tableau of shock and pain. The terrible attempts of the man on the ground to live, the whimpers of the man on my right to support his, probably broken, arm and the stunned silence of the third man while Alice stands, still and calm over his dying friend.

After a distressingly long time, the man on the ground stops moving, and Alice, with the briefest of glances around, steps over the body, stands directly before me, her eyes blazing, and I am left with absolute certainty that there is a part of her that wishes it were me on the ground. Her gaze is a warning and, once it is clear, she turns and walks away, giving no thought to the dead man or his comrades.

I follow in silence and the day passes.

The Way Station is still sealed. We pass my pestilence markers, which are

RETURN

still plain and easily visible. Alice walks up to the building, looking around as she does, checking the shutters and doors and I watch gently running her hands over the woodwork and pressing the side of her head to the door. When I finally arrive, she looks towards me. "I can hear nothing inside." Her voice is almost accusatory.

I am breathing heavily from the walk, and it takes a while to get enough air into my lungs to speak. "Go and see to the horse, make sure he is ready to travel. I shall open the house."

Alice stands still for a moment, and then stalks past me towards the stable block. I bend down and recover the pliers, brushing the dust from them and then grasping a nail, twisting and pulling. With a set of teeth-grating squeaks it comes free.

A Maggypy chatters away to my left. I have never subscribed to the folklore about birds, but the line *a lone Maggypy calls for pain* flashes into my head. I pull the second nail, leaning close to the wood, filling my sight with it. The chatter comes again, closer, and I manage, with a fight, to pull the final nail.

I pocket the nails, thinking that I will either need to hammer them home again or give them back to Matthew as, although they are blunted now, they may still be useful and they are not cheap to buy.

When I push the door it swings open easily into the dark Inn, looking much as we left it two days ago. The room is quiet. There is a particular kind of silence when a house is empty, unlived in. It is a silence that craves company, swallowing every noise made by a single person. Only the movement and speech of more than one can defeat it, and I am alone so the sounds of my footsteps disappear instantly. I try and make less noise, giving the house less opportunity to swallow my presence.

Moving to the kitchen, dark and cold, I stop in the doorway. Matthew is slumped on the floor, the fire has gone out, and the little shrine to The Queen has been smashed, bone white fragments on the floor. Matthew is still breathing, his skin covered in pocks, red, painful blisters with white centres. There is nothing I can do so I turn away, slowly climbing the stairs. The shutters are all closed, and I regret not bringing a lamp. When I reach the top, I stand still, catching my breath and then holding it, listening to the house. Listening to the silence.

Turning to the left I push the door to the child's room.

Jess.

The smell, when I open the door, is so familiar that I no longer reel from it. Mother and child share the bed.

When I return to the door to the house, Alice is waiting for me. All I need to do is shake my head in response to her raised eyebrows. Pulling the nails from my pocket I push them back into the holes they came from and then ram then home with a piece of wood.

"How is Harrold?" I ask, turning away from the door.

"Fine."

I sigh. "Good. We need to get going. We shall sleep on the road."

Later, as the sun drops and the sound of Harrold plodding accompanies the creaks and clattering of the cart. Alice is sitting in the back, her knees up and her back to me. There has been some traffic, but the road is empty now and I decide to try and clear the air.

"I had no choice." I turn my head back to see her, but I can only see the top of her head. Her hood is pulled up. "When I marked you, I had no choice. It was all I could do to protect you." She does not move, and it takes a long time for her to answer.

"You could have asked before you cut my face." Her voice is quiet, but there is oak behind it. "You should have asked. Told me what you were doing."

I am slightly taken aback, and for a minute do not know how to respond. When I do I can not keep a slightly exasperated tone from my voice. "Asked? You were unconscious."

Her response is immediate, furious. "I was not. I was awake." She thumps her fist onto the wood, turning towards me and shouting. "I was awake the whole ficking time. I lay on that stinking cot with that foul thing next to me while you cut into my face. And not once, not once, did you talk to me. Not once did you consider me. Like you did not consider the results of your choice to come here. Like you did not see Jess as a person." Her anger is rising, and flecks of spittle are bubbling her lips. She is shaking with rage.

She manages to get herself under control, and repeats, "I was awake when you cut my face", pushing back her hood so that I am level with the scars I made.

"If I had known…"

"That seems to be your mantra." She turns and slumps back into the cart. After a while she lies down and I am left alone with the moonlight and Harrold.

I stop after a few hours and settle the horse, allowing him time to rest. I stay awake, sat on the cart, enjoying the peace. I have not bothered to set wards. We are next to the Emfie and I have good sight in all directions. The sky cleared briefly and stars filled it, but clouds are coming in from the west again, sheets of darkness that promise rain. We should reach Erthcott later today, and then two days, possibly less, to Gloster.

And then to see what damage that crate has done.

Gloster

We take turns driving, resting Harrold less than we should but ensuring he has plenty to drink. The road gets busier as we head north and I am constantly listening for any news of pestilence, but there seems to be nothing. Even the station just to the north of Bristol is free of such news. It is full of travellers and we stop only for food and to water the horse. Alice has gone inside to pick up supplies and it gives me an opportunity to think. My arm is healing at last and it itches, my leg aches, my skin is tight and my mind is a mess. The one positive is that I recognise the fact, and I need to get it back on track before we reach Gloster.

I cast my mind back to the time we were here before, when Alice sensed the stones, and to the meeting with Lockwood. His view of the old standing stones was similar to mine. Avoid them, be wary, ward against them. And yet, Alice sensed or heard those stones, walked among them and touched them. And all with no ill effects. And I could not follow her.

Could not, or chose not to?

And then, in the hut, with the wind howling and screaming to get in, the pale thing that appeared, squatting on the dirt floor. I had taken it to be something of Fear, but it made no movement to get close to her. What was it she said earlier?

I lay on that stinking cot with that foul thing next to me while you cut into my face.

She could see it. She knew it was there. She could feel me cutting and she knew that thing was there.

Who in the name of the Queen is she?

Maybe it is unimportant. After all, she is not my enemy, at least, I do not think she is, and there are more important issues to consider than her feelings over my work on her face, or her reaction to the stones. Something has set its sights on Gloster, has killed a family and a hamlet, and is sat in town, presumably sending its foul tentacles deep into the population.

Alice throws a sack into the cart and then climbs up to take the reins. With a soft whicker Harrold steps forward, his huge feet softly thudding on the hard ground and we continue our journey. Heavy clouds now cover the sky and, as we begin the long haul up the hill which will take us closer to the Bristol Glass, raindrops begin to fall. Before long there is a loud crack of thunder and the downpour begins in earnest, quickly turning the dry dirt to mud. Harrold shakes his head but continues his steady pace and I pull my hood up. Of all the sounds a man can hear, one of the most dispiriting is the sound of rain on a hood. That flat, constant patter with no rhythm is one that I loathe, and I hunker down. Movement behind me suggests that Alice is also trying to make herself as small a target for the deluge as possible.

The storm does not let up. By the time we crest the hill the world has turned grey and contracted to little more than a few hundred yards. The magnificent view we enjoyed on the way down has vanished, to be replaced by grey moisture.

The rest of the day is a collage of rain, silence and slowly passing scenery. Rain, silence, slowly passing scenery.

We decide to settle for a few hours some five miles beyond Erthcott. I have guided Harrold off the Emfie along one of the small tracks which feed the villages, and pull him to a stop in a pasture sat in the middle of banks of trees. It offers some protection from the elements and, now that the rain has finally stopped, provides a rest for the horse that is not mud. Alice has been dozing and wakes when the cart starts bumping over the ground.

When I bring the cart to a stop I lower myself to the ground, unhitching Harrold and allowing him to walk a little way off. There is a small dew pond towards the trees, probably dug for cattle, and he slowly makes his way to it before lowering his huge head and slurping loudly.

"Try and get a fire going," I tell Alice and, as she busies herself with a spade to clear away a patch of grass, I pull the large tarpaulin from the cart and begin setting it up. The cart has brass eyelets on the back and these are used to secure one edge of the canvas, while a frame of interlocking tubes can be clicked together which stretches it tight, doubling back on itself to form a tent with canvas on the ground. Another, smaller, tarp is then attached which forms a side so, when complete, we have a sort of triangular room attached to the back of the cart with one side open to the fire.

By the time I have finished, Alice has got a fire going, and she builds it carefully. The flames produce deep, deep shadows around us. I settle down in the tent, close to the cart, and stretch my leg out. After a few minutes I begin to feel the heat in my foot. Alice looks up, her face strange and mask-like from the firelight, and I gesture to the space beside me. I can almost hear her considering which she hates more, me or the prospect of sitting on wet grass, and, eventually, I win.

When she has settled next to me, as far away as possible within the confines of the tarpaulin, I speak.

"I understand that you are raging at me. I understand why. But tomorrow we should reach Gloster, and I…" I can not finish at first. The thought of what we may well be going back to is almost overwhelming, and I have not allowed myself to examine it whilst we have been moving. So I change tack.

"I have failed you. I wanted to keep you safe, and all I have managed to do is guide you to harm. The runes I have given you," and at this she runs her hand over her face. It is an unconscious action and when her hand falls she looks at me through the corner of her eyes. "The runes I have given you will protect you." She keeps her eyes on me, and they narrow. "I am aware of the irony, and I regret it."

With a deep breath, I continue. "What did you see in Wood Bay?"

She continues to stare at me, and then sighs, her shoulders falling. "The pain in my head had been building for some time and it finally got too much. I felt sick. When I felt it was like the outside world vanished. All there was pain and heat. When you took me into the house I knew what was happening, but I was separate from it, insulated. And then you started cutting, and I could feel every scratch, and it burned. "

"I could not scream, I could not move, I could not fight. And then it was there. It appeared next to me."

"Did it do anything?"

She shakes her head. "No. It was thin and pale, out of focus. And it did not feel threatening." She suddenly inhales and turns to me, "There was something outside. There was something trying to get in."

I nod. "There was. I carved runes to stop it."

She sits, thoughtful. I watch the fire. I have always loved fires, particularly when outside. There is something deeply civilising about a well-maintained fire. It marks the difference between us and animals. One of the curious aspects of the Fearful is that they never build fires. I have hunted them in the depth of winter and found them with frost-bitten hands and feet, fingers and toes black or missing, because they will not build fires. I remember talking with Campion about this many years ago, and his belief is that when Fear possesses a body it's main concern is to cause distress to those around it. Even for us, encountering a body that has suffered such damage and is still taunting us is terrible. What it must do to close family is beyond my capacity to understand.

After a period of silence, Alice lies back, pulling her bedroll around her. I wait for a while, banking up the fire and following sparks as they rise into the sky, and then I settle down as well.

I wake to early pre-dawn light, cold and damp with dew. The fire has gone out and the sound of crunching chewing indicates that Harrold is clipping the grass nearby. I pull myself out of the tent and realise that I am alone. My arm is stiff, but the pain has gone, and when I roll up the sleeve, the scars have almost healed.

A light mist has risen, sending the world to grey. Not only has the colour drained, so has the sound. There are a few birds, but the cacophony of the full dawn chorus has either already happened, or the mist has silenced them. Alice appears from the woodland, moving quietly. As she comes into view I am struck by the surety of her movement. She walks like a dancer, steady and with a quiet, reserved power. When she sees me she nods, and I feel that something has changed.

Her tattoos have settled, even the redness around them is fading, and the marks are visible but subtle. She reaches into the back of the cart and pulls the sack to her, reaching in to remove bread and smoked pork.

While we eat, Alice asks, "Will Gloster be bad?"

With a deep sigh, all I can do is say, "I think so."

A couple of hours later the Emfie begins the long run down to the flat plain between hills that houses Gloster. The road cuts through the land in a deep, wooded scar of Old World construction and slowly, slowly the great curve of the Severn comes into view. The hills which rise up behind Stonehouse darken the mist to the right and, if I peer, I can see the dark smudge in the distance that is Gloster. I can make just out ships on the river.

I am heartened by the fact that we are not seeing a huge amount of traffic bypassing the town, but the feeling in my gut is growing more unpleasant the closer we get.

Meetings

It takes another few hours to reach the walls of the town and I confess that I am looking forward to sitting on something that does not rumble. Harrold is looking tired, and I feel that I will be in for a stiff talking-to from Master Evenright. I wonder whether he has completed making Alice's knife?

Alice has moved to sit next to me. I am not sure whether she has forgiven me, but she has, I think, come to terms with what I had to do, and that is half the battle.

"Could you take the horse back to Master Evenright? I need to speak with Campion, and I would rather tell him about your…" I do not know what word to use, so I gesture to her face.

"Mutilation?"

"Tattoos. So that he knows what to expect."

She nods.

Gloster's noise and smell hits me almost as soon as we pass through the gates. Harrold's great head nods, whether from recognition or discomfort I am not sure, but he plods on regardless and soon we are at the northern end of Southgate Street and into the market square. From our elevated position I can see over the heads of the multitude of people and along Queen's Wharf Road to the river. There is a ship docked and, even as I watch, it pulls away from the wharf, and my stomach sinks just a little. The only ships that use the Queen's Wharf take the dead over to the opposite bank where they are burned. The ships sail once a week, on Fridays. Today is Wednesday.

A sudden pain in my side pulls my concentration away from the Wharf, and I realise that Alice has been poking me.

It takes my mind a while to come round to the fact that she is trying to get my attention. "What?"

"Time to get off. Go and break the good news to my uncle." There is a little humour in her voice.

I watch as she flicks the reins and gently nudges Harrold away, actually wishing I could go with her rather than where I have to go. With a sigh I turn and head towards the Town Hall.

The building is its usual, bustling self, with Clerks moving quietly around the lobby and a short, quiet queue of aggrieved people waiting to air complaints. As I walk through the lobby, my stick clicking on the floor boards, I realise that I am attracting looks. A couple of acquaintances nod to me, but for the most part, the looks I get are of slight distaste.

Out the rear of the hall and into the quiet of the offices, I knock once on Campion's door and then open it without waiting for a response.

Inside, and looking slightly annoyed, is my old friend and Alice's uncle, Cecil Campion. Always tending towards the portly, life in town has done nothing but increase his girth. He is not fat, but another couple of years will change that. He is sitting at his desk, which is, as ever, covered with papers. The room is dark, shutters closed and a single lamp provides the light which casts light poorly. Campion is also not alone. Sitting across his desk is the gaunt figure of Deacon Mustaine.

When they see it is me, both men stand, scraping their chairs back on the floor. Campion, although large, is spry, while Mustaine looks frail, surprisingly so given that I last saw him about a week ago. His eyes, however, are sharp little pinpricks in the yellow light, and his smile is genuine. Campion, too, looks pleased to see me.

"Hobb," he says by way of greeting, but his smile quickly disappears.

"Master Grey," says Mustaine, holding out his hand which I take. His grip, I am pleased to note, is still firm. As I enter the room, the two men settle back down, and Campion points me in the direction of another chair which sits, almost hidden in shadow, against the rear wall.

Seating myself next to Mustaine I am acutely aware of how grubby my clothes are. The glances of the Clerks have worked on me and now that I sit against Mustaine's quite beautiful robes and Campion's smart Judiciary clothing I am actually pleased that the lighting is so poor. Campion will have noticed, Mustaine, probably not. Or if he has he will not mention it.

A groan escapes my lips as I sit, and my leg suddenly twitches. It does this when I have not taken due care of it, and I suspect I will be suffering tomorrow. Ah well.

"How are you?" Campion asks.

"Tired."

"You look rough."

I can only agree. "We need to talk. It is probably best if you are here for this." I turn to the Deacon as I speak. The two of them share a look and I have a horrifying feeling about what will follow.

Campion leans back. "Come on then. Do we need a drink?" He says that last with a smile which fixes and he reaches behind him to a bottle and some goblets. Once we all have a splash of brandy I tell of the events of the last few days, missing out the parts involving Alice. I shall break those to him later.

As I talk the mood in the room deepens, and the Deacon and Campion exchange glances frequently. When I finish there is a pause, and it is broken by Mustaine.

"We have had two cases of the disease you described. A woman and her son. Both have died. I decided to send the Queen's Barge out yesterday to dispose of them rather than allow them to wait for the scheduled crossing."

Campion is staring at me, his mouth thin and his eyes glinting. He has always enjoyed a challenge, and I get the feeling that he views this as little more than a project, a possible exciting chase through the town hunting Fear-Ridden.

I turn to Mustaine, "When did they come to light?"

"They were found two days ago."

"And there have been no more cases?"

"Not that I am aware of." He looks questioningly at Campion, who shakes his head.

That surprises me. The speed of infection at Wood Bay was frightening, and I expected to see many tens of cases here by now. Maybe I am being too pessimistic. Still, that gives us time.

"So, Hobb," Campion, starts, "how bad do you think this could be?"

The lack of cases is a good sign, but there is something that prevents me from believing it is anything other than a pause. "Possibly terrible. I think that the Church needs to prepare for a truly awful number of cases, as does the town itself."

"If you can, be discreet," rumbles Campion. "It might yet come to nothing."

"Well," says the Deacon, pushing his chair back as he stands, "that will give me something to keep me busy." He reaches over the table and shakes Campion's hand, and then places his hand on my shoulder. "It is good to see you again, Master Grey. Come and visit when you have a minute."

I smile and nod. "I shall."

After he has left, I turn back to Campion. "I have not told you all, yet."

"Oh?"

This will not be an easy conversation.

"Something else happened in Wood Bay. Alice became sick." His face loses all colour. I quickly raise my hands, trying to diffuse the thoughts that are now cluttering his mind.

"She is well, now. She is returning the horse and cart to Master Evenright. But I had to protect her. Have you ever experienced the Fear in the wind?"

He exhales deeply, and he is shaking slightly, but rallies well. Shaking his head he replies, "No, but I have heard of it."

"Aye, well it found us, or was drawn to us. I carved wards but she had already been hit. This disease is Fear driven in a way I have never seen before, and I had to work quickly." I pull up my sleeve, showing the ragged scars and thickened skin. "Thanks to my attempts to protect the child I was in no state to work with her wyrd, so had to do the only thing I could, and I tattooed her."

"Gods!" He looks shocked, but I can see his mind working behind his face.

I decide not to mention the episode at the stones. I need to try and find information, and it seems to have done her no damage. Campion has more than enough to consider, anyway.

"I am sorry, but without it she would have died."

"How did she take it?"

"Poorly. At least, at first. I believe…I hope…that she has accepted it now. Luckily I could not do proper tattoos, and the marks are not easily visible. But they will protect her." I do not mention the error in the cuts. It might, after all, mean nothing.

Campion nods slowly. I was afraid he would become angry, but it seems as though he has accepted the need for my actions. We shall see whether that acceptance remains after he sees her.

"We need to trace every crate that was removed from the Lady Jennifer. I have to find what was brought from Wood Bay."

He nods again, more firmly. "Yes. I did make some enquiries, but it was such a mess that it was impossible to track the cargo being brought off the ship, and I have since been busy. Speak to the Harbour Master. I shall talk to the Aldermen, get them prepared just in case."

He looks at me again. "You need to clean yourself up before you do anything else."

The Harbourmaster

An hour after my meeting with Campion and the Deacon I am lowering myself into the hot water of a freshly drawn bath. Secretary Reddick has managed to keep the boiler going and it does not take long to heat the tank for Master Evenright's incredible contraption to provide me with plenty of water. I add a good cupful of the oil I use to soothe my skin, and a good soak will ease my burns and the cuts on my arm.

As I settle I close my eyes and allow the privations of the last few days to ease. I used to love travelling, and have spent most of my life on the road, but as I age I find that home has distinct attractions. I am concerned about the way my body has reacted to the cutting when I tried to save the child. *Jess*. I have not had to work that deep into a person's wyrd for a long time, and the way my arm has reacted is troubling.

I have had to Test people on a fairly regular, but with Testing I am concerned simply with uncovering truth, and the way of cutting is light and purposeful, aiming only to pull and guide. With Jess, I had to fight my way in, working against her own wyrd which was trying to protect her, and then to unwrap and disgorge the thing that lurked there.

A thought occurs. Jess was very sick, and that was as a result of limited exposure to whatever had passed through the way station, and the thing that I fought to extricate was also a remnant, an echo of the real thing.

And yet, there was the stone in Wood Bay. I wish I had somehow copied the runes as I do not know what that stone did, other than provide a focus for Fear. The sickness was brought to Wood Bay, it came with the travellers, so what was the need for the stone? What was taken in the crate?

I am not sure how the fact that there have been only two cases here makes me feel. A small part of me is feeling hopeful. Maybe whatever was planned has simply not worked, or perhaps they have succumbed to the disease they brought with them. I am, by nature, not possessed of a particularly positive outlook and what I suspect to be the truth is that terrible things are brewing.

Finding that crate, and quickly, is paramount.

I finish my soak and feel considerably better, at least physically, and I apply a good amount of the emollient before dressing.

Downstairs I find Secretary Reddick, sitting in her chair with the small window behind her, a glass of brandy and a book by her side. She looks up when I enter her room.

"You came back, then."

"I did."

She nods and takes a sip, the light from the grubby window allowing her to read without the need for a lamp. Dust floats around her.

"There is something I would like you to try and find for me, if possible."

She sighs, and closes her book. She will make a fuss about the amount of work I am asking her to do, but she will secretly relish the challenge.

"Find out about the standing stones and stone circles. Not what is written in the official records, go deeper. Older."

She stares up at me, barely blinking, and says, "That is not going to be easy."

"I know, but I have faith in you. Try speaking to Edward Madikane."

She huffs. "I know how to do my job."

I turn to leave and her voice, quiet stops me. "This goes against the Judiciary. And the Church."

Without turning I reply. "I know. It is important, however. If you do not wish to do this, I will understand."

"How important?"

"In truth, I do not know."

"But you have a feeling?"

"I do. And do not mention it to anyone."

There is a snort of laughter. "Mention it? This could get me excommuni-

VISITATION

cated and I am too old to starve. I shall think on it."

"Thank you."

I head along The Wharf, upstream towards the Harbourmaster's Office, which sits in a row of buildings between Silk and Spice and Boat Yard's Wharf. There are people along the length of The Wharf, and ships are being loaded and unloaded. Porters shout and gesture. The Lady Jennifer has been removed from Ropemaker's, but the damage to the wharf is extensive. Workers are sawing and replacing the splintered oak, hammering wooden pegs to secure the massive beams they are using.

The barge used to convey the dead is berthed at Queen's Wharf again, looking suitably regal in her black and white trim. I note that the paint is scuffed and peeling, and I wonder when her next voyage will take place. Hopefully it will be back to weekly.

The Harbourmaster's office is a small building set slightly proud from the row it sits within. Well maintained, half-timbered with shingled roof and with leaded glass windows looking out across the river and up and down The Wharf. It has a tower rising from the roof, in which a lookout sits, logging the comings and goings of the trade ships.

A huge air-boat rises from the boat yards beyond the walls to the northeast, its propellers biting the air as it slowly turns towards the south. I understand that the Harbourmaster also logs the air traffic, which has been steadily increasing over the last few weeks. Winter sees an almost complete cessation of flights as the winds are so unpredictable, but the hot, still days we have had recently have been perfect for them. Personally, I am yet to be convinced of their real value, as they are not capable of carrying the same loads as the ships, and they seem to be terribly temperamental. There is no denying their grace and beauty, however, and I take the time to watch as the huge, fish-shaped machine picks up speed.

Once it has disappeared behind the rooftops I enter the office. Inside are a couple of desks, large chests with thin, wide drawers against the walls, and shelves full of ledgers. The room is getting light from the windows, the sun beginning to show itself more towards the west now, and there is an air of quiet busyness. Three people are at work, two men sat at the desks, poring over books and checking data, and a woman with grey flecks in her hair standing at a large table on which lie several maps that occupy almost the entire surface.

It is she who looks up when I enter. She immediately walks towards me, covering her eyes with her hand and issuing the greeting, "May the Queen guide your journey." I cover mine, "And may she guide yours."

"I am looking for the Harbourmaster."

She extends her hand, and I take it. "Master Evelyn Scornsy."

"Master Hobb Grey."

"You are the Watcher for the town, I believe."

"I am."

"Well, come through to my office, sir."

She turns and leads me through a door, stopping to ask the young man at one of the desks to bring coffee. We turn right and head up a flight of steps to a room that occupies the entire frontage of the building. It offers wonderful views across the river.

The room is also full of ledgers and chests. Sitting in front of the window, facing the door, is a long desk with leather inlays. The room smells of wood and paper and ink, and I find myself instantly comfortable.

Scornsy settles in a leather covered chair behind the great desk and she offers me an almost equally grand seat opposite.

"Now, how can I help the Judiciary?"

"I am not sure that you can, but I need to try and trace the whereabouts of a crate that was carried upon the Lady Jennifer, which crashed last week."

Master Scornsy is a slightly built woman and her face displays an intelligence and quickness. Immediately she stands, walking swiftly to a large, loose bound book on a shelf close to the desk. This she places onto the desk and, still standing, starts flicking through. The pages are full of close-set lists, headed by date and ship name. After a short while she alights on the appropriate page.

"Here we are, the manifest for the Lady Jennifer. Do you know where the crate was bound?"

"As far as I am aware it was here, but the only thing I know for certain is that it was picked up in Wood Bay."

She runs her finger down the list of data, until she reaches the final entry. I note that the words "wrecked in port" are written in red ink below the line. She turns the book so that it faces me. The line of text reads:-

13th June - Wood Bay, Devon - One Case Skins and Salted Pork - PP - D.Tanney, Fleece Row - 130lb - 0

The page is finished with two signatures, one of which is Scornsy's.

"How is this information collated?" I ask.

"Each entry is taken from the ship's manifest and shipment dockets. It is then written up here and the appropriate tax calculated. There was no tax charged on this as it contains food. The entries are then checked and signed off. Any that require tax to be paid are held in bondage until the debt is settled."

"But as there was no tax on this crate?"

"It would be free to be collected. The docket stated that it was pre-paid." She points to the *PP* on the ledger.

"And do you check where it then ends up?"

She shakes her head. "Really not our business, I am afraid, Master Grey. If something which is ordered does not arrive, then complaints are made to the shipping company. There are also cargo that the shipping company or captain buys en route in the hope of selling, but they are marked separately and any duty paid on sale."

Looking down the list I can see that the ship carried a wide range of goods, including fleeces, flour and wine in bulk, along with fragile or high worth goods like glassware. I suppose that ships like this which hug the coast are often gentler transport than carts.

"Are there any goods from the ship that have tax owing?"

Scornsy scans the data before answering. "Yes, two items. A barrel of wine and a crate containing cones of sugar. The sugar should have been taxed as it came into the country, but sometimes the correct paperwork is missed."

"And I assume you check the contents of the crates on which any monies are owed?"

She nods. "Of course. We do this with either the captain or a representative of the owners present."

All of which means that D. Tanney is my only lead now as to the whereabouts of the crate.

"You look disappointed."

I give a small laugh. "Disappointed? No." And then I sigh, "This is as I expected."

Scornsy closes the ledger. "Well, I am sorry I can be of no more help."

A sudden wave of exhaustion hits me. My lack of decent sleep over the last few weeks along with the nagging thoughts over what may be about to happen swarms through me, and it must be evident as a look of concern crosses Scornsy's face.

"Are you well, Master Grey? "

"Ach! Just tired. Well," I say as I stand, "I had better go and see Master Tanney."

When I leave I realise that I have not eaten since breakfast, and that seems like half a lifetime ago. The sun is lowering in the sky, spreading red across the low banks of clouds and Tanney can wait until tomorrow.

Entry One

Record of Helen Cready, Clerk
 I was approached by Master Campion today, whilst I was compiling the Bills of Mortality, and asked to add a new category, that of Yellow Pox. I was to prepare two copies of the Bills, one for Town records, with the correct number of deaths included, the other to be posted for public consumption, with a much reduced number recorded.

I questioned him as this is irregular, but he was most adamant.

And so, under his guidance, I recorded 12 deaths to Yellow Pox, but wrote only of two on the public Bills.

Warehouses along the docks are being cleared in order to cope with goods needing storage from quarantined ships.

Tanney

When I return to the Excise Committee I have the simple aim of finding something to eat and then to sleep. This aim is thwarted as soon as I enter the building and turn to the kitchen. I can see soft light coming from beneath Secretary Reddick's door and assume that I will therefore have the place to myself.

The kitchen, however, is occupied. Alice is sitting at the table. She has a large pot of stew before her and is ladling some into a bowl, which she places opposite her. She has a similar bowl before her, and looks up at me, gesturing me to sit with her eyes. I do not argue.

The stew is rich and thick, with a deep flavour of paprika. I know it is beyond Reddick's abilities to produce, and I suspect that it has been bought from the tail end of the day's trading. Food is often sold off cheap come the close of the stalls.

We eat in silence, and I actually find that I am enjoying the company, because of, not in spite of, the lack of conversation. Alice reaches down below the table and pulls up half a loaf of bread, which she places between us, ripping a hunk off. I follow her example, dipping the crust into the broth.

As we finish, and I begin to feel slightly more human, she reaches down again, this time placing a knife, complete with beautiful leather sheath, onto the table. She unclips the clasp and slowly draws the blade out. The blade is small, only three inches, but it is bright and sharp. She gently places it flat, and I can have a better look. It really is a thing of beauty. The hilt is made of two woods, oak and beech at a guess, and the dark and light are curved around each other, smooth and perfect, held in place with a bright brass butt.

Alice says nothing, so I break the silence. "I take it I owe Master Evenright some money."

"He says not. He says it is a gift from you to me, and that he is pleased to have made it."

I am quite overcome, and find it impossible to respond. Indeed, with all that I have put this woman through I am surprised she is willing to sit here, yet here she sits.

"Thank you," Alice says, very quietly. I inhale roughly, a little shudder breaking the sound. "Will you let me teach you how to use it?", I ask.

She thinks for a long while, and I honestly do not know what her answer will be. Eventually she sheaths the blade, stands, attaches it to her belt and, as she walks around the table to leave, she stops and says, "I shall."

When I hear the door close behind her, the tears finally come.

Sleep is restless. The deformed, nameless city is my home again, but this time it is populated by terrible, diseased creatures that fill the streets and block my progress, grabbing at me as I try to run through the streets. The dark light gives them a truly appalling countenance and seems to highlight the pustules which cover every exposed area of flesh.

When I wake, I wake in sweat, again. I also wake to the sound of rain on the shingles, a sound that I have not heard for weeks and it takes a few seconds for me to realise what it is. The cooler weather suits me better than the heat, I can think and walk freely, wearing my robes and scars in more comfort. It is with a slightly easier mind that I apply the oil and then get dressed. Today I shall visit Master Tanney and see what has happened to that crate. The fact that there have been only two cases is something I should take as a positive, for it at least gives me time.

The smell of bacon seeps into my room, and my stomach rumbles.

Reddick is standing with a pan resting on the fire. She looks round when I enter the kitchen, and grins. "I thought that this might rouse you."

I smile.

"We have eggs as well, and fresh bread," she says happily.

"You seem happy," I say, and she nods. I think that giving her a project has brought a little spark of life. The kettle is sat on the coals and begins to sing, so I reach around her thin little frame to make coffee.

As we eat I ask about the stones, but she shakes her head. "Too early," she mumbles through heavily buttered toast. "Need more time."

After breakfast I don my robes, pick up my stick, and venture out into the rain.

The ground is so dry after weeks of heat that the water simply pools or runs into the gutter trenches, where it quickly collects all the dry material that has accumulated. The ground is extremely slippery, a thin covering of slick mud where the water has not yet had time to soak in. If the rain continues the paths will soon become thick and cloying.

In the market square heavy tarps are being raised over stalls and people are taking cover in doorways until the market is fully ready. There is quite a little gathering under the portico of the Town Hall.

Southgate Street is a little clearer, but the rain increases its efforts and I am finding it more difficult to walk. My stick slips occasionally, once into the path of a man who trips on it, almost falling. He turns to shout but stops himself. I raise a hand in acknowledgement and he continues on his way.

Fleece Street is off Oxbode, another wide radial street which runs between Southgate and Eastgate. Oxbode was originally where cattle were brought for slaughter, but it is now one of the more affluent parts of town. The wide street, once full of cows and stench is now a mix of merchant-class residential and the sort of businesses which can be done quietly and cleanly. In particular the area, including Fleece Street, which heads off Oxbode towards the east wall and then turns sharply, is home to small trading and mercantile companies. These are often run by families, and trade and import small quantities of goods which the mighty Spanish Trading Company ignores.

The fact that they are situated far from the docks means their rent is lower, and, as long as they steer clear of the goods controlled by the STC, they can make a decent living.

Tanney's business, announced by a small carved plaque next to a bright yellow door, is half-way between Oxbode and the sharp corner. The little streets in town are generally in shadow and, as a consequence, many people use colour to brighten their dwellings, with yellows, reds and oranges often being mixed into the lime wash.

The little plaque reads "D. Tanney, Things of Worth", which points to something I suspected - that the shipping note was false. I open the door and step inside. A little bell announces my entry.

The room is lit by several oil lamps, which create a soft, pleasant space. There are a few shelves on which are beautiful vases and exquisite mechanical apparatus, clocks are very common. A polished desk with a large, bound book upon it sits close to the back wall. The floor is smooth oak, polished and clean and, from a door at the rear, a young man appears, well dressed in a dark blue tunic. His face is open and friendly, even when he sees my robes. He performs the Queen's Greeting and then says, "Good morning, Master Watcher, how may I be of service?"

"Unfortunately, I think you will only disappoint me."

He frowns, and I realise I have probably made him think I mean to question him, so I keep speaking.

"I am following a crate that came ashore on the Lady Jennifer, and was registered to you"

He shakes his head a little. "That was the ship which crashed? I do not think I have received anything from her. How large was the crate?"

"Around three feet square, I think."

He shakes his head. "I am sorry, but I rarely get anything that large, but let me check."

He steps to one side and sits at the desk, opening the book and running his finger down the entries. He turns several pages, shaking his head as he does so.

"I am sorry, Master Watcher, but I have not received anything like that for months. Can I ask what it contained?"

"You can, but I am unsure. The docket said skins and salt meat, which," I look around the shop, "would probably not sit well in here."

He smiles as he closes the book. "Probably not."

"What is your business?" I ask, as the collection of items, although all of high quality, is diverse.

"I act as an agent between clients and craftspeople. I have inherited good connections across Urope for talented people who are in need of a market, and people with the money to spend on quality items that might be difficult to locate."

"Inherited?"

"From my father. He set up the business twenty years ago, and I have taken it on following his death."

I move closer to one of the shelves in order to inspect the wares. There is a small vase, perhaps two inches tall, whose walls are so thin as to be translucent, the pattern on it cleverly exploiting this to form a woodland scene that appears to have depth, with trees appearing to be in mist. Next to it is a small clock, all polished brass and rich enamels , which displays the date and moon phase.

"The items in here are for sale. Most of the time I deal with commissions, but occasionally either the goods do not meet the brief or the craftsperson makes something for their own reasons and sends it to me. When it sells, I pay them."

"And how much would this little piece set me back?" I ask, indicating the little vase.

"That is thirty pounds."

I stop my finger from touching it and slowly withdraw it. Two of these vases would be enough to buy a house in a less salubrious part of town.

"Are you not afraid of thieves?"

He gives a little laugh. "This shop is well protected. I have one of Master Evenright's fiendish infinity locks," he points towards the door, and I can just make out the bolts in the frame header, " which seals the door and window, and that is the only entry. I also have insurance with the Spainish Trading Company."

I look at him, surprised. "Insurance with the STC?"

He gives a small laugh, "Yes. I am no competition to them, but yet they still manage to take money from me."

He then says, "May I ask what you were hoping to find?"

"That is more difficult to answer than you might be expecting. In truth, I am not sure."

Master Tanney does not press, presumably because tact is necessary to his work.

His mention of Evenright does prickle my mind.

"Well, thank you for your help, Master Tanney."

"I am sorry I could not be of any."

Blessings

Madikane's Old World Curiosities sits in a small side street away from the hustle and bustle of the town. Inside is is dark and peaceful, and I sit with Edward, a cup of coffee in hand, and he listens to the tale of my recent trip.

Over the months I have known him he has managed to gain a license to sell Old World books and documents, and has converted a small room behind the main part of the shop into a storeroom. It is extremely secure, and, as per the terms of his license he is extremely careful with who he sells goods to. He is just as careful as to who he buys from.

The trade in the Old World is frowned upon by the Church, hence the regulation. The world is too big and the Judiciary too small to effectively stop all interest, so the Church has introduced a method of control. Those wishing to trade register with the local Judiciary and are, after extensive vetting, granted permission, with different levels of license available for different levels of goods. Those caught trading without a license are dealt with extremely harshly.

Edward is proud of the trade he does, but I admit that it makes me uneasy. I do not understand the fascination that it has upon some people. The engineering feats are certainly magnificent, the Emfie being a prime example, but their world failed, and it failed in fire. Its collapse led directly to the creation of the Glass and the rise of Fear. However, I trust Edward, and he is aware of my feelings.

After a while he sips his coffee and looks at me over the rim of his cup and in his deep, soft voice says, "I had a visitor last night."

"Someone interesting?"

He nods, sipping again. "Your Secretary Reddick."

"Ah!"

"Ah indeed. Tell me, why was she asking about old tales of standing stones?"

In my telling of my travels over the last few days I have omitted the details about Alice and the sickness, concentrating instead on telling him about the journey. He does not get to leave the town much now and he loved travelling in his youth. When I spoke to him he closed his eyes and I could almost see his mind imagining our travels.

Now he is watching me intently.

I down my drink, and say, "Did you manage to help her?"

He shakes his head. "I did not. However, I did say that I would put discreet feelers out."

I look around the shop, at the strange tangles of metal, the broken toys, the wheels and all the other remnants of a world that burned, and the sight of Jess, lying in pain on her bed, covered in pustules sits before my eyes.

"I think something is coming. I think it is already here. And I can not find it."

"And this is a bad thing, I assume."

I nod, slowly.

Edward looks closer at me, and leans forward. "It is that bad?"

"The Great Conflagration cleansed the world, and from it rose The Queen, who brought swift mercy to those in pain."

"So begins The Redemption."

I look directly at him. "Lock the shop." He purses his lips and then stands. He locks the door and then, before he sits, says, "Should we have more coffee, or would something stronger be appropriate?"

"It is too early for me and I really need to speak to Campion later, but please, do not let me stop you."

He taps his foot on the floor, and then fires up a small oil burner, onto which he places a freshly charged coffee pot.

"There are two parts to this, and I can only tell you one, and it is the one that does not involve Secretary Reddick and the search for stones."

"Well," he says, gently moving the pot so that it sits square on the flame, "wait until we have coffee and I shall be a rapt audience."

A few minutes later the pot gurgles and Edward refills our cups.

"This had better be important, I am losing potential custom." He grins around his cup. I laugh, "Indeed, you may have a rush of a customer. How is business?"

He shrugs, "I make enough to keep myself in good coffee, and I meet some interesting people."

I sip the hot coffee. Edward likes it bitter, I would prefer a little sugar but he has none, so I try and take it as hot as I can bear. This means that it does not sit on my tongue for too long.

"When we reached a small Way Station, some way south west of Bristol, we encountered a family who had succumbed to disease. The child was extremely sick and I did what I could. Both mother and father fell ill soon after."

Madikane does not interrupt.

"I have not seen anything like it. It produced a mighty headache, fever and then an eruption of spots which rapidly filled with pus. The child was unconscious when I got to see her, and there was Fear there, but almost as a residue. Something had passed through and left the sickness. When we moved on to our destination, it had beaten us and wiped out a small hamlet. It had killed all but one person."

Edward puts his cup down and stands, telling me to wait. He unlocks the door to the rear room where he keeps his Old World documents, the complex lock clicking and whirring. He is gone for a short while, and the sound of rummaging is punctuated with occasional muttering. Eventually, with a quiet, "There you are", he returns, locking the room again. He is carrying a book. It has obviously been re-bound and, when he hands it to me, I note how incredibly fragile the pages are.

I carefully open it, and marvel at the neatness and small size of the writing. I have no idea how they managed to get such regularity, but I can see the attraction of the texts. This is titled "A Treatise on Smallpox."

"Take this and read it."

This book would be worth a lot of money to a buyer, but Edward nods firmly when I look at him. "What you describe sounds very much like this disease, which was apparently wiped out long before the Great Conflagration. If it is, you are right to be frightened."

I stare at the book, and then look up at Madikane, who still stands by me. "Smallpox? It does not sound that bad." I try and inject a little lightness, but it does not work.

He sits again. "A name is not a thing. Read the book."

"Erm....My reading is not good."

"I know. This will be an ideal time to improve." He leans in. "Seriously though, you should try. There is more information to be had here," and he waves at the room behind him, "than in all the minds of the modern world."

"Yes," I bridle, "and it is information that the Church has deemed necessary to restrict."

He waves a dismissive hand. "And why is that, do you think?"

"The Redemption is very clear." Edward has, I feel, spent too long with his Old World books and he is falling into the trap that is the very reason why the Church is wary. The Old World has an allure for some. Whether it is for technology or knowledge, the pull of our ancestors and their heresy is strong. I like Edward, but he and I will need to have a talk if he persists down this path.

He watches my face intently, before dropping his eyes and saying, "It is."

We sip coffee, me and my friend while a book from five hundred years ago sits at my feet and warns of…what?

"The thing is," I say, "this disease, Smallpox or whatever it is, is being driven by Fear. Whatever is or was in that crate will guide and intensify it. In Wood Bay, the village that had died, there was a stone, carved with runes that I do not know. Whether it was there to summon an aspect of Fear or to concentrate whatever had been brought to the place I do not know. What I do know is that whatever it was in that crate is in this town. It has caused the deaths of two people, three if I count the captain of the ship, and I believe it will soon raise itself and set itself free."

Edward sits back in his chair, the soft light from the window casting deep shadows on his black skin. A little glint sits in his eyes, a bright pinprick against the dark.

"I have seen what disease can do to a town. I lived for a while close to a fishing port on the south coast, Osminton. This was, maybe, thirty years ago. One summer, a hot one like this, Black Death came. Have you seen what it can do?"

I shake my head. "No. I have heard of it, of course, but never seen it."

"It is a hard killer. There is no dignity in it. It spread rapidly, and within two months half the population were dead. The port never recovered, it was abandoned during that winter."

I nod slowly. "Ay. I have seen similar, with Cholera."

"Yes, Cholera can rip through a village like nothing else, but with good water it is contained. Black Death has no such mitigation, it is a visitation from the Queen herself." He briefly covers his face with his hand. "If this is the Smallpox, I may be in the privileged position of seeing Her twice in one lifetime."

He places his coffee cup down on the floor and stands again, this time walking to the large desk and opening a drawer, from which he returns with a bottle. The top is uncorked and he pours a large amount into his cup before offering it to me. I refuse, and he shrugs and places the bottle next to him.

When he speaks again, after gulping a mouthful with a shaking hand, his voice catches. "I am not sure a man should be blessed so."

Thoughts and Remembrances - The Church

My dealings with the Church have been sporadic. As a Watcher I have spent most of my life unsettled, moving from village to village and not having a strongly rooted base. I have met with many priests and lay-members, and even the occasional Bishop, but in villages where there is no official presence, I am the representative of the Queen.

However, there are many things I may not do. Whilst I may conduct funerals, it being a regrettable but necessary part of a Watcher's life, I can not perform any other duty otherwise conducted by the clergy. I may report infractions of Church doctrine, but acting upon them is out of my sphere. There was a time, long passed, when a Watcher could act as a priest and perform marriages and namings, but the Church has slowly pulled such things back within its purview.

I may be called upon to act as part of a jury, either in legal or ecumenical issues, and have done so several times, not making doctrinal decisions, obviously, but weighing in on whether corruptions of religion are Fear related and, if so, what punishment, if any, is appropriate.

I know my place within these courts, and rarely have any cause to query or question the proceedings.

There was one time, however, when I did argue. It could have gone very badly for me and I was introduced to an aspect of the Church that makes me uncomfortable still.

I had stopped at a village, this was many years ago, you understand, and I can not remember the finer details. Villages all melt into one. I do remember that I was returning to Statfield to see my father, who was settled back into his life following the death of my mother, but exactly where it was is lost to me now.

I had spent one night close by, camped on the outskirts and enjoying company after many days lonely walking. The priest was a young man who had only recently been installed. Where an older man might have worked slowly to settle himself into the community he took the path of the firebrand. There are always some who take this route, and I generally avoid them, preferring a more mellow and thoughtful approach to religion, but I can see there is a place for such forthright and definitive belief.

However, things came to a head early in the morning when he accused a young woman of blasphemy. She had apparently struck him without provocation. Usually in cases such as this it is a requirement that there are witnesses before a case may be brought, and in this instance there was but one, a young lad who can not have been more than six years of age.

I was called by the priest to Test the girl, as she was screaming and full of anger. I could see nothing that suggested Fear, but performed a very basic Test, which conclusively showed that there was nothing to really concern me. However, as I had been brought in I was bound then to sit upon the jury, a jury presided over by the priest.

The evidence, such as it was, was laid out and the girl brought before us. She was fiery and forthright, and her story painted the priest in a poor light. According to the girl the priest made unwanted advances to her and she slapped him back. During her testimony the priest became extremely angry, shouting her down, and I remember watching him and finding her the more reliable witness.

However, I am always subordinate to the Church.

In such cases, all the jury can do is suggest courses of action to the Church representative, and I knew that there was no way he would listen to my views.

The decision was not a surprise. She was excommunicated. When she was taken away to be branded so that none could offer her succour, I took the young priest aside and spoke to him. I was firm and angry, seeing his decision as a blatant abuse of his power within the community. We argued, and I suggested at the end that I felt his actions could be read as being those of Fear-Ridden, which silenced him and possibly made him think.

I stayed a further two days, watching with great sadness as the girl was cast from the village and they turned their backs on her.

It was on the morning that I had decided to leave when a deputation arrived, headed by a Deacon, who met with the priest and, after a deep, intense talk, summoned me. I met with him in the hall that was used as a communal space.

He was older than I am now and less fiery than the priest, but he was also very certain of my position in regards to the Church.

When it became clear that I was in danger of becoming the subject of a trial myself, I explained my reading of events, of how it was my belief that the priest had tried to assault the girl and that she had merely defended herself. It soon became apparent that, not only were my arguments to be ignored, but that the actions of the priest were unimportant.

"Be very clear, Watcher," the Deacon said to me, calmly, quietly, "the authority of the Church is all that matters in these backwater places. It is not your place to challenge either the way it operates, or its representatives. Tread carefully, Watcher, for you would be a powerful example for it to use."

When he left I remember shaking uncontrollably. I packed hastily and walked away, looking back once to see the priest watching me go.

This event stayed with me for many months, and I actively avoided settlements where I could see the Church had a presence.

As I have got older I understand more the position the Deacon took on that day, although I will never accept the reasons behind the actual case being brought. If I encountered such a priest today in a backwater village, I would issue no warning, my test would be positive and my judgement swift.

The Lightness of Pigment

I stayed with Edward a while later, talking on lighter subjects so that, when I left, he was less melancholic. The book he has given me sits inside my robes, I can feel it bumping into my stomach as I walk through the crowds in the market square. The coffee has made me hungry, and I pick up a pie on my way through. As I settle on a bench and take my first bite, I am joined by Campion, who stands in front of me.

"I am glad to have found you." My immediate worry is that cases of the disease have been reported, and I stop chewing as I wait for him to continue. "I have arranged a meeting with some of the Aldermen tomorrow morning. I want you there. Nine O'clock."

I relax a little, and continue eating, but he does not leave. After an uncomfortable time I indicate the seat next to me. "Please sit, you are ruining a decent pie."

He huffs, but does join me.

"I have seen Alice." He is tapping his knee with his fingers, and I nod.

"And?"

"She told me her version of events." I look round at him, and he holds his hands out placatingly. "I believe you acted correctly, but she is wounded."

With a sigh I reply, "I know, and if there was another way I would have taken it."

His knee is now jiggling, and he slaps his hand onto it to stop it. He leans in so that he can speak softly.

"She told me something about a stone circle."

Ah! "I am looking into that."

VISITATION

"Looking into..." His voice is a mix of quiet fear and anger. "You and I have chased enough Fear Ridden to know what the ability to touch worked stone means."

"And yet she is perfectly lucid and calm. Something happened there that I have never seen, never suspected. She is not Ridden - I would have seen that when I marked her. I am making enquiries."

Campion was always too ready to get caught in the emotion of events, which is why the Judiciary suited him far better than being a Watcher. He needs time to weigh up evidence and, if forced to react, does so from the heart. A little voice, unwelcome, reminds me of my actions in chasing the origins of the crate, something that could certainly fall into the same category.

Campion slowly calms down. In truth, I have no idea whether to be nervous of Alice or not. Nothing feels different, and, as I have just said, I am certain that I would have picked up Fear when I marked her.

I turn to him, and say firmly, "Do not worry about her, at least not for this. If you must worry about something, worry about what may be coming."

With a deep exhale he says, "You may be right. Nine tomorrow. And clean your robes."

He stands and takes a few steps away, and then turns back. His expression has gone from anger to concern. "Should you need to act against her, tell me."

"Of course. But I am making no plans to do so."

Campion stands, undecided for a short while, before saying farewell and leaving. I watch him walk away, heading off towards the Town Hall. Should I need to act against Alice I will do so on my terms.

I turn back to finish my lunch, but it tastes flat.

Some time later I find myself standing in Jacob Perez' studio on Ness Row, and breathing in the smell of paint and sweat. I have found that this is a good place to come and think and, if Jacob is busy, he is quite happy for me to sit quietly in a corner.

He refuses to let me see what he is working on, which is not unusual. I have not known any other artists, but from what Inigo Evenright tells me, most people with an imaginative pursuit are there own critic, and hate the idea of their work being commented upon, even when complete. For an artist who relies so much on parody and the ability to shock through wit it would be a terrible thing indeed to be critiqued on an incomplete work.

He greeted me warmly and we chatted briefly about the past week's events, although I was careful to spare him any information which might cause him distress, and then he went back to his canvas, working quickly and with vigour, the sound of his knife scraping the surface as he applies thick paint providing a rhythm that I find soothing.

As he works, and when I am sure he is absorbed in his task, I pull the book from my pocket and start flicking through. As I have said, I am not adept at reading, and it takes me a while to find what I am looking for. I must make for a comical sight when reading, as I am certain that, should my index finger be somehow removed I would be rendered illiterate.

The disease followed a standard pattern, with fever and general feelings of being unwell lasting for a few days. Some days after this a rash appeared and rapidly spouted pustules, which, over the course of two days covered the entire body. Death, if it came, occurred some days later, with roughly one in three succumbing. There were other variations which were invariably fatal.

What made it particularly terrifying was the chance of permanent scarring and the fact that it spread incredibly rapidly. What gives me a knot deep in my stomach is the similarity to what I have seen, but also the speed with which it hit Wood Bay. This did not happen after a week and a half, but a couple of days. The child's parents were hit within a day of each other. If this does come to Gloster, it will strike so hard that it may be impossible to contain.

I am unsure just how long I sit staring at the pages of this ancient book, but when I look up to the window opposite the sudden bright light hurts my eyes.

Sight of a World Long Gone

I am standing on the top of a hill, on a wide area of stone. Before me, the land falls away, an area of grass with trees to either side, to a large, white building about a mile away. The building is wide, with long, covered walkways extending from either side. There is a wide, slow river curving just beyond. The building and its setting are elegant but what I stare at is the city behind it, a city so vast I can not see its extents, even from here. A faint yellow fog sits over it.

Rising from the haze is a collection of truly astounding constructions. They crowd on the horizon, hundreds of feet tall, with glass and metal glinting in the sunlight. One of these buildings is topped with a pyramid of grey.

As I stare, I see something flying. This is no boat, there is no envelope or propellers, this is something solid with wide, narrow wings. It drones with a discordant whistle, rising into the air from my right and turning away, with a speed that makes the huge boats over Gloster seem positively sluggish.

I can hear the life in this town, the constant buzz of people moving.

With no warning, no preamble, a flash of white, brighter by far than the sun, sears my eyes, and I bring my hand up to cover my face, mirroring the greeting of the Queen.

When I lower my hand and slowly, so slowly, open my eyes, the town has gone. In its place is a waste of black, gnarled molten stone, a sea of glass. Rising from it, no, fading into it as if it has been there all along but out of focus, is the place of my dreams, the strange angles and impossible buildings illuminated by two black suns.

There is another flash

The Darkness of Pigment

The light slowly fades, leaving me disoriented and nauseous and, as my eyes clear I am confronted by the face of Jacob Perez, concerned and close. As I open my eyes and shake my head to try and get my vision to settle, he exhales noisily.

"May the Queen rattle my corpse, but you gave me a fright."

I am on the floor, my left leg bent painfully beneath me and my head feels as if it is full of sand. Perez, is kneeling before me, his hand on my shoulder.

"Are you able to stand?"

"I think so." He stands, pushing himself up with a hand on his knee, and then offers that hand to me. With a grunt and a stab of pain I manage to put weight onto my leg, rubbing it as I stand. Jacob gently eases me back onto the chair.

I begin to feel better as I sit. The room comes into focus and, as the smell of paint and oil works its way into my nostrils, I realise that it is supplanting the stench of burning.

"What happened?"

There is no way that I can explain, so I make up something about being tired from the journey. He looks at me with, if not disbelief, then the surety that he is hearing but part of the tale. His hands, I note, are shaking, slightly but constantly. My gaze obviously rests for longer than I realise, for he pulls his hands away and folds his arms. When I look up at him with a raised eyebrow, he smiles and says, "You and I could both do with some sleep, yes?"

I smile. "I have been doing my job, what is your excuse? I know how you artistic types love to show off to impressionable clients."

Jacob laughs. "Ah! Such times we have." His face falls rapidly, and I catch a look, briefly, of pain.

"What is it?"

"You tell me yours and I shall tell you mine."

"I am afraid I can not."

"Official business?" His tone is exaggerated, slightly sarcastic, and I reply with an overly definite nod.

"You?"

He walks away, taking a seat close to his easel. He looks up at the painting and stares at it for some time. Eventually he turns back.

"One of the greatest joys of being an artist is when inspiration hits in such a way as to leave absolute clarity. It can destroy rest, sleep and friendship, but the end result is something that defines what you are."

"Then there is the opposite."

"When inspiration does not come?" I interject.

He shakes his head. "No. That is frustrating, but there is little to be done. No, the opposite is when inspiration comes but the hand is incapable to translating it to one's ability. It festers and burns and will not let you go. If it is particularly strong it precludes the production of other work until it has been exorcised."

He sighs deeply, and then shakes himself. "Listen to me, complaining about having an indoor job with no heavy lifting. You are out in all weathers fighting something which most people here," he waves his hand towards the window, indicating the town beyond, "simply have no concept of."

"And I fail in my work if they do gain knowledge of it."

Jacob returns to staring at the canvas on the easel. He grunts, and I can see that his mind has returned to whatever drives him. I stand, and am relieved to see that my legs are sturdy enough to use.

I bend to pick up the book that has fallen onto the floor, tuck it into my robe, and say goodbye to Jacob. He does not answer for a while, eventually tearing his eyes from the canvas to look towards me.

"Sorry, sorry. Are you well enough to go?"

"I am well enough. Thank you. Do not allow that," I point to the canvas, "take over your life."

He sends me a slight smile and nods but, when I turn back as I step through the door, he is staring again and does not notice that I have gone.

Aldermen

I spend the evening reading Edward's book with a large glass of wine and a chunky ham sandwich. Secretary Reddick is already back at the Excise when I return, but will not be drawn on her enterprises. Instead, it is she who pours the wine, stating that I "look like an ambulatory corpse".

The book is fascinating, but unnerving. It goes back into times so far before the Great Conflagration that I have difficulty understanding that such a world existed. As with all such texts, I am unsure how much is true and how much is propaganda. The Church holds that all Old World texts are untrustworthy, that they seed their lies with aspects of truth, and that the real danger lies in the inability to tell the difference. Given the contents of this book, I can not see the danger, unless it proposed treatments or cures that are false. One thing that has surprised me is the mention of red cloth being used as a preventative that was deemed useless. It seems that there is little new under the sun.

It takes me a long time to sleep. Every time I start to drift I am in the vast city from my vision, jostled by people, assaulted by noise. Thousands of people all going about their lives completely oblivious to me. And every time I drift the city is obliterated in a flash of white.

Eventually, a large brandy keeps the visions away long enough for sleep to come.

When I wake it is with a headache, a terribly dry mouth and nausea.

The nausea is fixed with breakfast, the rest will improve over time.

At a quarter to nine I leave the Excise to walk to the Town Hall.

It only takes a few minutes, and when I arrive, skirting around the square to avoid the mass of people trying to get early goods at the market, Campion is waiting on the steps. He nods a greeting but says nothing, his lips are thin and he turns when I get nearly level with him. He stalks through the foyer, scattering clerks and public alike.

When we leave the foyer, we turn towards the room where Hester Carr was broken by the yellow vastness of the King . It is lit by oil lamps on the walls and, after our entry, the door is closed and the bolt shot to lock it. A table has been set up in the centre of the room with papers piled upon it. Alderman Colston, her grey hair nearly as severe as her drawn face, is sat next to three other officials. One is the Harbourmaster, Evelyn Scornsey, who greets me with a little nod. With them is Deacon Mustaine, who stands to shake my hand warmly. He looks grey and when he sits he lowers himself slowly, a hand on the arm of the chair. The third is a severe looking fellow I do not know, wearing black robes. He looks slightly nervous, but is doing his best to hide it by projecting an air of importance which, unfortunately, merely makes him appear arrogant.

When we are all seated, Colston clears her throat and says, "Thank you all for coming. I assume we all know each other, so let us get straight to the business of this meeting."

"I am sorry to bring things to a halt so soon," I interrupt, "but while I know nearly everyone, I am afraid this gentleman is new to me." I turn towards the black-robed man, who smiles thinly. He puffs himself up before answering, and his voice is suitably deep.

"Doctor Wynter, Master of the Guild of Apothecaries and Doctors." I can almost hear the capital letters falling into place. I smile at him. "Master Hobb Grey, Watcher of Gloster."

"I know well who you are, sir." His tone suggests that he is unimpressed.

Colston clears her throat, "Now that we have established who we are…" She looks to Campion, who picks up a sheet of paper, looking hard at it before laying it down again. From where I sit I can see it is a Bill of Mortality, the monthly page which is attached to the front of the Town Hall, recording the many forms that the Queen may choose to visit the population of the town.

"Following the cases last week of this new disease, we," he nods towards Colston, "took the decision that any further incidences should be recorded as "Yellow Pox". Given the nature of the infection we were unsure as to whether or not to notify them on the Bills, for fear of inducing panic within the populace, and then a possible exodus. We eventually, after much discussion, decided that they should not be so recorded. It seems, however, that the clerks who compile the Bills were not informed of our decision." He sighs, and I feel my stomach flutter as I wait for him to continue.

"This is the latest Bill, which is due to be displayed today. On it the Yellow Pox is noted to have taken eight to the Queen. Now, the reason for calling you here is not to discuss whether or not to post the Bills. Given the fact that the disease seems to be making its presence known our hands are forced. No, we need to decide upon an upcoming course of action."

Colston takes over. "Which means we need to know what we are dealing with." At this she looks pointedly at me. I glance around the table. Campion is staring at the page before him, Mustaine is looking at me with concern and Scornsey with interest. The Doctor is leaning forward on his elbows, his face a picture of assumed intelligence.

"This disease is driven by Fear, but it is my belief that the infection itself is natural. It strikes hard and fast and care will need to be taken when dealing with those struck by it. The death toll will be high."

The silence that greets my words is broken by Wynter, who chuckles briefly. "Come, come, Master Watcher. You are knowledgeable about the Fear, but disease is my speciality. I am sure that we shall find a remedy for this malady soon enough."

"I hope you do, Master Wynter, for the little I have seen of it gives me no cause to hope for a good outcome."

"A little positive thinking is needed, I believe." He smiles. I know that he is speaking simply because he wishes to make a good impression to the people assembled here, but I find his attitude flippant. It is not my position to comment, however.

I continue. "What I can say is that if there have been eight fatalities, there are many more sick. How are they tracked?"

Colston speaks up. "That is one of the things we must decide. I do not recall another disease that had the potential to hit the whole town. We have the usual winter fevers, but they pass with the spring and most people recover well."

Mustaine addresses me. "What steps did you take when you encountered it in your travels?"

"The first place was a Way Station. I tried to offer assistance, which is how I know the nature of it. When it was clear that even with my intervention the sickness had spread within the house, I sealed it and placed Plague Markers. I did not want other travellers spreading any infection." There is a quiet murmur of agreement.

"You mentioned that you believe the disease is driven by Fear," Mustaine says, "what led you to that conclusion?"

I tell them about the thing lurking within Jess' wyrd, and then continue. "But of itself that would not be enough, merely a piece of colour to the picture. No, what sealed it was what I found in Wood Bay."

I take a deep breath.

"Wood Bay is a small hamlet, home to only some ten to twelve people. It is a functioning port with a secluded cove, but the access from land is steep, so it is rarely used. When I arrived, Wood Bay was essentially dead. The travellers who came through the Way Station had ended up there, and the infection begun. I found a stone tablet, inscribed with runes I am unfamiliar with, buried beneath the floor of one of the hovels. I believe it was used to summon an aspect of Fear that was bound to something which was then sealed into the crate which has been brought here, but what that something is I do not know. What I do know is that it tried its skill upon the people of Wood Bay, and they all died."

I do not mention the old man, it seems a false distinction to list him among the survivors.

"What may be to our advantage is the size of Gloster. If, as I suspect, it is Fear-driven, it will spread slowly and in disparate locations, rather than run riot through the town. It will need to be sown rather than spread. However, it will be difficult to contain it either way."

Colston nods, but then says, "How would you attempt to do so?"

I shrug. "Normally I might try and contain it by hemming it in with runes and markers, but that is only effective when I can set up a perimeter. Here, I do not have enough skin or blood to stop it from spreading. We will have to rely on Doctor Wynter and his fellows." I look over to the doctor, who puffs himself up.

"We shall relish the challenge," he says. Colston's face displays the skepticism I feel, but she says nothing.

"I think it is important to gain as much information as possible about the path this disease takes." Colston says, "Master Campion, can you organise the collection of the Bills so that we may track the areas of town that are hit? I am minded to employ a quarantine on infected houses, but that will take some degree of organisation."

She turns to the Harbourmaster, "It is important that this is contained here, so there will have to be a ban on ships leaving the town until they can be shown to be clear. Is that something I can leave with you, Evelyn?" Scornsey nods.

"Meanwhile, Master Watcher, it is up to you to try and find the source of our troubles and deal with it as best you can." She does not try to keep the contempt from her voice.

"We shall meet again next week."

With that she stands and quickly sweeps from the room. Campion looks at me with a little pity, while Wynter barely hides a little smirk as he leaves. This leaves Scornsey, who, after the room has emptied, says, "Well, what have you done to upset Alderman Colston?"

With a sigh I reply, "I do not know. She had a little glimpse of my world when Hester Carr was Tested. Perhaps she finds it frightening."

Scornsey looks at me as I pick up my stick and walk around the table.

"Perhaps." As I draw close to her by the door, she adds, "Perhaps she resents you bringing it here."

The Decision to Cut

When I leave the room I find Campion in the foyer, talking with Colston. As I walk past he calls to me, asking me to wait. He and Colston continue talking quietly for a short while. When they finish she walks away without a backward glance.

"By the Queen," I say when he comes to me, "What have I done to illicit such rudeness?"

He shakes his head, smiling. "Do not concern yourself with her. She is worried, that is all. If it is any consolation she might dislike you, but that is nothing to how she feels about Wynter."

"Then why involve him?"

He looks at me, slightly exasperated. "Wynter is the public face of medicine. He can organise the actions of doctors to treat the sick as we are notified of them. He can cover the town with little copies of his arrogance which will do no good but provide a balm to the panic that will rise. He will buy us, you, time."

I slowly turn and look out of the doors to the the market square beyond, with its hawkers and food, its merchants and buyers, to the hundreds of people simply being themselves, surviving and hoping for better. The sun comes from behind a cloud, and the place becomes awash with colour.

"I do not know how to trace it." I say, the world beyond the foyer almost overwhelming me with its number of potential victims. My voice is quiet and Campion moves close. "The crate has been lost. It could be anywhere out there, with whatever is inside biding its time. We already have cases, many more, I am certain, than the deaths we have seen, and I am weak."

He places a hand on my shoulder and leans in. "This would be too much for you even in your prime. Enlist help. Speak to Alice."

I turn to face him and he nods. "I shall do what I can to help, beyond what Colston has asked, but I was never a Watcher. Alice could be."

He looks so serious, so certain, that I can not say anything so I nod. I reach up to grasp his hand, and then say.

"Keep track of where the cases arise. There may be a pattern that will aide us."

Slowly I make my way down the steps and onto the market square. When I first came here I found the noise and bustle difficult, it being so different from the places I had frequented and lived. Fear rarely reared itself in large towns, keeping instead to villages and hamlets, where its effects would be more keenly felt. After all, why waste time in causing a little strife when the same effort would destroy the lives of an entire community?

However, in my time here I have come to appreciate the market, and, while I still dislike the noise of the height of day, I love coming here in the early morning and watching the preparations, the quiet business of setting up the stalls, of unpacking the wares and the slow coming to life of the heart of the town.

Today, all I can envision is a sea of pain and sickness that simply believes itself to be healthy. I shake my head. I will be of no use if I can not shake this dark fog.

But Campion is right. There are things I can do, with a little help, and so I turn towards the Excise, in the hope, not only that Alice is there, but that I might find something in the archives, some use of runes perhaps, that can be applied to an area as large as Gloster.

As I walk it occurs to me that I am looking at this in the wrong way. If I can get notification of the cases as they arise then maybe runes can be cut to contain individual outbreaks rather than attempt to contain the entire town. It does depend, of course, on how many cases arise, but over time it should make a difference, and possibly enable me to narrow down the location of the source.

I turn back to the town Hall, walking as quickly as my leg will allow.

VISITATION

Campion is in his office, looking stressed and my appearance does not, it seems, provide any ease.

"I shall not take much of your time. Speak to Colston for me. There needs to be a much more rapid tracing of infection, and I need to see the cases and their locations daily."

His mouth drops open and it takes a few seconds for him to respond.

"Have you any idea what you are asking? This will take more people than we can currently muster."

I shrug. Of all the problems in this world, this is not one of mine. "Then muster them. Resources are the perview of the council, impress on them the need. If this can be made to happen I think there is a way of tracking and containing it, at least in such a way as to slow it and make it more difficult for the Fear behind it to act freely. Maybe, even, a way for me to hunt it and face it."

"And if the council refuse?"

I round on him, frustrated and angry. "They must not be allowed to. If they do, the only thing we shall be able to do is watch Wynter and his followers bleed and purge the sick while it spreads unchecked, and the town will die." I see him bridle. His position within the council has meant that he is unused to instruction, and I calm myself a little. "Cecil, this is unlike anything we have dealt with before. It killed Wood Bay within two to three days. My guess is that it has already taken hold here, but the speed of reporting is too slow to be of use in any way other than preparing carts to carry the dead to the dock. Believe me, the Queen's Barge will be sailing every day and the fires over the Severn will spread even with the efforts we are planning. Without them, we have no hope of doing anything other than watching."

We talk a little more, and I impress on him the urgency of swift reporting once again. I leave him preparing to see Colston and re-trace my steps towards the docks.

By the time I reach the Excise, a plan of action has formed. It relies on Alice being swift and efficient, and me being ruthless. Playing to our strengths, perhaps.

It also relies on Alice learning some basics, and learning fast.

As luck would have it, she is there, sat at the kitchen table, turning her rune-knife over in her hand slowly, thoughtfully.

She looks up as I walk in and the redness of the skin around her tattoos catches the light. She looks up and says, "You look rough. Good meeting?"

I try and force a smile, but it slips away. When I sit she looks down at the knife again, and I sigh.

"What was discussed?"

"Not much, in reality. There is not much known for certain as yet. But, I think I have a route to follow to try and contain things." She looks up at this, her face open and interested. "It relies on getting swift knowledge of new cases and the two of us working together." Alice raises her eyebrows and brings her hand up, unconsciously, I think, to gently scratch at her scars.

"There are runes that can be carved which will ward against the Fear being used to control or power this disease, providing it is the same as in Wood Bay. There are others that can be used to trace it, track it, but they only work within a small area and are dangerous to get wrong."

Alice says nothing, and I pause, almost afraid to ask her outright.

"I will work the Trace, but I need you to cut the wards."

She leans back in the chair, holding her knife lightly, twisting its point against the table and her eyes narrow. Not once does she look away from me, and it is I who break away.

"You want me to cut runes?" I nod.

"In sick people's houses?" I nod again. She continues playing with the knife, and then asks, "Will these," she uses the point to indicate her tattoos, "protect me?"

"Yes. They should. I can not make solid guarantees. But the work I need you to do is not dangerous, that is for me."

"Why do you need my help?"

In response I pull up my left sleeve. The scars have healed, but the skin is tough and ridged. "There are two reasons. One is that we will need to work quickly, and with two of us in conjunction we can do just that. The other is that I am old and battered. I have not the strength or blood to see this through on my own."

"What will I need to do?"

Rune work can be complex, as the shapes may be combined in many ways to perform different tasks. When runes are combined they are known as Bindrunes. The simplest are those for Warding, as they are often needed to be cut and marked in a hurry. The simpler runes also tend to be those that are more forgiving in the way they are cut. It is more important to put feeling into the marks than it is to cut them exactly. While the shape is important, it is secondary to the desire. Alice should be able to cut effective Wards with but a little guidance, whereas the Trace runes are technical and complex, and need to change and react to circumstance.

In all cases, however, blood is the catalyst. For the Wards a light smear is enough, whereas the Trace requires a fluuidity that can only be gained through a fresh wound. I am hoping that I shall not need to do more than one Trace a day - even that will be taxing.

And so I explain to Alice, and she listens and remains very, very quiet.

Eventually, when I think I have said all I can, she sits back with a heavy sigh. When she does speak, her voice cracks ever so slightly and I can almost see flashes of Stonehouse pass behind her eyes.

"You are asking a lot of me."

"Too much?"

There is a pause before she says, "Possibly."

I can not do this without her, so I say, "I do understand, and I can not pretend that there will be no danger. The things we are ranged against are not what I would choose as your introduction to our fight, but it is what it is."

"Our fight?" She looks slightly incerdulous. "*Our* fight? You *chose* this life. It is something that you thrust upon me."

My patience is running low. What with Colston's dislike, Campion's political concerns and Alice's fear it appears that only I see the threat for what it is.

"I am aware of that, but this is not the time to squabble. I need your help. I am not actually asking for it."

Her whole face drops and then hardens, and I hold her eyes with mine, waiting for the explosion, but it does not come. Rather, she contains her anger, and I can see her burying it. No dubt it will resurface at some point, and I find that I hope it is not directed at me when it does.

Entry Two

Record of Helen Cready, Clerk
    Yellow Pox cases have risen sharply, and the deaths are frightening. Again I have been told to change the numbers on the Bills, something that I questioned, but was told in no uncertain terms to do. The true numbers are in the hundreds.

Carts have been requisitioned to carry the dead to the Barges.

There is a great movement of carts carrying soil out of the town, I suspect to enable the burial of the dead until such time as they are put to the fires.

Practice and Application

Over the next two days, while I wait with increasing impatience for the data from Campion, I instruct Alice in the way of carving Wards. We sit in the open yard behind the Excise, with old scraps of wood, as Alice repeatedly practices the simple shape of the Ward bindrune. Although the shape of the rune is simple it is good practice to make each carving as controlled as possible, so that it becomes natural to do, a process that requires no thought. That way it can be carved swiftly and marked, moving on to the next in order to throw up a wall of protection.

Her first attempts are crude and uncontrolled. Using a knife takes time, and there is little I can do other than provide encouragement, as her knife differs from mine and will feel and balance in a way that I would find difficult.

Over the course of the next few hours she improves markedly. Her focus is extremely good, and by the time a Clerk arrives with a package, she can produce a passable bindrune. I am actually pleased with her, and make efforts to tell her so. Her mood softens a little. I think she appreciates being useful, regardless of the direction that use is put.

When the Clerk arrives it is close to sun down, and I take the pack from him. Inside the officially sealed envelope I find rather more than I was expecting and I am pleased to see that Campion is taking this seriously. I have a copy of the official Bills of Mortality, supplemented with a list of addresses of those afflicted. It is a horribly long list, counting thirty dead and over fifty sick. I am heartened by its inclusion, however, as I am not strictly interested in the dead, as there is nothing more to be done for them, but the list of the sick is very useful.

Also included, neatly folded, is a large map of the town, with all streets named. This will be extremely useful as it will enable me to track cases as I am notified of them, which will then inform where best to begin the work that Alice and I must do. There is also a note, which I pass to Alice. I have had enough of reading. I have tried to work through the book that Edward gave me, but it is so alien that I have managed to read but a little and what I have read does not give me comfort.

She clears her throat and then begins. It does not take long.

"I have roped in Wynter's doctors to search properties and given them authority to enter houses and seal them if needs be. I suggest you work by night. We do not want to terrify people more than they will be. It is signed by Alderman Colston."

Colston is clever. Using the doctors to search houses is a good move. It will make them feel important, they will be diligent as they will believe they are helping, but the workload should prevent them from treating too many people. The little I have managed to read of the "Smallpox" book showed clearly the disdain the authors had with the attempts to treat the disease, and I feel that they would hold similar thoughts about the current state of medical intervention.

There are some, of course, who do some good. The Church is home to some very adept surgeons, who can work delicately and swiftly. The knowledge of the Old World is made available to them and, although there is no method of removing pain, they do, at least, have the expertise to identify and work on problems. I have never seen one working, but I understand that they are quite a spectacle.

That knowledge is closely guarded, however. I have been told that the Old World doctors treated ailments with potions and powders, much like our doctors do, but that these worked and were not accompanied by such terrible after effects. I am lucky, and I have never needed the ministrations of the medical profession - my burns were dealt with by Campion and Margaret, my housekeeper, and the lotion I use is currently supplied by Campion. I have no doubt that had I been handed to the local doctor I would have been bled and purged and sweated and cooled until there was nothing left of my original self.

In this instance, however, I am happy to see the doctors being used. If nothing else it keeps them out of trouble.

Colston's directive to work at night makes sense. The Warding may be designed and placed to seal more than one house providing we can gain access to each window, and I can cut a Trace within a block of cases. It will be hard but over time I should be able to build up a good map of the Fear in the town.

Alice and I lay the map out on my desk, hastily clearing it of the detritus of my time at the Excise, and then, as she reads out the addresses I mark them. At first there is no pattern. A case in Swan Street, another in Pound Lane, a third in Milton Square. Thus it continues, until we have exhausted the original cases. Then there is a break in the dates, and a cluster of eight in Bellgate, a small set of alleys that spurs off Dark Lanes. The houses there are small, poor, and Bellgate itself is a narrow street of three storey buildings that are crowded and poorly kept. The people there are manual labourers, dockers, seamstresses and, of course, prostitutes.

Alice and I can lose ourselves there. There will be people walking the streets, but the majority will keep themselves to themselves. Those seeking the night-women will be keen to remain quiet, and the dockers administer swift justice to those that step out of line.

While we wait for darkness and the town to quieten, we drink coffee and talk about the everyday. No mention is made of my coercian and the time passes pleasantly. At one point Secretary Reddick joins us for some food, and the three of us chat. Reddick, I think, relishes the Excise being full of talk. For so many years it has been silent, and I wonder whether she sees Alice as a new hope for the building, for the establishment. Personally, I doubt it, and I am almost certain that I shall be the last Watcher to work here, but this evening is not about the future. This evening exists solely in the present.

The clock in the kitchen finally strikes ten, and Reddick yawns. Alice and I look to each other, and as the old woman rises and bids us good night, we also stand, and with a final gulp of coffee, we step out ont the wharf, picking up my case on the way.

Fog has settled, and it muffles what sounds there are. The docks are rarely completely quiet, as the rhythm of the days are set by the tides, and if a high tide coincides with the darkest hours there still need to be workers available to tie the ships and secure them. The Harbourmaster's men are always available, of course, to log cargo and calculate taxes. Tonight, however, the water is low and the docks are quiet.

Bellgate is close to the market square, Dark Lanes running off Southgate Street but a hundred yards from the southern edge of the square. While the buildings along Southgate are quite large and colourful, with reds and yellows mixed in with the lime wash, those on Dark Lanes rapidly become poorer and when the turn is made into Bellgate the houses are narrow and tall, jutting out into the street. At its narrowest they almost meet at their apex. Lines are strung from building to building to help dry washing, although they are all empty. Looking up they appear net-like, web-like, trapping us and preventing even dreams from finding their way in.

There are few people around, and those that are abroad pay us no heed. The ground is damp, whether from rain of waste I can not tell. The night-soil collectors rarely make it into these narrow streets and I do not wish to examine what is underfoot. This whole area of town smells ripe anyway, so it is not as if my nose could give me warning.

The houses we need are at the place in the street where it turns sharply left, looping around to meet back with Dark Lanes. When we reach the corner, I set my case down and withdraw my spirit lamp, flicking the lighter. The soft yellow light haloes us within the fog. The door has been nailed shut, and the doctors have painted the bone-white mask on the door.

These buildings back straight onto others, so there is no possibility of windows at the rear of the properties, although I suppose there might be doors into them. However, given that these will be the grand buildings on the market square, I doubt that, even if there are doors linking them, they would be used.

I hear a soft cough from inside, and I cast a glance towards Alice. She has heard it also, and the same thought flashes through our minds, which is a brief horror at what it must be like in there, almost worse for those that are healthy, knowing that their fall into sickness is, in all probability, but a matter of time.

Alice has removed her knife, keen not to get started, but, I believe, to finish.

"This house, next door and another two doors in that direction." I point along the alley, away from the corner where we now stand. The fog has settled so thick that I can not see the end of the houses.

"Carve the runes into the uprights of both door and windows, and then move onto the next. I would complete the carving and them mark them, if I were you. It requires but one cut and you can easily mark this number before the flow stops."

Alice nods, and then asks where I will be while she does this. I tell her that I will be close on this occasion, but in future we may well be separate, as the Trace is best done from as close to the centre of a Warding as possible.

She begins to carve into the oak of the upright, struggling with the uneven surface of the old, heavily weathered wood. It takes her a long time to carve anything like a good enough bindrune, but I do not chastise her. It is very different carving in the real world when compared to sitting calmly in the kitchen, and I am pleased that she is not quick to give up. When she is happy, she moves on to the next, and, although the cuts are a little crude, they are better than I had expected they might be. The test will be when I start the Trace, as I should be able to see the changes in Wyrd easily. As it is, all I can do is keep lookout while she works.

When she is on the third cutting, a figure appears at the end of the alley, half hidden by the deep shadows. It is tall and almost conical, and approaches smoothly. I step forward, between it and Alice. I can not make out what I am looking at until it is picked out by the light from my lamp, and I am not overly eased by what I see. It is a man, certainly, but dressed in outlandish garb. He wears a heavy coat that touches the ground and hides his body completely. His arms are free, but are sealed with heavy gloves. His head is a mask of leather, smooth and round with great round eyes of glass. Little slits either side of the mask allow for the passage of air. When this monstrous thing is standing before me, it reaches behind its head and I hear the snap of clasps. With the sound of a deep breath the mask is removed, and Wynter is stood before me, grinning.

The Doctor and the Mark

"Master Watcher, how good to see you."

I can not say the same, so I simply nod in greeting. Alice has stopped carving and is staring at the doctor, knife in hand, unsure as to whether to greet or attack this strange vision. Wynter, who I see is sweating, looks towards Alice, and then back at me.

"What is this? Some sort of Watcher magic being performed?"

Before I can answer, he blusters on. I get the feeling that he is so pleased with his task of organising and managing the searches that he is simply over excited.

"Well, I have no time to waste watching you and your little carvings. I am here to check that the afflicted houses are properly sealed. Busy, busy, busy."

As he raises his mask back to his face, he gives a little sigh. "I will admit to a degree of jealousy, however. You are able to go about your work easily, staying outside as you are. This mask is terribly uncomfortable." With a series of slight grunts he manages to pull the leather over his face and, with a little circled wave of his hand, he stalks off down the alley.

I watch him go, and Alice puffs a wordless exclamation. "Pfah! Who, in the name of all that is good and proper, was that?"

"Ah! You have encountered Doctor Wynter."

"I should like to tie that mask firmly in place." She turns back to her work. While carving I hear her mutter "Busy, busy, busy."

"Keep your mind on your work, these are not pictures. You need to feel them." She stops, takes a deep breath, and then continues.

The rest of her cuts take a good time, but they are done well, and I watch over her as she makes a small incision in her forearm from which blood trickles. She sheaths her knife and rubs her fingers against the cut, smearing blood into the nearest carving. Slowly retracing her steps, she marks each bindrune and then presses her hand hard against the wound to stop the flow. When she finishes she stands back, and I see a wave of fatigue go over her. I take her arm and ease her gently down to sit against the wall. "Rest for a while. The tiredness is a sign you have done it well. You should recover soon. Can you keep a watch?"

She nods, and raises herself a little. She is young and strong, and the fatigue will pass. She reaches into the pouch she has brought with her and pulls out a length of cloth, using it to bind her arm.

Once I know she is unlikely to fall asleep, I begin to settle myself, rolling up my sleeve and unsheathing my own knife. Tracing is difficult and requires a high level of concentration, something not easy to achieve in the middle of a dark alley, blinded by fog. Luckily, Alice is more than capable of giving me time to react should someone decide to take umbrage at our work.

The first cut I make slides me into the darkness behind the everyday. I have never liked Tracing, as the initial sensation of falling always makes me nauseous, and now is no exception. As the world rushes past and my wyrd pitches me forward, I fight the rise of bile, knowing that once I get past this initial unpleasantness I shall be fine. With the second cut the pitching motion ceases and I have sudden sight of the bindrunes, their influence already wrapping around the wyrd of the people sealed within.

Cutting deeper, the lines become more distinct. There are four people in the house, three are sick, their wyrd curled in on itself.

Before I go hunting, I quickly turn my attention behind me, to see Alice. The runes on her face are clear, a network of lines that enmesh her, and I am satisfied that she is as safe from this business as I can make her.

Turning back to the task in hand, I extend my view, and begin to see the bindrunes Alice has carved on the other houses. Yet again, I make out the pain within, but little else. Their wyrd is so inward-facing that I am not at all certain this is being driven by Fear at all.

And then I see it, a little bit of something wrong with the world. It is difficult to describe, as everything touched by humans has a trace of their life on it, so even while looking at this strange version of the world I can make out buildings. Their lines are faint, but they still hum with pale lines of light.

And there, to my left, is a little area that makes me feel sick when I pass it. It appears little different from everything else, but the feeling it induces is extremely unpleasant. It feels as though something has slid into me and is churning my guts. I actually retch, and I sense that Alice has stood behind me. I can hear her asking if I am well, but I can not answer. I am intesely grateful that she is there, as I am almost incapable of doing anything other than trying to control my stomach and locate the source of this corruption.

Leaning against the wall in front of me, I slowly edge my way along the alley, sliding my hands over the surface rather than walking them. As I shuffle along, I become aware of a figure at the end of the alleyway. If I was not caught in the web I might just be able to see it, but as things are I can only get a sense of it. It watches for perhaps two seconds, and then turns and leaves, heading back towards Dark Lanes.

My attention is drawn back to the terrible knot of bile and pus that is, I sense, trying to hide from me. With a few twists of my knife, I cut a bindrune into my arm which clears the path for me to see clearly. It lies down close to the ground by the neighbouring door to where I started, and I reach down to place my hand close before I stop the Trace. It is always disorienting when moving from one view of the world to another, and I do not want to run the risk of losing it.

When the Trace is severed, the cold, fog and dark flood back, and I fall to my knees. But my hand stays steady, and I jam my fingers against the wall. "Light," I grunt, and Alice brings the lamp close.

There is a small hole in the plaster, probably simply a result of wear and tear, and my finger sinks into it.

I am in no position to reach around myself for my everyday knife, so I whisper, "Your usual knife," holding out my hand and clicking my fingers. Alice scrabbles at her belt and pulls her short, heavy knife out, passing it to me. It is the work of but seconds to drive it into the plaster and gently scrape out what it contains.

A small, perfectly smooth oblong of stone falls to the dirt. In the light of the lamp I can see that it is marked, but so finely that I can not make it out, and I am not prepared to lift it close to my face.

Instead I manage to balance it on the blade of the knife and drop it into my pocket. As I raise myself, my left leg shaking badly when I put effort through it, I ask Alice whether she saw the figure at the end of the alley.

"I did, although he was not there long."

"Could you make out who it was?"

She shakes her head. "Not clearly, although by its silhouette I took it for that doctor, Wynter, was it?"

I grunt. It would not surprise me if he had decided to come back to check on me.

Still, I am not going to concern myself with him now, not when I have something so evil in my pocket.

"We need to get back to the Excise, now."

As I turn, my stomach loses its fight and I lean forward and vomit painfully. I loathe being sick, and it takes me a long time to get my body under control and by the time I start walking I am shaking badly. Alice offers me her arm and I take it readily. I do not think I have ever felt so old and fragile as I do now.

It takes much longer than it should to get back to the Excise. At one point three dock workers pass us and one of them says something I do not catch. His friends laugh and something within me snaps. Without thinking I stop, draw my rune knife and prepare to drive it into my arm, knowing that if I do one of them will likely lose his mind. A soft, but strong hand closes over mine and firmly eases it down.

A sudden panic overtakes me and I start looking around wildly. "Case?"

Alice reaches down and shows me my case. She has it with her and had dropped it when we stopped. By the time we reach the Excise my mind is racing, constantly flicking from noise to noise, from though to thought, impossible to quieten.

I am led into the building and I hastily slip my robe from my shoulders.

As it falls to the floor in the hallway I breathe deeply and blink hard. It takes time for my eyes to focus. As I look around I see Alice reaching into the pocket for the stone, and I shout, "No! Do not touch it."

Alice pulls her hand away sharply, looking up at me. "Make sure no one else touches it. I shall need to prepare things." I pick up my case and head into the office, where the map of the town is still laid on the table, but turn before I enter. "Thank you." She nods, a faint look of surprise crossing her face.

I carefully fold the map, placing it onto the floor, and lift the case onto the desk. The soft clicking of the Infinity Clasps is comforting, a sound of mundanity that my mind clings to, savouring every little whir.

Of all the things I keep in there, the one I have used least is, in some ways, the most powerful I have. I wish I could have someone make a large version of it, but that would be impossible, which is why I still need to rely on wooden Wards.

It is a frame of brass, which unfolds and pivots to create a complex seven pointed star. At each point is a small threaded sleeve, beautifully cast. Into these I screw iron rods, flattened and inscribed with warding bindrunes. In the centre I attach a little pedestal, and slip a magnifying glass into a seventh sleeve.

Once this is set I take a set of iron pliers from the case.

Using the pliers I extract the stone from my robe, and take it through to place it carefully on the pedestal. Alice stands at the door, and I motion for her to come in.

Peering through the lens, it takes a little while for my eyes to adjust, to focus. I have not used this apparatus for many years and I always found the glass difficult. After much slight adjustment I can see clearly onto the stone. It is a nondescript grey, very smooth, with clearly defined, almost sharp, edges.

The stone is covered in a thick, sticky mucus, yellow and drying to a crust. I swear under my breath and then ask Alice to look.

"What is it covered with?" she asks.

"It looks like pus, but there is so much."

When she looks up at me there is grim determination in her face.

"Would you go and rouse Campion? He needs to see this."

Alice leaves without a word. The Warding frame is doing its job, and I can no longer feel the corruption before me. In truth, I doubt that I would have felt it were I not attempting a trace, but I feel much more settled now that I know it is trapped.

I can turn my thoughts to the purpose behind this little piece of evil. My first guess is that it is a marker, placed to keep track of the spread, but that makes no sense when the Bills of Mortality are posted regularly. And why would whoever is behind this care about the specifics of infections? Even the idea that it could be aimed at a particular target does not work as this family was not important. I focus again on the little stone, looking carefully at the foul substance covering it, and something strikes me. Perhaps this is not a marker. Perhaps this is the opposite of a Ward; a curse.

My ruminations are stalled by the arrival of Campion and Alice, the former looking unkempt and flustered, the latter, grim.

The King and the Promise of Iron

"This had better be important" Campion growls.

"Not in the mood. Sit…look." I push the chair away and stand, stepping aside and glaring at him, and he at least has the decency to look slightly embarrassed. He attempts to smooth down his hair which is ruffled from sleep.

Campion sits and, after a little adjustment, peers into the glass. He remains there for some time before looking up. "What is it?"

"I am not sure. I would probably not have even found it were I not Tracing."

"Where was it?"

"In the wall of the house we Warded on Bellgate. What worries me is that this must be what was contained in the crate brought from Wood Bay, and there must therefore be many hundreds of them."

Campion sits back, linking his fingers across his belly. "There is nothing about it other than the stone? The substance itself is not Fearful?"

I shake my head. "Not that I can tell. It made me sick, but, as I say, that was more to do with what I was doing. Can you feel anything?"

Campion looks down at the Warding Frame and closes his eyes. Using the pliers, I retrieve it from the clasps and hold it a foot or so from Campion. After a couple of seconds, he shakes his head. "No, nothing." With that, I place it into the frame again.

I turn to Alice and raise my eyebrows, to which she responds with the tiniest of head shakes.

"It has given me an idea."

Campion turns to look at me.

"But I need to destroy that thing first."

Campion vacates the chair and I pick up the pliers again, gently lifting the little stone from the Frame. I carry it out of the door and onto the wharf, picking up a heavy cleaver. The wharf is constructed of heavy oak beams pegged securely together, and it has been there for many years. As a consequence, there are gaps between some of the beams and I place the stone across one. One smart hit with the cleaver and the thing splits. When it does, I feel nothing. The two halves skitter away and I retrieve them, picking them up in my fingers. Again, there is nothing other than the uneasiness of dressed stone.

When I return to the Excise, Alice and Campion are sat in the kitchen, and I drop the pieces onto the table. Water is heating on the fire and Alice is spooning coffee into a pot. I sit next to Campion and sigh heavily. My left arm is throbbing again. I should bind it and give it proper time to recover, but I feel that this is a luxury I can not afford. Time and age are against me, and there is little I can do against either.

"So," says Campion, "if there were ever proof that this is not simply disease…"

Alice is sitting opposite me and is watching intently. When she is sure I am looking at her she slowly lowers her gaze to my arm. When I follow her, I see blood seeping through my sleeve.

"What do you need?" she asks gently. I turn my arm and slowly pull back the sleeve. As I do so, and the wounds come into the light, Campion gasps. He reaches over without a word and takes my wrist, gently but firmly twisting the arm so that he can see clearly. While he is doing this, I say to Alice, "Bandages and my ointment, please. Both are in my room, on the small table." Alice stands and leaves immediately.

I pull my arm from Campion and draw some water into the sink. Once again I am extremely thankful for the wonderful machinery Evenright has installed, and bathing my arm in warm water feels wonderful. Alice swiftly returns with bandages and a pot of emollient and places them both on the table.

When I sit back down and start working the cream into my arm, Campion speaks up.

"Your arm is in a bad way."

I look down. Perhaps it is because I see it every day that I have not noticed how terribly scarred and mangled it has become, but now that it has been mentioned I can only agree. The scar tissue covers almost the entire underneath now, mixing with the burns to create an appendage that appears almost made of pink and pale bark. It is little wonder I have had to cut deeper to draw blood, and that it now takes so much longer to heal. With a sigh I begin to apply the bandage.

"Hobb," Campion using my name is a sure sign of trouble. "Hobb, you can not continue the way you have."

"Then suggest an alternative." I continue wrapping. He opens his mouth to argue, but I cut him off, angrily.

"I know." The anger leaves me almost immediately, and the truth settles instead. "We have allowed ourselves to be left open, Cecil. The Watchers are gone and the Fear is back, not that it ever left. I can perform perhaps two Traces, perhaps two Tests, and then what?"

"That is a question for after this disease has gone," is his response. Ever the pragmatist. "The question for now is, how do we get to that stage?"

I continue binding my arm and we sit in silence. Alice, who has poured boiling water onto the coffee, picks up the pieces of the stone and examines them thoughtfully. She pours us all coffee, and then asks, "Why are our knives made of iron?"

I sip the drink and it is Campion that replies. "Iron warps wyrd. It bends it to the will of the Watcher and pulls it to his story, disrupting the power it gains from the world."

"And blood?"

I answer this one. "It depends on what work is being done, but for anything requiring power, be it Warding, Testing, Tracing, a sacrifice to Wyrd is required. Nothing is free."

She turns the little stones over in her fingers.

"So that is why the little frame you used works? It disrupts and blocks the Wyrd of the stone?"

I nod.

"So these," and she holds up the broken stone, "are being used to change Wyrd over the town, almost the opposite of our Warding?"

I nod slowly. "That makes sense, yes."

"You can find them using a Trace, but your arm is too damaged to allow more than a couple?"

I nod again.

I can almost see her mind working as she thinks, staring intently at the little thing of evil she has in her fingers.

"So let us make our own version of this. With iron and blood."

Campion opens his mouth, but no sound comes out. He closes it and then looks at me.

"Is that possible? Would it work?"

Thoughts are rushing through my head now, and Alice is watching me intently. She begins to grin at me.

"Possibly. It would need a fair bit of iron, but Warding bindrunes could be cast into the surface and then they could be slipped into each house where the disease strikes, negating the stone."

"Blinding the King," says Alice, and I nod.

"Hold on, wait," Campion interjects. "There is still the blood. Your arm will not yield more."

He is right, and I cast around for an alternative.

"Wynter." Alice says the name without feeling, simply as a statement of fact. "Wynter is good at drawing blood. He could take enough for it to be used to douse the iron rather than cutting for each one."

I am staring at her, and Campion mutters, "Would that work?"

When I answer it is quietly and with thought. "Enough for me to recover. If they are used carefully they should act as Wards to start hemming it in."

I keep my eyes on Alice. "That is good thinking. Could Master Evenright cast the iron?"

She shrugs.

"Does he have enough iron?" Campion asks, looking between us. She shrugs again.

"Well," I say, stretching, "I think that we should sleep now. Alice, tomorrow, please ask Evenright about the iron and the practicalities of what we plan. Cecil, keep the council updated. Can you speak to Wynter?" Campion nods.

"Good. Ask him to come round to see me. Make no mention of the reason, I do not want him suspecting that I am weak."

He nods again. "And what will you do?"

I look directly at him and say, "Hopefully, sleep."

Long after they have gone I lay in bed, sleep coming and going, and with every visitation the city returns. Black stars and dark suns are reflected on a mirror lake that stretches to the horizon. And voices that mutter and mumble, rising and falling as though on the wind. At first they are soft, almost musical, but each time I visit the voices become clearer and more strident. The voices shout in unison, thousands of them, screaming but distinct and the sun brings light to the world outside my head.

"Along the shore the cloud waves break,
The twin suns sink behind the lake,
The shadows lengthen
In Carcosa."

Fires on the Shore

I wake in full daylight. I must have slept during the night, but my body refuses to believe it. I spend a long time using the oils, working them into every crease, fold, cut and ripple of my old, burnt and scarred skin. My left arm is of particular concern. One of the benefits of being a Watcher, possibly the only one, is the ability to heal rapidly, particularly from the self-inflicted wounds necessary to do the job.

My arm is a mess. It has been the subject of cuts since I was sixteen, and the scars run wide. However, up until recently, I have had to make only shallow cuts, intricate and details with the point of my knife only. And now, the cuts I make are deep, into fat and muscle. They lack subtlety and beauty and they scar deeply, meaning that even if I could heal as I used to, I could not Test again. Testing requires quick and elegant movement, precise and definite, and now hardened tissue will change the run of the blade.

Ah well, it comes to us all eventually. In many ways, I am lucky to have been able to retire, albeit briefly, and I am fairly sure that Campion will allow me peace once this is over. Most Watchers die young, or at least, younger. To live to this age is a privilege not afforded to many.

The ointment helps ease the pain, and the ritual of its application allows my mind to calm itself.

I can hear clattering from downstairs and when I finally don some clothes and ease my stiff legs to the kitchen, Secretary Reddick is standing at the fire, and the smell of bacon is beginning to fill the room. She is whistling to herself and I note that she has not cleared the coffee from last night. My mug is still half full, and I pick it up and drain it before taking the pot outside to empty the dregs into the river.

Looking across the water, smoke is rising from the far bank, and I can just make out flames. The burning of bodies is ramping up.

On my return, Reddick looks up and her face falls. "You look like you've been touched by the Queen."

I can only nod in agreement as I ease myself into a chair. She points to the slab of bacon on the table, "Cut yourself some slices, I shall cook them for you."

Reddick's skills at the cooking fire are less evident even than mine, but I am in no state to refuse, so I cut three slices and she slips them into the hot fat. I note that she has got eggs waiting on the side. While she cooks, I cut some bread and draw water for coffee.

When we sit to eat, and I bite into the mouth-shattering crispness of bacon, there is a knock at the door and I shout for whoever it is to come in. There is no way I am moving yet. A young Clerk from the Town Hall enters warily and presents me with a rolled and sealed set of papers.

It is the new list of cases compiled by Wynter's doctors, and it makes grim reading indeed. One hundred and thirty new cases with eighty deaths. I put the leap in numbers down largely to more efficient tracing, but, given that it will be some time before I can start to seek the cause, those numbers will surely rise massively.

Reddick looks over, wiping a dribble of fat from her chin, and points at the pages with her knife. "That the numbers of the dead?" she asks.

"It is."

She chews thoughtfully. "Going to get bad?"

I nod. "Yes, I think so." She grunts and takes a sip of coffee.

"What are you doing about it?"

I load my fork with bacon and egg before answering. "My best," and then I eat. She grins and nods.

"So, how are your investigations into the old stones going?"

Reddick chews thoughtfully. "Interesting. There is, from what I can find, a lot of old lore around them, a mixture of good and bad. They seem to be the remnants of religious sites from thousands of years ago and have been held as sacred since they were made, certainly until the Great Conflagration. After that, well…" She shrugs.

"Well what?"

"They are not mentioned."

"What?"

She shakes her head and starts mopping up egg yolk with a piece of bread. "Not mentioned again. The Redemption is silent on them, and they appear in none of the modern texts I have looked through. Almost as if they do not exist." She pops the bread into her mouth. "I shall keep digging."

That is strange when the Redemption is so clear on stone in other circumstances, and I must admit that I can remember no mention of them. I can only assume that those who live close to them either actively avoid them or ignore them. I am interested to hear what she discovered regarding the old lore.

Reddick is not an elegant eater, but she is efficient, and by the time I finish my eggs her plate is clean and she is on to her second coffee.

"Do not forget to write your work up in the Journal."

"It is completed every night," I lie. I have been very remiss recently, and owe the Journal at least a week of entries. I neither read nor write for pleasure and see little point in doing so as a chore, so I change the subject.

"I noticed the fires on the shore are burning."

She nods. "The Queen's Barge sailed last night, and I understand it is due to sail again today."

"It will be busy. I am not sure it will be enough to carry the numbers I expect."

Reddick nods slowly and I expect her to leave the table, but she stays while I eat. Only when I finish does she speak again. "Am I safe here?"

The tone of her voice shocks me. Secretary Reddick is self-assured and generally unconcerned about what others, including me, think of her. She has almost been a model of what I aim to be, and yet her voice is quiet and frightened. It strikes me that I have never checked the Warding around the Excise, something that should have been a priority. I shall ask Alice to do so at the first opportunity.

"You are," I say confidently. "You are."

Reddick smiles and stands, pulling her old self back to cover the fear and picking up her plate to wash. "If you say so, I shall act as though it is true."

After we have cleared the breakfast things I take a coffee out to the wharf, looking out across the river to the smoke. It is not long before I am joined by a figure I had hoped would give me more time. Loping towards me from the direction of the square comes the tall, thin figure of Doctor Wynter. He breaks into a wide grin when he sees me, and hails me loudly from a distance.

"Master Grey, how good to see you again."

I guide a smile towards him, and he claps his hand to my shoulder when he reaches me.

We head back into the Excise and I turn him to my office room rather than the kitchen. I settle myself in my seat and he, after a flourish of his robe, sits opposite me. He looks with sparkling interest around him, and his eyes eventually settle on the Warding Frame. He reaches out to touch it and I gently shake my head. His hand stops and hesitates for a moment, but he withdraws it and smiles at me.

"Quite right, quite right. Never touch the tools of another man's trade without invitation."

I am uncertain as to what to make of him. He is clearly intelligent, but his manner is arrogant and condescending. Beneath it is an uncertainty, and I wonder whether his bluster is a method of distraction, as much for himself as for his audience. Like Watchers, doctors rely on a certain amount of theatre for their professional credibility, and I suspect that Doctor Wynter has not understood when to drop the facade.

"Doctor, I need your help," I say, and I can see that even these little words make him puff his chest a little.

"This sickness is driven by something evil and with purpose. I have a method of combating it that will enable you and your colleagues to do their work effectively, but it will most likely require an amount of my blood that I am unable to safely take."

He looks at me with interest, mixed with a shadow, a flicker, of disappointment. I imagine he thought he would be helping directly with the fight. To some the Watcher's work is glamourous, and he is the sort of man who will happily put himself in a little danger for the stories it might provide.

Of course, it is entirely possible that I may be wrong.

"How much, might I ask?"

I shrug. "As things stand, I do not know. I hope to find out later." He nods.

"Will the blood be used immediately?"

"Not all of it, I suspect. Why?"

"It congeals rapidly. It might be best to draw a smaller amount on consecutive days rather than a large amount on one."

That had not occurred to me. Stretching the draw out will weaken me for longer, but might make my overall recovery faster. It might also enable Evenright to produce better castings.

Wynter can see that I am mulling the idea over and, before I answer, he asks to see the arm I want to open. With a little grimace, I roll up my sleeve and rest my left arm on the desk. Wynter leans over and draws breath in through his teeth. He looks up, bringing his hand up and raising his eyebrows before he touches me. I nod and he begins to gently, but firmly, press the scars. He surprises me in being absolutely professional. At one point he takes my wrist in one hand and presses firmly on my arm with his other. He makes soft "Hmmm!" noises.

After a while, during which time I do nothing but allow the sounds of the docks to filter through my mind, he lets go and straightens up in his chair.

"The scarring will make it difficult. Can I persuade you to open your right arm?"

"Absolutely not."

He smiles a little. "I thought that would be your answer." He purses his lips while he considers his options, and then says, "Normally I would make a small incision in a vein and draw what was needed, but I think, given the extended time over which this is likely to happen, I would like to try a different approach."

"Go on."

"Well, I think that it would be best to make a wound that can be kept accessible. It will be less painful and, hopefully, more efficient."

I shrug. "The pain means little to me if that is your concern, but if you have something in mind that can make the whole process easier then I have no complaint."

His ebullient manner returns in a flash, and he beams at me. "Wonderful. Let me know when my services will be required and I shall exsanguinate you."

As he prepares to leave, fussing over his robe at the door, I ask how the searches are progressing, and he responds quickly without facing me. "Very well, very well. I have procured more of the masks I designed so that my fellows will be instantly recognisable, and safe."

As he takes the door handle, however, he does turn to me and, in a low voice, says, "Master Grey, if I can assist you in controlling this disease I shall. I fear it will get much, much worse in short order." He hesitates and I feel that there is something more he wishes to add, but he straightens his back, opens the door and says loudly, more to the world than to me, "let me know when I might be of assistance."

With that, he leaves the building and I am left alone, standing in the doorway, watching this strange, insecure man walk briskly away towards the square.

Entry Three

Record of Helen Cready, Clerk

The Barges are sailing every hour, but many are disguised as trade ships. They travel a circuitous route down river and then back up along the western bank where the fires have been extended further in land. I have heard that a village has been cleared and the houses used as fuel.

The soil removal has stopped as the capacity of the fires has increased.

Night-soil men are charged with collecting bodies at night.

Curfew

It is not until the following day that Alice gets back to me, accompanied by Inigo Evenright. During the time between Wynter leaving and them arriving I walked the town. To my eyes it looked little different than normal, traders were still shouting, ships docking and being re-stocked, people in the streets, but after a while, I began to see subtle changes to the everyday.

Standing in the market square the first thing that works its way into me is the lack of chatter. The town breathes gossip and today there is almost none. The square is busy, but the people in it are intent on doing rather than being. They move from stall to stall, shop to shop, purposeful and direct. There are, of course, little pockets where friends gather and laugh or argue, but they are rare and at the edges. Where one forms spontaneously in the square itself, it moves away from the crowd of its own volition, almost as if the group is an organism trying to hide from a predator. Occasionally I see one of Wynter's doctors stalking, and the little groups disperse rapidly when they approach. Strangely, as I watch one head into one of the dark alleys off the square, I think about how lonely a life that will become.

There is a small crowd at the steps to the Town Hall, milling around where the Bills of Mortality are posted. As I pass, one man is reading the figures out loud to the silent watchers.

I spend the afternoon just walking aimlessly. At one point I head to see Jacob Perez, but his door is locked.

By early evening, the town is quiet and still.

Reddick and I chat about nothing, and I sleep fitfully again.

VISITATION

And now I am back in my little room with Alice and Inigo opposite me, explaining exactly to the craftsman what I want. He looks dubious, but I know that the challenge will eat at him.

After outlining the plan and showing him the broken stone curse I collected from the house, we talk over the practicalities.

"How many of these things will you want?" he asks.

I have actually decided to take a slightly more cautious approach than I initially had imagined, and suggest that perhaps we should make five to start with, as we can position them in a small area and I might be able to do a Trace to see their effect. Alice looks hard at me, and shakes her head.

"You are in no condition to do a tentative Trace, not if we need you to sacrifice more blood. Your arm will not take more damage, and you might be required to work something harsher." I am about to explain about my meeting with Wynter when she surprises me and shocks Inigo by saying, "Teach me."

"Teach you?"

She nods emphatically. "Yes. We can set the pieces around the Excise and you can guide me here."

"That will not work. The Excise is Warded already." She opens her mouth to argue, but I hold up my hand. "However, that is a good idea. I wonder if we might use a warehouse instead? If we can find one with space we can set the pieces out and see how they fare." In truth, I am relieved.

Training Alice is something I know I have promised but, when it comes to it, it is also something that I am reluctant to do as this is not the life I wish for her. However, Tracing these curse markers is something she should be able to do and it does not involve the deeper, nastier aspects of the work that, for example, Testing entails. It will, as she says, enable me to focus on preparing to face whatever we encounter at the end of this.

Inigo places the stone pieces onto the table. "Well, each of these will need about thirty grams of iron, so if I can get about a kilo from a bloomery then that should give you around thirty pieces. A bit is lost in each firing in impurities."

"And how much blood will be needed to quench them?"

Inigo noisily draws in his breath. "I honestly do not know. I have never done this before and I do not know how it will react to the heat. It may be that it clots very readily and therefore needs to be refreshed frequently, although I would have thought that the heat might help prevent that. All we can do is test it."

I am about to say that this answer does not help when he speaks again. "A pint per firing, perhaps. Can we dilute it in water? Even a little would help."

"We can test that as well," says Alice.

"Very well. A pint," I say. That sounds like a lot to me, but I have never been bled before.

"How soon will you be ready to try?" I ask.

Inigo thinks. "I do not have that amount of iron available, although I am certain I can get some more. I shall talk with Madikane, he can probably donate some. Failing that, I can buy ore, but that will take time."

"Time we do not have. Do what you can and let me know when you are ready."

He nods. "Can you draw the designs you need cast upon the surface?"

"I can. They need to be clearly defined. Are there limitations to the process?"

"The main one is that a mould may only be used once, so it will be time-consuming. How many designs are required?"

"That will not be an issue. I can create a single bindrune that will serve, so only one."

Inigo nods happily. "That is good. In that case, I can create thirty in one go using the same master. I was afraid you would need a set of differing designs before you could start which would complicate the manufacturing."

"So we could have a hundred within a day?" Alice asks.

Inigo shakes his head. "No, no. I can not re-use the bloomery. The process essentially bakes the clay used into stone. I can use it perhaps twice before it starts attracting Fear. You are looking at perhaps a week to create a hundred. Besides," he looks at me, pointing, "you will need a few days to recover between each blood-letting."

I sigh and huff slightly. "I need to let Wynter know when to stick me.

When might you be ready?"

Inigo taps his fingers on the table, thinking, and then says, "I shall speak with Edward now. If, between us, we can pull together enough iron to work, then…the day after tomorrow. I need you to draw the rune thing now. I can make a master and you can check it tomorrow."

I get a sheet of paper and draw the bindrune. It is quite complex, being constructed of three separate runes intersected and elaborated upon. It is one I have used for protecting camps and I know it is effective at driving Fear. Inigo looks at it, his brow furrowing. I guess it is more complex than he was expecting, but he takes the drawing and, with a smile and a handshake, he opens the door, almost walking into the young Clerk who is poised to knock. After a little confused mumbling, the Clerk steps aside and Inigo leaves. The Clerk wordlessly hands me a sheaf of paper, bows slightly, and also departs.

As I sit back down, I hand the papers to Alice, who breaks the seal and casts her eyes over them while I roll up my sleeve and inspect the skin on my arm. I do not think I have ever felt my years as keenly as I do at this moment in time, sitting in my office, young Alice poring over the papers and with the sounds of the dock filtering in.

I am not thinking as such, more wallowing, when a little gasp rouses me and I bring myself back into the room. Alice looks up from her reading.

"A curfew has been imposed, beginning tomorrow at sundown. The Aldermen are trying to limit what they class as "unnecessary contact" between people."

I grunt. It does not surprise me, and I am secretly pleased that they have acted so swiftly. Alice is reading further. "The town gates will be locked between sundown and dawn and all shipping will be required to undergo quarantine. All boats are grounded and no flights are allowed to berth."

"That makes sense. I am still unsure as to how this disease is spread and it is wise to try and limit it."

"I suppose," says Alice, "but this will infuriate the traders and merchants."

"It will," I reply, but I am absolutely certain that such a decision is well outside my concern. "What are the case numbers."

She looks down, finding the Bill. "Not good. A further one hundred and fifty sick with ninety dead."

"The Queen's Barge will be running constantly."

"It will if we do not make a proper plan."

I nod in agreement.

"I was wondering whether these stones are the method of primary transmission," I say. "Placed in a house, they allow the disease in, from where it can spread." Alice nods slowly, and I continue. "And in which case, finding and replacing them with the iron Wards will effectively stop the spread, if we can work quickly. It might also weaken the thing behind it."

"Possible, I suppose, although I gather from your tone that you are uncertain as to the truth of this."

With a small laugh, I respond, "I have no idea whether this is correct at all, but it seems logical. What is certain is that these things," I flick half a stone across the table, "are not our ally and that removing them can be nothing but a positive action. Which leaves the issue of finding them."

Alice leans forward, "I meant what I said. Teach me."

"I shall. Thank you."

She smiles, but looks uneasy. "Does it hurt?"

"At first, yes, but not as much as you might think. Make sure your rune-knife is very sharp."

"How will I know what to cut? I do not know the runes."

"Do not fret. We shall go slowly and carefully. By the time we are ready to begin you will be more than ready."

The Queen Calls

The screaming in my dreams repeats the verse from a few nights ago, multiple voices all in unison. It should be impossible to hear the words, but when I wake I hear myself saying "Carcosa".

I feel exhausted. Sleep is coming, but it is not accompanied by any meaningful rest, and my mind is constantly in motion.

I manage to take my breakfast early on the wharf, and, although I do not doze, it is restful as I am able to switch my mind off by watching the river slip past. It gives me a sense of peace, and not a little fatalism, as I watch the unceasing movement of the vast body of water. Nothing that happens in the town behind me will have any bearing on the river, and that brings comfort tinged with futility.

The food I have, bread, honey and strong coffee, is almost tasteless.

The sun rises behind me and I am in the shadow cast by the Excise, wrapped in my robes and a blanket against the early cold. I am uncertain of the time, but I guess it is close to five. As the sun has risen I am not breaking curfew, but it is only by minutes.

The docks are quiet. The tide is on the way out and, although there are ships berthed, they are either unprepared or quarantined, and no porters are fussing and swarming.

As I sit, leaning against a thick post with my feet dangling over the edge, I hear footsteps approaching from the left. Turning, I see a doctor, case in hand, heavy cloak and masked face concealing his identity. I first take it for Wynter, but he does not acknowledge me as he passes, and I hear his heavy breathing behind the leather. It must be hard wearing that mask, and,

I suspect, from the weariness of his steps, he is on his way home after a long night.

Some time later, after the town has woken and is going about its wary business, Master Evenright and Edward Madikane call on me. As there is little I can do until the iron blocks are ready to be cast I have taken the opportunity to rest, becoming as sedentary as Secretary Reddick and napping in my comfortable chair. When the knock comes at the door I start and it takes a few seconds to ground myself.

The three of us head through to the little yard behind the building. The high sun warms the space and we sit and talk in the pleasant quiet. Evenright has made a sample and he hands it over.

The iron is grey and smooth, and its weight feels deeply comforting. The bindrune is beautifully crisp and any worries I may have had about his ability to create such fine work rapidly dissipate.

"This is a thing of beauty," I say, turning it over and over in my fingers. Inigo allows a little smile to show.

He and Edward share glance, and it is Edward who speaks up. "There is a potential problem."

I sigh, "Of course there is."

"We do not have as much iron as we had hoped, and obtaining ore quickly will be impossible."

Evenright begins to explain that the issue is with the quality of the iron he and Madikane have. Apparently a lot of it is covered with other materials, paints and other protective substances that will have to be removed, and there is a certain amount of an iron alloy which will not succumb to the heat of the bloomery.

"We can prepare the pure iron we have, and that will yield a little under a kilo of cast pieces. My estimate is that I can make twenty five pieces."

This is a blow. I had hoped to create a lattice of Wards that would tighten around the source of this evil, but twenty five will not be enough. Waiting for more ore is out of the question. I swear quietly, but there is little to be done. Iron is required to be registered and is extraordinarily expensive. Even if we could sequester every scrap from the town it would not add much to the total.

"Make what you can, we shall devise a plan to make best use of it. How quickly can you cast them?"

Evenright looks at Madikane, "With some hard work we can be ready tomorrow."

That at least is good news. "In that case I shall get Wynter to empty my arm in the morning."

Evenright nods, and then says, "I will drop a container to you first thing that might help with keeping it in a usable state."

I raise my eyebrows but he says nothing else.

A little while later, after they have left with instructions to ask Wynter to bleed me in the morning, Alice arrives. I am still in the yard and have lost track of the time, so it is a pleasant surprise when she walks in carrying two bowls of hot mutton stew and bread.

"I have given some to Reddick."

"I have not seen her today."

"I think she quite likes town being quieter, and she has taken the opportunity to stretch her legs."

As we sit together and eat it strikes me that, were the terrible disease not running through the town, I would possibly be at the most content I have ever been. I am still concerned about Alice and her reaction to the huge stones, not to mention the fact that I had to tattoo her against her wishes, but her resilience is inspiring.

The food is distressingly tasteless, and I assume that it is largely due to my fatigue. I hope that, when this is done, I can go back to enjoying those things that make Gloster such a pleasant place to live. Being a Watcher, I am painfully aware that hoping for a good future is something that I should curb.

As we eat, she asks, speaking through a mouthful of bread, "Will this idea work?"

I pause before replying. "In truth, I do not know. Warding is usually done in situ, with the blood being applied as each bindrune is completed. My guess is that the fact I am mass-producing them will count against them, but that the iron will help to mitigate against that. All we can do is try."

"And what of my part in this?"

I wipe a piece of bread around the bowl. "Do not worry. We shall go through everything when we have the pieces." I can see that this does little to settle her, so I try to help. "Tracing is usually difficult, as one is trying to separate one strand of wyrd from the mass of life around it. In this case, all you are doing, at least initially, is seeing what is wrong in a place. Now that I know what to look for I can guide you and you need not get too close. All we need is the general location of the stone."

She nods. "What if there are more stones than bindrunes?"

"I am sure there will be. I think we will run a couple of practices, and then sit and examine a map, try and see a pattern."

Alice finishes her food, and then smiles at me. "What?", I ask.

"You look terrible, your arm is a mess and you disfigured me. You are relentlessly grumpy and I know you are not sleeping."

"Is there more to this, or are you simply going to find fault with everything I do?"

"There is, for despite all this you are risking yourself to bring an end to this evil. Not for yourself, but because it is correct."

I smile a little. "You give me too much credit. I do this because it is what I am, what I have lived to do since I was a child. In truth, I can do nothing else."

She leans forward, speaking slowly and carefully. "I see that I was wrong. Especially at the Way Station. I have no desire to be a Watcher, not after seeing the toll it has taken on you, but I will do my best to help."

I am surprised and deeply touched and am unable to reply. Alice collects our bowls and takes them inside, leaving me to collect myself. I had not realised how deep my affection for her ran and find my mind wandering to how proud I would be if she were my daughter.

My ruminations are stopped when she reappears, simultaneously flushed and pale. "Reddick…"

I am standing and moving as quickly as I can behind her. I smell the vomit before I reach the kitchen. By the time I reach them, Alice is kneeling next to Reddick, who has collapsed and is twitching, mucous pooling from her mouth and sweat glistening on her skin. Holding my breath I kneel as close as I can get, and see tell-tale spots.

After a few seconds, she stops twitching and opens her eyes, making a low murmuring that tells of pain and discomfort. Alice and I carefully lift her and carry her upstairs to her room, which is full of files and papers. Nestled deep within is a bed, almost like a nest, on which we lay her. Alice turns her onto her side and covers her with the blankets. She looks up at me and whispers, "You said the Excise was Warded."

"It is, but she has been out a lot recently."

Alice rests her hand against Reddick's forehead. "She is burning. Can you bring some water?"

I leave the room, relieved to be away. I do not deal well with sickness and am useless when it hits.

Over the course of the day and the following night we take turns in sitting with Reddick, doing what little we can to ease her suffering. The sickness is terrible and she twitches and moans constantly. She has never looked overly robust, but the toll it takes in such a short time is horrible. She quickly takes on a sickly yellow tinge and sweats profusely. When I take over duty from Alice in the small hours, I can see that there is little hope and I make the decision to do what I can, and cut into my arm yet again to seal her away from her pain. She falls, at last, into a deep sleep, finally succumbing to the Queen as the sun rises.

When I go back downstairs, Alice is sitting at the kitchen table, head resting on her crossed arms. I am not sure whether she is asleep, but she slowly lifts her head when I enter the room, her eyes dark and red-rimmed. I pull out a chair and sit heavily, before standing again, heading back up to Reddick's room and, with a nod of thanks, picking up the bottle of good brandy she kept next to her bed. In the kitchen, I pour two measures and pass one to Alice. We raise them in silence and drink. The burn of the liquid as I swallow is the only sensation outside fatigue that I feel. Even the pain in my arm is but a dull ache.

Alice drains her cup and places it softly onto the wooden surface. "Who will conduct the Rites?" she asks.

This question poses a problem that has only just occurred to me. I am capable of doing the required ritual, and I think that Reddick would prefer me to officiate. She never expressed a deep fondness for the Church, although her body will need to join the Queen's Barge at the earliest opportunity. The problem is that I need to alert the Church and the town to her death, and that will mean that the Excise will be required to quarantine, being shut by Wynter for ten days, and that will prevent us from fighting the infection.

It is with this realisation that the thought this was a direct attack first hits me. Whilst Alice and I are, it seems, immune, this is a good way to frustrate our actions.

"I shall perform the rites, but we have a problem." I outline my thoughts and Alice's eyes widen.

"The only thing we can do, I think, is tell your uncle and hope that he sees the importance of not following the protocols for infection control. Would you be so good as to fetch him? I shall care for Reddick."

Rite and Fire

After another small measure of brandy, Alice leaves, heading out into the early morning drizzle that is dampening the world. I probably have half an hour to prepare Reddick before Campion comes blustering in, and then I will need to ready myself for Wynter. That thought brings my attention back to my arm, which I take care to bind well.

Nestled deep in the room Reddick used as her place to sit, surrounded by the files and ledgers of past Watchers, is the small household shrine to the Queen that all properties, by decree, must have. Ours is dusty and half-hidden, and it takes me a while to move enough paper and books out of the way to reach in and grab the Bone White Mask.

It is a long time since I have had to perform a funerary rite, and the words do not come freely. My thinking is hampered by the Mask, which smells musty and warm, and I stand by her body for a while before my memory wakes. I spread my hands, holding them open and welcoming, as I was taught. The first part of the rite is general, and is intoned at every death.

First there was fire, and from that fire was the world born anew
And in that pain and was the Queen also born
She walked among the people
And understood their fear
Taking it from them and
Driving it into the stones.
But only when she comes to us
in the last of our days

will we be granted the peace of her arms

The words are spoken easily, but the feelings they used to engender are not there. Still, Reddick would be happy to know that they are said. The second part of the recitation is specific to Watchers. Officially she should not be afforded this as she was not a Watcher, but as the senior representative of the Excise in town, I feel that this is a call I can make. The words I speak are old, older, I believe, than the lines from the Redemption

The Watcher thinks about the Fear
And deeply considers this dark life.
From times far away the Watcher recalls
The deep-wyrd cuts and says,
Where is the horse? Where is the warrior? Where is the gift-giver?
Where is the wine hall? Where are the sounds of joy?
The cries for the wine! The cries for the Watcher!
How those moments went,
Grayed in the night as if they never were!

When the words end I am in complete silence. I realise, as I finish, that tears are wetting my face behind the mask. How long I have stood there I am unsure, but I hear the door open and Alice and Campion talking softly. I pull off the mask and drop it, wiping my face with my sleeve and bowing to the thin, pale, lifeless body of the last Secretary of the Excise in Gloster.

When I enter the kitchen, both Alice and Campion are stood waiting for me. Alice gives me a look of empathy when she sees me, but Campion simply looks worried.

"What has gone wrong now?" he asks. "I need more sleep than you are allowing me."

Alice sees my anger rising at his words, the insensitivity and sheer selfishness of them grates me and my own lack of sleep has shortened my fuse drastically. Before I can gather enough sense to launch into him, she places her hand on my arm and says, "Uncle, Secretary Reddick has died and we need your help."

Campion looks shocked, switching his gaze between me and Alice and then apologises.

"I am sorry. Would you like me to fetch the Deacon?"

"No. The issue is that she died of the sickness that we are trying to fight." His concern flashes into fear, and he steps back.

"I should alert Wynter…" He is agitated and makes to walk around me to leave, but I step to block him.

"And he will seal this building and we will be unable to fight."

He stops. "Then what do you expect of me?"

"I have performed the Watcher's rite for Reddick, so all we need now is for her body to be taken to the Barge, before the town wakes and questions are asked."

"And before Wynter arrives," says Alice.

I had forgotten about this, and I swear under my breath.

Campion looks from me to Alice and back again, thinking. Eventually he says, "I shall collect my cart. We can use it as a bier. With the number of bodies now being carried, one more will make little difference."

"Thank you. Do you know when the next sailing is?"

He snorts. "This is why I am not letting Wynter shut you in. There are no sailing times any more, the Barges go when they are full, and they fill rapidly."

I am taken aback by this answer, and say so. Campion is silent for a few seconds, and then visibly sags. "The Bills are under-reporting, by order of the council. We have had around a third more cases than they show."

Both Alice and I exclaim "What?" simultaneously.

"How am I supposed to track cases when I am not told where they are?" I am furious with this deception, and my anger vents at his flabby face. "What exactly do you think we are fighting? This is no little case of Flew that will disappear in a few weeks, this will kill the town."

He is taken aback by this, but rallies, keeping his voice low, "Do you think I am unaware of that?"

"Well someone is, and is playing with the lives of everyone here."

"The decision was made to prevent a mass exodus."

"And the decision to hide the details from me?"

He pauses, unwilling to go further.

"Was not mine," is all he says.

"Then whose?"

He pushes past me and opens the door, turning back before leaving, his manner softer. "I am sorry about Secretary Reddick. I shall make sure she is given respect."

As he turns back and steps outside, he almost walks into one of Wynter's shrouded and masked doctors, and he backs away hastily. The doctor says nothing but continues along the wharf, towards the narrow streets by the wall.

After Campion has disappeared from sight, I turn back, still fuming.

Alice is no happier and is pacing back and forth. When she sees me she erupts.

"The Queen damn them! This is political. Someone has decided to keep us, you, from doing your job." She controls herself, but then raises her finger, wagging it stiffly in my direction. "This puts a new light on Reddick's death - someone wants you out of the picture."

I think that is a stretch, but she could be right. And that would mean one of two people.

"If that is correct it could only be Colston or Wynter," I say.

"Colston dislikes you, but she would not act against the town. Wynter?"

I shake my head slowly. "Wynter is relishing his new-found importance, that does not make him an agent of Fear, or the Yellow King, or whatever we are fighting. Still, he is due here later, maybe you should stay, just in case."

"With a knife at his neck."

I am not sure whether she is joking.

She resumes pacing and I suggest that she needs to control her anger before Campion returns and we need to maintain a dignified silence. After a degree of growling she takes a few deep breaths and forces herself to be still.

Some minutes later the rumbling of wheels announces Campion's return, and I raise a finger to Alice.

"Keep your calm." She nods, and then, when I keep looking at her, she says, "I am calm." I smile at her and there is a brief answering curl of her lips.

Campion does not knock, but opens the door. He is carrying a large, folded cloth. A shroud in which to wrap Reddick's body. The fact of her death suddenly hits me, and a weakness rolls across my body, starting deep in my stomach and making my knees shake. I manage to control myself quickly enough, but where the sadness touches me it changes to anger. If Alice is correct, then Wynter shall pay dearly. The church and council have no jurisdiction over the actions of a Watcher investigating the murder of a member of the Excise.

Alice and I clear space on the floor next to Reddick's body. We decided that it would be best if we handled her as we know that we are protected, at least to a degree, by the tattoos we bear. Campion waits by the door, ready to open it so that Reddick may be loaded straight onto the cart.

We gently pick her up, which is easier than expected as she weighs little, and lay her upon the sheet. We bring the cloth over her feet and her face, and then wrap her tightly, swaddling her like a newborn.

With as much dignity as possible, we carry her down the stairs, Alice going backwards and softly telling me which tread she is on with each step. After we reach the bottom it is easy to gently slide her onto the cart. Campion closes the door and locks it and the three of us climb aboard and within a couple of minutes we are at Queen's Wharf. There are three other carts, each with similarly wrapped packages, although where we carry one, they carry many.

Deacon Mustaine is there, officiating and directing laymen as they, wrapped in black cloaks and with cloth wrapped around their faces, slowly lift the bodies from the carts and place them onto the Queen's Barge.

Mustaine sees us and makes his way over. I disembark and go to him, meeting him before he gets to the cart. He covers his eyes, but I can not bring myself to do the same, so I raise and lower my hand briefly. The Deacon looks exhausted.

"It is good to see you," he says, "how are you keeping?"

"Not as well as I could, but better than many."

He smiles briefly.

"Are you here often?" I ask, looking at the scene behind him.

He nods, looking around, and says, "Every day."

"Every day? You can not be overseeing every barge?"

He shakes his head wearily. "I did to start with, but I need to sleep occasionally."

We watch the laymen unloading bodies, the gentleness of their movements is affecting.

"I have just discovered that the numbers are much worse than I was led to expect."

He looks to me, and then back at the barge, and he sighs loudly.

"Did you know that I was being deceived?"

"No, I did not. I have not been in a council meeting since the day you returned from your travels. My time has been spent, first treating the sick, and now dispatching the dead."

I believe him. There is a weariness to his voice that is impossible to feign. He sounds unsurprised but resigned.

"I am sorry to add to your burden, but…" I turn and point to our cart.

He looks over. "Who?"

"Secretary Reddick."

He covers his eyes and mutters, "May the Queen guide her journey."

I lean in and speak quietly. "She died of the sickness last night. By rights, I should be in quarantine. If that happens this disease will run rampant. If you take her you will be going directly against the orders of the council."

He looks up at me, across to the cart, and then back to the barge. He signals to the laymen, and two jump down from the cart they are on and walk towards us. He walks round to the back of the cart with them, and supervises while they remove the tightly bound body. As they walk past me, Mustaine stops.

"If it is in your gift to end whatever is doing this, then do it. And do not be gentle, that is my job."

We wait in silence, Campion, Alice and I, while the last of the bodies are loaded. Once done, the carts leave, clattering away over the boards, no doubt resting before starting their rounds again.

The wharf is coming to life, people slowly opening up the warehouses and bringing supplies to the ships lined along the docks.

With no fuss or signal, the Queen's Barge slowly pulls away. I guess that there is a Sterling engine deep in the hull powering water-screws. For the short journey across the river it is not worth raising sail.

We stay until the barge is but a dot, and then leave. The fires are burning constantly and there is little point in staying. I shall miss my brittle, spiky Secretary.

Blood and Iron

Campion drops us off at the Excise. Strangely, even though I rarely actually saw her, the place feels a little colder and emptier without Reddick and I stand in the hallway, just looking up the stairs for a few seconds. Alice gently ushers me into the kitchen and begins making coffee.

We sit in silence, drinking and, in my case, mulling over the coming events. I am not looking forward to the rest of today, not just the fact that I will be putting my health into the hands of Wynter, but the idea that the process will leave me even weaker than I am now.

My ruminations are interrupted by the arrival of Inigo Evenright, who informs us that he has constructed the Bloomery and asked Wynter to meet us at his workshop in an hour. Alice and I exchange a glance, and we leave the Excise. Alice, I note, checks to make sure she has her rune-knife with her.

There are notably fewer people on the streets today, and our journey to Evenright's workshop is easier than it would otherwise be.

When we arrive he leads us down Archer Street rather than into the main entrance and then unlocks a small, narrow door that sits within the yard of a cooper's shop. The door is hidden behind barrels and is not visible from the street. As he thumbs the infinity locks he looks round, "I thought this would be a more appropriate entry given what we are planning. The fewer eyes the better."

The door opens directly into the yard behind his workshop. The yard is fairly large, probably fifty feet in each direction, and surrounded on all sides by other buildings. I look behind me and realise that the wall I have just come through is, effectively, false. It rises to the height of the first storey of the workshop but is only the thickness of the oak supports. I look down to the ground and Inigo stands next to me, smiling. He points to thick brass tubes, each about a foot high, that nestle in the corners between the pillars and the wall. There are three on each pillar.

"Hinges," he says. "I can open this entire wall if I need to. It folds back on itself like a fan."

I smile, shaking my head slightly, and then turn to look at the contents of the yard.

Against the two actual walls that are not part of his workshop, tarpaulins are stretched on frames, providing cover to the collection of half-finished projects and pieces of interest. In the centre is a huge structure, mostly covered by a tarp. What I can see is made of brass and leather, and looks almost organic. As I begin to move towards it, he gently takes my arm and steers me away.

"This way, Master Grey. That is to remain secret for the time being."

He leads me over to a clear area, where Alice is kneeling next to a clay funnel approximately four feet tall. A fire has been lit within the open base and smoke is rising. Alice is gently pumping a bellows that extends to one side.

A high-backed chair is set close by, which I assume is meant for me. Indeed, Inigo ushers me to it and, while I settle, ask Alice to start pumping harder. I can see flame in the furnace and, as Alice starts working, it whooshes, changing colour with each loud breath of the bellows.

Inigo stands close by and periodically pours charcoal from a large sack into the top.

"How long will it take to get to temperature?" I raise my voice to be heard over the noise.

"Around an hour," is Inigo's reply.

"Excellent!" I look around to see Wynter standing at the back door of the workshop, looking on with interest. He is not wearing his somewhat sinister regalia, but does carry his case. He steps closer to me.

"How are you feeling today, Master Grey?"

"Better now than I shall soon, I imagine."

He laughs. "Very possibly. Might I suggest you drink a pint or so of water before we start? It will make the shock of losing your blood easier to bear."

Over the course of the next hour or so, I alternate between watching Inigo and Alice taking turns pumping the bellows and wandering around the yard, peering at instruments and half-formed mechanical devices. Occasionally I find something which I can pick up and examine closely, and I lose myself tinkering with clock movements and articulated "things". I sip water constantly during this time.

I also chat with Wynter, asking how the searches are progressing.

"Oh! As well as can be expected, given the circumstances. I have employed non-medical men to search properties, in the hope of speeding up the discovery of cases. But it is proving rather more difficult than I expected."

"I can sympathise with you on that score."

He chuckles softly. "Managing a disease, I can do. It is managing people that is difficult. Do you know, I have had three doctors simply not show up."

"Doctors or people simply employed as searchers?"

He smiles mirthlessly. "Quite right, quite right. Searchers, not doctors."

I watch Inigo for a while, his busyness is in complete contrast to mine.

"I am not surprised," I say. "That people do not show. It is a grim job."

Wynter thinks for a while and then nods.

Eventually, Inigo calls over. He has brought a wooden box close to the Bloomery, which he stands, carefully, on its long side. It is filled with packed sand and I can see a hole in the top. This, I assume, is the mould. He bends down, peering into the bottom of the clay pillar, moving his head from side to side to get a clear view into the heat. He gestures to Alice to increase the rate of the bellows and then looks up at me and nods.

With a sigh, I turn to the chair, where Wynter is waiting. He pats the seat and I sit, rolling up my left sleeve as high as it will go.

Alice, I note, is watching him carefully while maintaining the airflow through the furnace.

Wynter, thankfully, becomes completely professional. He opens his case and withdraws a belt, a length of waxed cloth tubing, a glass jar and a short, bright copper needle.

He wraps the belt around my upper arm, doubling it through a buckle, and pulls hard, constricting so much that I feel my fingers tingle. He places the jar on the ground and pushes the tubing onto the needle. He takes a small jar from his case, opens it and dips the needle in. I am watching him carefully, and he looks up, seeing my expression.

"Almost pure alcohol," he says. "Better than a flame at cleaning." He offers the jar to me and I sniff. It almost strips the inside of my nose.

He asks me to rest my arm palm up, and then starts gently but firmly pushing his fingers into the skin. Eventually, he locates a vein and, swiftly, inserts the needle into my arm, using his thumb to hold it in place. It stings initially, but after a couple of seconds all I can feel is the pressure of his thumb.

With his other hand he releases the strap and blood starts to flow into the jar. He watches intently, dividing his time between me and the jar. After a while, I am not sure how long, my head starts to swim. Sounds lose their brightness and the world turns black.

I wake instantly to the sound of screamed verses, looking up at a white sky with dark stars. I also wake to pain, deep, intense, blinding pain in my left arm. Curling up to a sitting position, I cradle it and cry out, adding my voice to the throng.

I eventually dare to look down. My sleeve is soaked in blood and I can not move my fingers. Whimpering, I try and roll back my sleeve, but it is sticking to the blood and the pain, the pain is flashing light at me and spinning my head.

I stand, staggering, to get help from the voices I hear. Stumbling into walls that slope at terrible angles I crash from building to building, trying desperately to shield my arm. Narrow alleys disappear into darkness on either side of me, and the voices take on a direction, always before me regardless of where I turn.

I come out into an open area, with a great lake before me, glowing a sickly yellow in the fading light. Casting around frantically, the city curls around the edges of the lake, buildings rising from the ground as it forms itself, growing and massing like fungus, barring my return and blocking any route but forwards.

Two suns, black holes in the white of the sky, sink slowly beyond the lake and, as they fade I see something in the sky, something vast and hateful, yellow-tinged, stretching from horizon to horizon, moving wetly and with terrible intent.

The voices scream their verses, adding to the one in my dream, and I collapse to their sound.

Strange is the night where black stars rise,
And strange moons circle through the skies,
But stranger still is
Lost Carcosa.
Songs that the Hyades shall sing,
Where flap the tatters of the King,
Must die unheard in
Dim Carcosa.

Angry shouts rouse me and I blink my eyes open to a white sky which slowly turns to blue. A voice, panicked and harsh is shouting. I feel warm, tingling pain in my cheek and, as I slowly bring my eyes to focus I see Alice kneeling over me. She sinks back down as I try to sit. My left arm stings and, when I look down, there is a small tear where Wynter's needle had been. It is bleeding freely.

I feel rough, and the world spins around me when I raise my head.

"By the Queen herself," Alice explodes, "I thought he had done for you." I manage to sit, leaning against something that gives little support which, I realise, is the chair I was sat upon.

Looking around, I see Inigo is pouring molten metal, bright red, into the mould. Wynter is sat against the wall, looking terrified.

"What did you do?" I ask Alice.

"Reacted. I saw him draining you and then you slumped and cried out. I

VISITATION

hit him."

I start laughing and find it impossible to stop. Through tears I see Wynter slowly and unsteadily get to his feet, and I try to speak to him, offering an apology, but I can barely breathe through my laughter.

Eventually, I control myself and turn to him. "Forgive us, Master Doctor. My colleague and I have had more than enough attempts on our lives and she reacted to save me."

He looks uncertainly towards me, trying desperately to pull the old, blustering Wynter back. I look down at my arm. "Did you get enough, do you think?"

Alice picks up the jar which, thankfully, survived the fracas, and holds it up for Evenright to see. He thinks for a while and then shrugs. "We shall know shortly", he says.

Wynter steps warily closer, and I hold out my arm. "Would you be able to see to this?" I ask. He kneels and looks closely, his eyes flickering to Alice, who backs away, hands held out placatingly.

"The wound is small. Keep some pressure on it and it should stop soon."

"Thank you. And thank you for your help."

He rallies a little. "I have seen people faint before but few go down as quickly." It occurs to me that if he was of a mind to exhibit my weakness, he has the perfect example to use.

"You need to take more care of yourself, Master Watcher," he says. "Make sure you drink and eat well this evening, and rest. You will probably sleep well and long tonight."

As we talk, Inigo walks over and collects the jar, the contents of which he pours into a metal bucket. Rapidly, he dons thick leather gloves and picks up a mallet, striking the wooden case of the mould until it falls apart, and then using it to scrape the sand away. He reveals a tree of metal, and he skillfully snaps it into small pieces using the mallet and gloves to separate the little casts from the whole, which he then drops neatly into the bucket. There is a brief sizzle as each one hits the blood.

I look at Inigo's face. He is studying the process very closely and, after each piece has hit the bottom of the bucket, he picks up a pair of long tweezers and fishes the cast out. It drips thickly, the blood falling from it with soft splashes, and he peers closely.

Eventually, he walks towards me, a slight smile on his face. He takes the metal from the tweezers and drops it into my hand. Most of the blood has fallen from the surface, but it sits in the Bindrune, which is clear and well delineated.

It looks good, and I smile. All we need to do now is see whether they actually work.

Testing

Wynter was correct. I slept deeply and long, with no dreams. I went to bed before dusk and woke in full daylight, feeling more refreshed than I have for many weeks. I am not one for omens, but I hope this bodes well.

Alice stayed in the Excise last night, on the pretext of needing to start early with her training. In reality, she had, I think, decided to keep an eye on the old man who seems to have partially taken over her life. I am grateful, although it is a little like having a young mother-hen clucking around me.

Wynter left us in, I think, decent enough spirits. Alice apologised, eventually, and I believe he accepted the reason behind her attack. If he knew how lucky he was to merely be bruised he might be more thankful.

After breakfast, we take a walk from Black and Tan Wharf along the whole length of the riverside, all the way up to Boat Yard's Wharf, taking note of which warehouses are being used. The latest Bills had been delivered to us, but I gave them no more than a cursory glance. Even in their amended form, they made depressing reading with over a hundred more cases and eighty three deaths. The truth will be worse.

I have a handful of Inigo's casts in my pocket. I am hoping that Alice will be able to see them and their effects so that she will then be able to understand what to look for when seeking the stones. I am, I admit, also interested to see what she will make of a Fear piece, when the time comes, given what happened at the standing stones.

We walk the length of the wharves twice, once in each direction, and settle on a building close to the Excise, opposite Tobacco Wharf. A sign, hastily scrawled, has been pinned to the door, announcing that the building is in the middle of a change of ownership. This is often done to ensure that no stock is kept within as it would become part of the assets of the building.

I try the door handle, and it opens, swinging inwards easily. This door is set into larger sliding panels which allow for crates and cargo to be carried directly into the building from the ships on the river.

The room is large, and largely empty. There are a couple of crates against the far wall, and large posts sit at regular intervals, supporting the roof frames. Timbers criss-cross the roof-space. In other buildings there might be flooring on the upper level, but here it is open all the way to the shingles. There is a door in the far wall, leading, I assume, to offices or the other buildings behind.

We slip inside, and I close the door. A plank is propped against the wall, and I drop it into the brackets in the door frame, locking the door. Light pierces the gloom from a set of narrow windows high on the wharf-side wall.

Alice looks around. "Will this do?"

"I think so. Come." I walk into the centre of the room, Alice padding softly behind. The floor is packed earth, hard and smooth, and quiet.

"Most people find it easier to sit while Tracing, it helps to quiet the mind." I lower myself slowly and with a complete lack of grace, stretching my leg out as straight as I can. Alice simply crosses her legs and folds them, ending up sitting neatly before me. I pull out my everyday knife and scratch a simple bindrune into the floor.

"Copy that with your usual knife. This bindrune opens you to wyrd, enabling you to see the web close to you. Once you can do this well you shall need to try cutting it into your arm with your rune-knife. But not yet. The shape is important as it acts as a focus for your mind and wyrd, so be as precise as you can be."

She looks down at the bindrune, withdrawing her small knife, and weighing it in her hand, finding the balance point. She begins to copy the rune, and starts well, but her third stroke goes awry and she tries to correct it. I stop her.

"It is important that the cuts are made correctly in one go. Mistakes happen, but never attempt to correct them. Remember, you are doing this in your flesh."

Alice nods, and I smooth over her attempt, and she starts again.

We repeat this time and again, each time she gets further into the rune. I tell her how well she is doing and she simply starts again.

Eventually, after perhaps twenty attempts, she does it accurately, twice.

"Well done. Now, take your rune-knife. Get used to its weight and balance as you did before. When you are ready, roll up your sleeve. The cuts should only just break the skin - I am sure you have suffered worse accidentally while working with Inigo. If you do it right, you will begin to see lines. After a while, they will coalesce around me. When they do, tell me what else you see. You may well find it easier to close your eyes."

She breathes deeply, not in a panicked way, but to calm herself, to gain control. She has told me she has a little routine she does before she works on something intricate, counting back from ten whilst breathing in and out on five.

She slowly, deliberately, rolls her sleeve up, turns her arm over, and places the point of the knife gently on her skin. Her eyes are closed and, with one more deep breath, she pushes lightly and a small point of blood appears. She begins smoothly moving the blade, and I am impressed at the control and feel she has. The knife moves swiftly and decisively, the cuts a little deep, but they always are at first, and she completes the rune in seconds.

"Well done. Talk to me."

She straightens her back. "I can see nothing."

"It can take a while. Do not try and rush things. Just relax."

She nods, breathes deeply and calmly again, and settles more comfortably.

After a few minutes, she moves her head from side to side, almost as if she is listening for something.

"There are silver traces, like spider webs in mist." I let my breath out slowly, relieved.

"Can you sense me?"

She moves her head, aiming in my direction.

"Yes." She smiles. "You are a mess, lines everywhere, coiled around you and through you. I can see your shape. You are…bigger than you."

I laugh, and then walk around the room, looking carefully at the wooden pillars, until I find one with a notch taken out. It looks as though it was originally designed to accept a shelf, and it is entirely possible that this tall, straight piece of oak was taken from another building before finding its way here. Whatever its history, I place the cast on it and move away, standing back where I was initially.

"See if you can find the cast."

She nods and I continue.

"You need to extend the web, push what you can see further. It will be hard, and it will fight you. Wyrd is private and the webs of others resist your attempts at seeing their shape, but you can do it. Take your time."

Alice's breathing deepens, and her mouth becomes a thin line.

"I can see it, although…"

"What?"

"I can only see it because it is not there. It pulls everything to it and there is blackness."

When I see a Ward it appears bright, shining with a purity that burns. Not everyone sees the same thing, of course.

I walk towards the rear of the room, into deeper darkness. There are two crates against the rear wall, both empty, their tops splintered at the edges where they have been levered off. I reach into my pocket and place a cast carefully onto the edge of one of them and walk back to Alice. She is still sitting facing the front.

"Next one?" I ask.

"Behind me, close to the back wall, but…"

"What?"

She frowns. "There is something else there."

I look around, into the gloom. "Probably whoever is in the building behind." She shakes her head.

"If so then he is really sick. There is something alive, but only just, behind the door."

VISITATION

It could simply be some poor soul locked in their house to die, but it is best to check. I try the door, but it is locked. "Wait here, I will be back soon. See if you can follow me."

"How much longer will the trace work?"

"Not much. When the blood stops the trace will fail."

I walk swiftly, for me, to the front door, lifting the bar and slipping through. The quickest way to the other side of the building is to turn down Goldman Street, which turns sharp left after a couple of hundred feet, and opens up to be a decent, expensive part of town. The building that sits directly against the warehouse belongs to the Spainish Trading Company. The front of the building is austerely grand, with smoothly planed oak and intricately carved beech panels. Windows with small, leaded panes rise either side of the double door.

It opens easily and I find myself in a small, but polished lobby. As I walk in I am approached by a lady wearing long robes so purple they are almost black. She smiles as she approaches, raising her hand to her face, and I follow her lead.

"Master Watcher, how may I help?"

"Just a simple question. Is this building linked to the warehouse behind?"

She shakes her head. "No. We use Kingsley Wharf almost exclusively."

I feel almost faint. "Thank you."

I turn so quickly that I almost lose my footing, and the woman steps forward.

It takes a few minutes to get back to the warehouse, and I am not cautious in opening the door. As light spears in, I see Alice lying on the floor, and I stop, slipping to the side of the door out of the light. The door in the rear wall is still closed, and there is enough light for me to see the whole room fairly clearly, and there is no one else here. I move to Alice, kneeling close and gently stroking her hair away from her eyes. She murmurs and slowly raises herself to sitting.

"Are you well?"

She shakes her head, more to clear it than to say no.

I help her back to rest against a post.

"Tell me."

She opens her eyes and blinks a few times, and then a great, racking sob makes her shudder. She cries, deeply and painfully, and all I can do is wrap my wrecked arm around her.

After a while, she calms herself, and I can feel it takes an enormous effort. She pulls away from me, and wipes her sleeve over her face, sniffing hard.

"There is something there. Something horrible." She glances towards the dark door. "It felt like Stonehouse. Like…him. I was trying to follow you, but it was too difficult. Too many people. And then I touched it. And it knew me."

She shudders.

"I need to look at something, will you be alright for a minute?"

Alice looks up at me with red-rimmed eyes and nods. I can see her containing her emotions, and am, again, impressed.

When I get back to the door I kneel down, and run my finger along where the wall meets the floor. There is almost no dust on the bottom of the wall. As I trace my finger along I notice a furrow, probably made by a crate being dragged over the earthen floor, which disappears beneath the wall. This wall is a new addition to the warehouse. I go back to the door, running my hands over the surface, particularly where it sits within the frame.

It is poor quality and, joy of joys, has leather hinges. They are thick, but with a little work, will cut.

Kneeling back with Alice, I ask her to go to Inigo and get a sharp, strong knife, suitable for cutting the hinges. She stands, a little shakily, and, with a slightly sickly smile, heads off.

While she is gone, I collect the casts and pop them back into my pocket. I will not risk running a Trace myself, but having a pocket full of iron Wards seems like a good idea.

When Alice returns, she is carrying a stout knife of unusual construction. The "blade" is wood, with beautiful rippled colours, alternating dark and light. Set into it, running the length from handle to tip, is a thin edge of iron.

I look at it, turning it over. "This is beautiful," I say.

Alice responds by saying, "It is laminated. Different woods are glued together with their grain running at different angles, making it extremely strong."

I raise it to the upper hinge and run it into the leather. It bites and cuts through.

Turning to Alice, I take her arm and usher her away towards the front door.

"Listen. I am going into that room, or whatever it is. I am going to kill what you felt, and I am going to end this."

Alice looks at me. She is shaking slightly, but her eyes narrow and she says, "not on your own."

The Masked Dead

The hinges take longer to cut through than I anticipate, as the leather is surprisingly thick. Alice leans against the door to stop it from moving. I start at the bottom so that the door will not swing out before we are ready. When the upper hinge is removed, we take places on either side and, on a count of three, gently ease the hinge side away.

Our plans to move quietly are destroyed when the bottom suddenly pushes towards us as something heavy hits the door. Alice is on the hinge side and she shouts as something rolls out from behind the door and slumps to the floor, falling towards her. She dances out of the way, but I am suddenly left holding the weight of the door, which twists in my hands and falls. Luckily, Alice manages to grab it before it hits the floor and we lower it as gently as possible.

Alice apologises quietly, and we both look to see what has caused our problems.

Lying half under the door is a figure, long cloak and leather mask hiding its identity.

Alice immediately moves towards it. "One of Wynter's doctors," she says, reaching out to help it out from under the door, but I bark a curt, "NO!" She stops, stock still, and I move around her, fishing one of the casts from my pocket.

When I am next to the figure, the smell hits me. Unwashed sweat, sickness and something else, something darker and mustier. Reaching out I gently pull the collar away from its neck. The skin beneath is white, flacid, tinged purple. Gently, I press the iron against the skin.

With a lurch, the figure flinches back and, slowly, raises itself up onto its hands. The iron slips from my fingers and I back away rapidly, scooting and kicking to stop myself from collapsing. Alice is also backing away.

The figure, moving smoothly and slowly, tries to stand, but the door is still on its legs and it does not seem to understand that this prevents it from rising. Seeing that it is pinned gives me the time to stand, but my stick is next to the post where Alice was sat. I reach into my robe for my rune-knife but, before I can withdraw it, there is a sickening crunch as Alice brings the iron edged wooden blade down hard on its head. It collapses but immediately starts to rise again.

I shout, "The iron must hit skin."

She looks up at me, and smacks the blade down hard again and, as it collapses, she straddles it, sitting down on its back, and is startled when it rises once more, albeit slower. She reaches down to the bottom of the mask, and pulls hard. After several tugs, the leather slips off the head with a soft, wet sound. Without pause, Alice brings the iron edge down hard and it cracks its way into the skull. The arms give way and it collapses again, this time remaining still.

As Alice gets off, swearing and panting, I kneel close to what I now see is a man, and turn him over. Both of us reel back.

Beneath the mask is a face that has been dead for days. The remnants of pockmarks are everywhere, but they are white, breaking through skin that is wet, thin, purple-veined and bloated. Its eyes are white and blank. Where the iron hit the skull, the skin is peeling back, trying to get away from the cut.

We stand, staring down at the thing before us. Alice tucks the blade into her belt and looks up.

"Wynter said that some of his doctors had disappeared." And then a thought strikes me, and I kneel again, this time searching for pockets, pouches, anything where things may be carried.

In a pocket inside the heavy cloak I find three small pieces of shaped stone and throw them onto the floor. Rejoining Alice, we stare at them.

"Use your blade on them." Scowling, she brings the heavy iron down on all three, breaking them easily.

She turns and points towards the corpse. "How long has that been dead?"

I shrug. "Days."

"And it has been walking around planting those?"

"Yes."

"How many of Wynter's doctors are missing?"

I shake my head, shrugging. After retrieving the iron cast I look at the doorway.

"Whatever is in there knows we are here. There is little point in delaying."

"Do you have a plan?"

I laugh. "I have no idea what is in there. I will use the casts I have and I will fight it with my blood. If you can give me the space and time to do that…"

I get an emphatic nod by way of response.

The doorway is dark, even with the light from the windows and front door, but I can see that the false wall is perhaps four feet from the real one. Stepping slowly forward, I wait, allowing my eyes time to adjust. If I am going to traverse the dark I want at least a fighting chance of not walking into something.

Leaning into the doorway, I peer to the left and right. To the right, the space between the walls stops but a few feet away. On the left, steps lead down into blackness. I can hear nothing.

Rolling my left sleeve up and making sure I have a casting in my hand I take the first step down. As what little light there is fades, I place the back of my left hand against the wall. Smoothly interlocking timbers line the stairwell. The stair treads are wood, and I am very careful to move slowly, toes first, muffling any sound as far as possible. My breathing is a little ragged, and I regret not waiting a little longer to ensure I am as calm as I can be, but it is too late now. Alice is about two steps behind me, managing to be quieter than I.

The steps descend perhaps fifteen feet, and the wooden walls become damp. We must be below the river level, at least partially, and the smell of damp fills the air, musty, thick, and tinged with something sharper. There is almost no light filtering down from the room above, and even if there were,

Alice's body would cover me in shadow.

The steps end and the corridor curves away from the river, boarded now on walls and floor and still damp. Alice gently taps my shoulder and I stop and turn.

"How long has this been here?" she whispers.

"I do not know. But the warehouse was empty, between owners, allegedly. My guess is that it will have been so for a couple of weeks, in time for the crate from Wood Bay to be delivered and hidden. At the moment, I do not care."

She smiles grimly and nods, and we press on.

A faint light begins to filter in front of me. The light is pale, yellow, like harvest moonlight. After but a few steps more, the corridor straightens, leading to an opening less than ten feet away. There is nowhere to hide should someone appear, and the light means that anyone looking from the room before us will see our approach. There seems little point in trying to sneak, but it is difficult not to.

I stop, straighten my back, and bring my stick down on the boards. I can feel Alice tense behind me, but I feel strangely free. If Alice sensed "it", then there is a good chance "it" sensed her and is waiting.

"Let us keep our distance no longer."

And we step into the room.

The Yellow Crown

My mind rebels at the sight, and Alice lets forth a cry of horror. Wet, naked flesh shivers and twitches, yellow, purple lined and swollen, leaking pus from pockmarks that are no longer discreet, but flow into each other. Limbs writhe within the mass, hands reaching, legs circling and padding the air, always moving.

Faces are visible, eyes round with fear or pain, mouths wide, moving.

There are sigils painted on the walls, that drip and run with the damp, but they will have to wait for examination, as I have to concentrate on not retching. The smell is appalling, like that in Jess's room but so many times worse. That stench emanates from the thing in the centre, which is being attended to by two figures clad in the long cloak and mask of Wynter's doctors. They pay no attention to us, but remain intent on their own tasks.

In sight of this I am unable to do anything but stare, breathing ragged and shallow, and, dimly, I hear a whimper of fear from Alice. That noise breaks the spell and I turn to her, gathering myself, pulling my mind back so that there is only me and her. Her eyes are wide, flicking around, trying both to make sense of, and avoid, seeing what is in that room. Her mouth hangs open. I move in front of her and gently, firmly, take her face in my hand, guiding her eyes to mine.

"Listen to me. This thing is Fear, nothing more." I try and steady my voice, make it sound confident in the assumption that I know is wrong. "It can not move, but it is alive and that means it can die. Can you help me kill it?"

She looks past my shoulder and then back at me, and her mouth closes and becomes set in a thin line. She nods briefly and I give her a smile. "Good.

Here."

I pass a handful of iron Wards to her. "Move slowly and carefully. Place these around the room. Use the cracks in the walls if you can, if not on the floor then tight against the wall."

I keep one eye on her as she moves off, moving slowly and smoothly, keeping her eyes on the monstrous mass in the centre of the room. While she does so I try and make sense of what I am seeing.

There are four faces, all male, within the thing. Four bodies, melted together, sick and in agony, constantly writhing. The faces are looking around, their eyes moving in all directions, but I believe they comprehend nothing, for even with the heavily shadowed light in this room, they must be able to see Alice and me, and yet they do not react.

Their mouths open and close, and I get the impression that they are speaking, but I can hear nothing.

The "doctors" are working on this mess of flesh, but what they are doing is beyond me. Slowly, slowly, and with as little noise as I can manage, I start edging closer. Alice is already heading towards the wall opposite the doorway. I am surprised the placing of the Wards has had no effect, but given the lack of any reaction to our presence, perhaps that is to be expected.

Another few steps and I have to cover my nose and mouth with my hand, for the reek coming from this monstrosity is so strong it burns my throat. By the time I am close enough to the doctors to see what they are doing, Alice is heading towards the third wall.

I realise, with a sudden flash, that, although I believe this thing is created of Fear, I can not sense it. When Alice cut herself to run the Trace, she knew there was something here, but I did not, and even now, so close to it I could, if I desired, step forward and touch it, I feel nothing but revulsion. I am sure that, should I take my rune-knife and open my arm, I would be overwhelmed, but without doing so there is nothing. Maybe this is how a Watcher's life ends, unable to feel, unable to sense anything without shedding blood.

Alice's journey around the room is almost complete, and now I see some change in the behaviour of the thing before me. The faces, although still mouthing their almost silent words, are looking around more wildly.

I am close to one of the doctors-figures, and I can finally see what they are doing. The one before me has a stack of the little carved stone pieces and is pushing them, individually, into gashes in the quivering flesh. It takes no notice of me whatsoever as it works, simply acting almost like an automaton.

I stand but a couple of feet away from the thing now, and slowly edge towards a face, noting how its eyes constantly move. It looks terrified, and there is no sanity in its eyes. And I can now hear what it is saying, in a voice that is a whispered scream.

Along the shore the cloud waves break

I know these words, they have been with me

The twin suns sink behind the lake

in my mind, constantly

The shadows lengthen

and my mouth joins these awful voices and I am powerless to silence it

In Carcosa

I blink and I am in the city by the lake, standing on the shore as the suns sink to the water.

No! Not now!

Looking wildly around, although an exit has never presented itself to me before, I become aware of noises behind me. They are different from the screaming choir of before, more panicked, terrified and fewer in number.

With no other course of action available to me, I turn away from that lake of absolute, appalling calm, and follow the voices.

The walls, leaning and curving above me, are glistening and wet, moist and dripping with something that is thicker than water. I recoil from touching them, but it is impossible as they seem to press in, breathing and gasping as I run as fast as my leg will allow. My scars are burning, and I can not move the fingers on my left hand.

With each step the voices become louder, screaming in pain and shouting for help. At one point I lose my footing and slip, throwing my hand out to steady myself. My own shout joins them, for when I hit a wall, it gives slightly, like pressing into a pig carcass. The city is alive, aware. This city is the Yellow King, vast, malevolent, cold.

I round a corner and find myself in an open square perhaps two hundred feet across. Tall "buildings" rise on all sides, and in the centre, horribly reminiscent of the place in Stonehouse where Alice was held captive, is a tall cross. At its base, struggling and screaming, are four bodies, and I rush to them, thinking that if I can help them it might, somehow, create a way for me to get back to Alice.

When I arrive, panting and limping, I see that any hope of freeing them is long gone. Each has partially melted into this foul city, becoming one with its flesh. Three of them are largely subsumed, writhing, but only as a fly writhes within a web as the spider feeds. The fourth, his head bent back away from the touch of this predatory place, sees me and shouts. There is nothing I can do, his stomach is wrapped in tendrils that pulse wetly, and his legs have all but disappeared into the mass of stone-flesh.

I kneel at his side, looking into eyes that are mad. I do not know whether he really knows I am there, but his screams have ceased, replaced by sobs, through which the words "Home," and "Wood Bay," are repeated again and again, and I understand who these people are.

This is Izaak, the man from Wood Bay. The others must be the men who took him, and who infected Jess and her family. If I can stop his suffering, this man dragged into the belly of this King, then maybe it will throw me back to Alice.

Shaking, I reach into my robe and withdraw my rune-knife. Acting swiftly, as I am sure there will be a reaction to the iron, I bring the point to his forehead. He screams as the iron touches his skin, and I quickly lean into the hilt, bringing my useless left hand hard against it, and driving it deep into his head. His scream intensifies, his arms flail at me, and he twists away, the blade pulling out with a wet, sucking noise.

I stumble back as his screaming continues. Why has this not worked? Why did the iron have no effect?

And then I realise: It comes down to blood. It always does. Killing for the sake of mercy will not work here, but maybe a sacrifice will. Here, perhaps, is where I can be a Watcher for the last time. I wipe the gore from the blade of my knife and roll up my sleeve.

You have taken my mind with your song.

I have a song of my own.

The Watcher thinks about the Fear

The first cut breaks the skin, opening my wyrd.

And deeply considers this dark life.

The second begins the Wolf-Hook, an ancient rune of pain and despair.

From times far away the Watcher recalls

The third seals the Hook, curving deep into flesh and dropping blood to the ground.

The deep-wyrd cuts and says

I drive the blade into my arm, between the bones.

Choke on me.

Turning the blade with a bellow of rage, I draw it from elbow to wrist, feeling tendons rip and my hand go limp. My wyrd curls around me, cradling me and burning bright as the Watcher in me dies on the Wolf-Hook, giving itself

VISITATION

to the Yellow King.

Sunset

I sit on the edge of the lake, watching the suns as they sit forever on the horizon, never setting, casting dark light across the white sky, illuminating the vast and beautiful face of the King. I feel no pain, no sorrow, no love, no hunger.

I am blessed.

Return

I wake to pain and loss. My left arm is on fire, useless and dripping, and I cry because I can feel again. The lake is gone, the suns have gone, and all I have now is the memory of them and the pain of a wrecked and butchered arm.

Sobs rack my body, taking my breath and shattering it against my chest. I am being held tight, but it feels more like a cage than comfort and I am so weak that I can not struggle.

Words slowly feed their way into my mind, words that should bring peace, but sound grating and harsh. Nevertheless, they continue, and slowly, slowly, they prick through my loss.

I become aware of movement around me, of figures walking and kneeling, of other voices querying and being answered, but they are outside my pain and mean nothing.

Eventually, I stop sobbing, aware that I need to get back to Alice, to protect her against the thing in the basement. The peace of Carcosa can wait, and suddenly I am fighting against the arms that hold me, struggling to be free, to stand between her and the mass of corruption that will surely take her.

Words, half-formed and blurred, are forced from my mouth, and are responded to by a clear voice, a voice I know. A voice that refuses to let me go as it repeats, "I am here, I am here," again and again, until it works its way deep into me and replaces some of the calm I miss.

I open my eyes, looking up into the face of the woman whose words pull me back to myself.

"Alice?"

RETURN

Short-hair, dark-rimmed eyes, bruises and deep, scratches, bordered with tattooed runes look down at me, and nod.

"Yes."

I am sobbing again, but with relief this time.

Gently, she pushes my head away, forcing me to sit against a wall, and I can regain control. My eyes finally focus on my surroundings, and the pain in my arm makes a sudden, and enormous, reappearance.

I am in the warehouse on the dock. Alice is sitting before me, looking battered and haunted, but alive. I look down at my arm, which hangs limp by my side, and see a pool of blood slowly creeping across the floor. Alice calls out and we are joined by a man, who rapidly binds my arm tightly in cloth. Wynter. His name is Wynter.

There are other people here, but I am unable to focus on them, as the room begins to spin. I hear Wynter say something and Alice places a small cup to my lips, urging me to drink.

I wake in bed, and it takes a long time to sit, as I can not seem to use my left arm. When I finally manage to raise myself and rest my back against the wall, I look down to inspect the damage.

My arm now stops at the elbow.

My exclamation of horror wakes the person sleeping in the chair across the room.

"Ah! Keep calm, Master Grey."

Wynter stands and takes a few steps towards me, but stops before he gets within reach. He looks less assured than is usual, but manages to maintain his professionalism.

"Deep breaths. Take a couple and I shall talk with you."

I follow his advice, and memories flash into my mind. Memories of a city, memories of peace. Memories of my knife slicing through my arm, and memories of needing to get away to find…

"Alice?"

Wynter sits on the end of the bed. "Alice is fine. A little battered, but other than that, physically well. You have done your job."

The words take a little while to sink in, but sink in they do, and I rest back against the wall. I raise what is left of my arm.

"Tell me."

"I was accosted by Alice after she dragged you out of that cellar. By the time I got to you, you were raving and had inflicted severe damage to that arm. I did try to save it, but after I repaired what I could it became rotten and had to be removed. It will be uncomfortable for a few weeks, but should heal well."

I blink hard. "I have no memory of any of that."

Wynter smiles indulgently. "I am not surprised. I have been administering Black Water to you for the last ten days. The time has come, however, to wean you away from it. You will feel rough for a while longer, but that will pass and you shall be back to your old self soon."

Even as he says these words, I know he lies. He knows he lies. I am a Watcher no longer.

"You will be very sleepy, and should rest as much as possible. Would you like to see Alice?"

As he says this, I realise that my body is exhausted, heavy, leaden, but I nod. He stands, resting his hand on my shoulder temporarily, and then leaves. Alice immediately enters the room. Her face is bruised, and scabbed scratches run down one cheek, but she smiles when she sees me, and sits on the bed where Wynter has vacated. She reaches out for my hand, enveloping it in both of hers.

"Hello, old man."

"Certainly more decrepit."

She looks at me, and says, "Wynter says you need to rest, so I shall leave you. We shall speak when you are more able."

The fatigue flows through me, and all I can do is nod. She starts walking towards the door but turns back to me, and says, "I do not know what happened to you, but I know you did it to save me. Thank you."

Sleep overtakes me.

I dream of Carcosa.

After many days of fighting sleep, and losing, I eventually make my way downstairs to the kitchen, realising that I am ravenously hungry.

RETURN

It is daytime, and the front door is open, allowing light and air into the building, and I stand and savour the warmth and sunshine. Voices from the kitchen draw me in, and I open the door to see Alice and Wynter at the table. They look up as I enter. I am pleased to see that Alice's face has, largely, recovered. The discolouration of the bruising has faded, and the scabs have largely gone. Wynter, with his back to me, turns and grins.

"Ah! Good to see you up and about. How are you feeling?"

"I am not sure. Hungry."

Alice stands and immediately begins hacking at a loaf of bread, slathering butter on it before putting it onto a plate, and starts to prepare coffee. I sit next to Wynter and try to rest my head on my left hand. It takes me a while to understand why this simple action is so difficult.

With a sigh, I pick up a slice of bread. It tastes of nothing, but feels good as I eat. Wynter watches me closely, and I offer him my left arm to inspect while Alice pours some coffee. I thank her and Wynter slowly, carefully, unwraps the bandages. I have not seen the stump yet, and I refuse to look while he prods it. Only when he begins to wrap it back up do I turn.

He has done a good job, but it is still a shock to see the heavy scars where the stitches were.

"Does it need to be wrapped?", I ask, and he stops, looking up. "No, not really. Would you prefer to let it breathe?"

I weigh up the choice. If it is bare I will have to look, have to acknowledge it, and that, perhaps, is not a bad thing.

"Leave it. If I change my mind I am sure it can be bound again." I go back to eating, but my eyes continually flick to the blunt end of my arm.

I look up at Alice, "How are you?"

"Better than I was. Better than you."

I laugh a little. "Will you tell me what happened?", I ask.

"I shall, but later." She looks pointedly towards Wynter, who is rolling the bandage up tightly and does not notice. When he has finished, he stands, and says, "Well, I should be on my way. If either of you need anything, please do ask."

As he turns to leave, I say, "There is one thing."

VISITATION

He turns back, his face open and smiling. "Yes?"

"How goes the fight against the disease?"

"Well," he replies. "There were no new cases yesterday, I am pleased to report. As long as those who have it are kept quarantined, I think we shall soon be rid of it."

"Little thanks to your doctors." His face falls and he begins to stutter. I hold up my hand.

"Three of your doctors were instrumental in spreading the infection, Doctor Wynter. Without them, it would have progressed much more slowly."

He flusters before finding his voice. "Now, look. I was in no way responsible for their actions."

I hold up my hand again. "You were responsible for *them*, though. They were under your direct employ, and you failed to keep track of what they were doing. You were complacent, if not complicit."

Wynter stands still, mouth opening and closing as his cheeks flush.

"If I need you, I know where to find you."

After he leaves, Alice looks at me questioningly. "He has barely left your side since you got here."

"You think I was harsh?"

"I do."

"I shall thank him tomorrow. I just want him to remember what happened. He *was* complacent. This might make him a better doctor. Now, tell me what happened."

Alice's story is frightful. She worked her way around the room, placing iron Wards on each wall and watching me as I stepped closer and closer. When I reached the mess of flesh, I collapsed, and things moved very quickly as the "doctors" suddenly became aware of her presence.

She fought them and won, but not before being severely hurt. Both were in the same state as the one we found at the top of the steps and proved equally difficult to despatch. She only managed by leaping onto their backs and pulling the masks off.

She had also realised that they were inserting the stone pieces into cuts in the flesh of the monster, and then withdrawing them, no doubt then using them as Curse markers, spreading the sickness wherever they were placed.

As soon as she had dealt with the doctors, she ran to me, to find me twitching on the floor. Apparently, I shouted her name and then stuck my arm with my knife, doing the damage that led to its removal.

When that happened, she made a decision and, reaching into her pocket, withdrew the remaining iron Wards and pushed them deep into the wounds where the stones had been inserted. Immediately, the thing began screeching, writhing to get away from the iron. A blackness spread, rapidly destroying the flesh, but then stopping. She pushed her hand into the wet, stinking mass and withdrew some Wards. Rapidly, she moved around, cutting slits with her rune-knife, before pushing them back into the monstrous thing.

Once she was sure enough damage had been done, she grabbed my arm and dragged me away, heaving me up the steps and into the warehouse. She was uncertain exactly what I had done to my arm at that point, and ran to get Wynter and Campion.

As she said this, I realised that Campion had not been to visit, and I asked why.

"He has been sick."

My stomach falls.

"He is alive," she adds, "and is likely to recover." Her statement finishes there, and by her tone there is more to come.

"But?", I ask, quietly.

She takes a deep breath, which is let out shakily. "But, he is blind. The pocks hit his eyes."

The world stops, and I have no words to offer.

Epitaph

I went to see Jacob Perez yesterday. This was the first time I have had to myself since I woke, and I decided that seeing a friend not involved with the events of the last few weeks would be a good idea.

The walk through town was pleasant enough. Things have returned to normal, at least outwardly, with crowds in the streets and the Queens Barge only sailing when needed. But there is a quietness to things now. The town needs a period of mourning, and there will be a vigil in a few days, led by Colston, who seems to have cemented her position in the council.

The makeshift cellar beneath the warehouse has been filled. Engineers examined it and proclaimed that it would have collapsed soon, which makes what happened in there to myself and Alice of dubious benefit. The remnants of the three "doctors" and the abomination were bustled away and burned.

Campion is recovering well enough. He is still weak and fatigued from the sickness, but that is passing with each day. The loss of his sight frustrates and angers him, and his temper is short. At the moment he blames me for it, and I am not strong enough to argue, so I keep my distance.

Alice is stronger than I, and spends time with him, being harangued and shouted at.

Wynter is wary of me, but has proved to be useful, and is helping Inigo design me a false arm.

When I reached Jacob's studio on Ness Row, the door was shut but unlocked. As I walked up the stairs, I could hear muffled words from the room above and, on entering, was astonished to see the place in disarray.

Boards and canvasses were strewn all around, untidy, piled upon each other in a manner that would have caused Perez extreme annoyance but weeks ago. Jacob himself was at his easel, painting feverishly, and did not look up when I entered. As I approached I realised that he was muttering.

Glancing around at the artworks, a terrible feeling washed over me, for each depicted the strange, unnatural angles and geography of the city that still haunts my dreams. Each painting showed different views, but each was instantly recognisable. Some even showed the vast Yellow King, squatting in His gown that was not a gown but tentacles that reached out into the minds of the pale inhabitants who writhed in the streets.

When I came to stand next to him, he was repeating the lines I knew so well, over and over. He was working on the portrait of me. In the painting, I am standing on the shore with him at my side. We are hand in hand, heads bowed to the hooded, yellow figure standing before us, rising from the still water.

Along the shore the cloud waves break
The twin suns sink behind the lake
The shadows lengthen
In Carcosa.

As he and I completed the lines together, he stopped painting and turned to look at me, his face gaunt and dark. I think he had neither eaten nor drank in days, and I could see that his mind was gone, but that he retained enough of himself to see me. Tears formed in his eyes, and I saw that he understood we had shared Carcosa, and that it was killing him.

A sob shuddered his body, and he returned to the canvas. I did the only thing I could to help him. With a swift push of my knife into the back of his skull I released him from this world.

I regret the need to do this, but I will not share Carcosa.

Notes and Thanks

The Emfie Road, currently called the M5, does run as stated, but I have diverted it to go south of Bristol, rejoining it close to Clapton-in-Gordano. Hobb and Alice finally leave it at what is now the A361 at Tiverton.

Gloster sits further south on the River Severn than its present-day incarnation, between Framilode and Epney. At this point the Severn is a couple of hundred metres wide. The fires are set on the spit of land that forms the loop around Rodley.

The title, "Visitation", comes from the name given to the Great Plague in London of 1665/6.

The lines spoken by Grey in "The Yellow Crown" are a re-working of the deep and beautiful Anglo-Saxon poem "The Wanderer". If you have not read it, I urge you to do so.

As ever, I must give thanks to my wife, Penny, for her support and willingness to listen to me prattle - and not necessarily about the book.

Thanks also to Cat Treadwell and Nimue Brown for reading early drafts and offering insight and corrections.

Printed in Great Britain
by Amazon